FINDING LANCELOT

D1519306

TAMARA PALMER

FINDING LANCELOT

Tamara Palmer

FINDING LANCELOT
Tamara Palmer — 1st ed.

ISBN 13 9798686044234
Copyright © 2020 by Tamara Palmer

Santel ePublishing
Santa Barbara, California
www.santelepublishing.com
Proofread/Copyedit: www.ProofreadNZ.co.nz
Book design: Judith Sansweet
Cover design: Catherine McDonough
Photographers: Annette Patko (back cover)
Rebecca Wachtel (About the Author)

Except for the purposes of fair reviewing, no part of this publication may be reproduced or transmitted in any form or by any means, electronic or mechanical, including photocopying, recording, or any information retrieval system, without permission in writing from the author.

Publisher's Note: This is a work of fiction. Names, characters, places, and incidents are a product of the author's imagination. Locales and public names are sometimes used for atmospheric purposes. Any resemblance to actual people, living or dead, or to businesses, companies, events, institutions, or locales is completely coincidental

DEDICATION

To the spirit (or perhaps my own past-life self) who whispered Keira's story to me at the Chalice Well in Glastonbury, thank you.
I hope I told it right.

"Tis all a chequerboard of nights and days
where destiny with men for pieces plays:
hither and thither moves, and mates, and slays,
and one by one back in the closet lays."
— Omar Khayyam

PROLOGUE

The room hummed with a palpable vibration of people, music, and energy. It was way more than Amanda Barnes would have chosen for her 25th birthday, but according to her cousin Roxie, it was a crucial marker in time. Twenty-five was the year that officially launched you closer to 30 than 20, and Roxie had insisted it was critical to celebrate these significant life events.

It was getting late, well after midnight. Ryan had disappeared probably an hour before, maybe more. He wasn't a fan of crowds either, so when he'd excused himself to go to the bathroom and then didn't come back right away, Amanda didn't find it all that surprising. She figured he was hiding in Roxie's room, playing games on his phone.

Amanda and Ryan's mutual level of introversion was the base ingredient in the glue that bonded them. They could have the best time sitting side by side on the couch — Ryan deep in a strategy game on his phone, Amanda scrolling Facebook or Instagram on her iPad — each lost in their own worlds, occasionally emerging for a "Check this out" or a "Let's order dinner in."

Amanda excused herself from a dull conversation about the pros and cons of the Keto diet with Roxie's upstairs neighbor and meandered her way thru the kitchen in search of Ryan, thinking, *Is it okay to leave my own party before it's over? I'll fake a stomach ache if I have to. I'm done. I'm ready to go home.*

Amanda found Roxie in the kitchen assembling strawberry daiquiris in the blender. A circle of rapt fans surrounded her, as if she was making a celebrity chef appearance on the *Home Shopping Network*. Amanda remembered the daiquiri incident five years before — they'd been so distracted that they forgot to put the lid on the blender before pressing Purée. Roxie's apartment had looked like a cotton candy factory exploded. Weeks later, she was still finding pink stains in odd places, like under the refrigerator.

"Rox, have you seen Ryan?"

"Yeah, maybe 20 minutes ago? He and Cassie were waiting in line for the bathroom."

"Oh? I thought Cassie was long gone. She said she was getting a migraine."

Roxie shrugged and turned to her audience.

Amanda played back the conversation: *I know I had a lot to drink, but I clearly remember Ryan asking Cassie if she needed help getting back to her apartment. Cassie said no, she'd take an Uber. Did he leave with her? No, he wouldn't without at least telling me first.*

I also remember that Cassie didn't think she'd be able to make it back in time for the party, and it was only because her TV show had an unexpected hiatus that she caught a last-minute flight from LA that afternoon, I felt bad about the cost of that ticket. But Cassie insisted her life was now on a whole other scale, and told me I really shouldn't worry. She keeps an apartment in Chicago while having a house in LA., so yeah. Whole other scale.

Amanda wove her way down the hallway passing single friends chatting with couples who were locked in standing snuggles on one side, the bathroom line on the other.

She gently pressed the handle on Roxie's bedroom door, as though she was nervous about waking a sleeping baby. Opening, it squeaked just slightly. She could see the bed piled with raincoats and sweaters, jean jackets, and windbreakers, the late spring outerwear for May in Chicago. Behind the breaker of coats, sat Ryan and Cassie, snuggled together among the excessive decorative pillows, their own private bunker. Her best friend since junior high and her boyfriend since college together — without her — she knew they shared an embrace that would exclude her forever.

Ryan looked up to see who'd entered the room, his head having been buried deep in the nape of Cassie's neck, his arm holding her tight, claiming her as his. Cassie's red lipstick kisses covered Ryan's cheek, neck, even the top of his chest.

Amanda no longer had to fake a stomach ache. She saw no apology in their body language. They didn't separate. They were clearly a unit. She took a step backward and heard both of them call after her as she slammed the bedroom door and flew out of Roxie's apartment into the damp Chicago night, crying as she ran down Clark Street.

****

"You should really be over it by now." Roxie sipped her latte and looked past Amanda, her eyes tracking the door, as if waiting for someone to arrive, someone who was better company than Amanda. "It's been what, six, seven months already?"

"Nine, actually — almost a year."

"Has it really? Wow. See? It's time to move on with your life. I never liked him anyway."

Amanda knew otherwise. Roxie liked Ryan. Everyone liked Ryan.

"You forget that it wasn't just Ryan I lost."

"I know, but you were kind of losing Cassie anyway."

Amanda glared at Roxie. They'd been through this before. Every year of success in LA had taken Cassie further from their suburban Chicago teenage years. Even though Amanda lived in the city now instead of the North Shore, she often felt her life was merely a continuation of high school, as though she hadn't actually grown up yet.

"The therapy doesn't seem to be working and you're just a mopey mess who's sick all the time. Have you at least considered setting up an online dating profile? You can shop even if you're not ready to add your purchase to the cart."

"I'm not shopping for a mate."

"That's kind of how it works. Of course, in my case, I'm always buying and returning. Wink, wink. That's the fun part of shopping. I love trying things on, giving them a test run and then exchanging them for something else." Roxie's laugh was infectious. Amanda often wondered what it would be like to have her sense of levity, to be so confident in her own skin.

"Did I tell you I saw a picture of them on Facebook with that actress from *This Is Us*?"

"Mandy, stop following them on social media!"

Amanda nodded. She had unfollowed them, but that didn't stop her from looking them up several times a week to see what Ryan and Cassie were up to in LA.

"I just don't get how I missed the signs. In retrospect, they're all so obvious."

"That's the way it always is."

"I keep telling myself that at least I found out before the engagement party, you know? Before the wedding. Before we had kids." Amanda's voice caught on 'kids.'

Roxie grabbed Amanda's hand, indulging her in yet another round of empathy.

"The path was so clear before, so laid out for me. We had it all planned out. The starter home in Evanston or Glenview was going to happen as soon as Ryan got his next promotion. Did I tell you that we'd even picked out the dog we were going to get? Irish Setter. Ryan had one as a kid named Big Red."

Roxie rolled her eyes and released Amanda's hand in the same motion. She was a cat person.

"Ryan always said that once he made partner, we'd be set for life, and then we'd probably upgrade to Winnetka or Glencoe. I was supposed to have the yoga-going, kid-raising, lunching-with-friends life that I wanted, that my sorority sisters were on track to get. This stupid job was only supposed to be temporary until his career took off."

"You hear how privileged this all sounds, don't you?"

"Of course I do, but it's a nice dream, isn't it? How could he flush it away? I thought it was his dream, too."

Amanda sipped her latte, her gaze drifting off to the corner of the room by the door, looking as inward as she was outward, trying to understand what was no longer understandable.

"Cassie isn't going to offer a suburban-wife life."

Roxie, in the midst of swallowing, choked a little as she laughed. "Nope, no suburban-wife life coming out of that one."

"So you say I should be over it — but that's a lot to frickin' get over. Now what am I supposed to do with my life? Find someone else to replace Ryan and start the whole process all over again? We fit together. We were such a 'sensible match,' you know?" Amanda used air quotes as though they could contain the dream within them.

"I could start on my feminist rant about how you don't need a man," Roxie offered.

"Just don't, please. Not today. Let me mourn my 1950s housewife fantasy a little while longer."

"You're something," Roxie sighed and glanced at her phone. Roxie's attention span was quickly waning.

"This buzz in my head is an endless loop. I can't stop asking these questions." Amanda decided it was better not to discuss the physical effects of the relationship stress. Her sleeping was now totally screwed up, and as a result, she'd started taking over-the-counter sleep aids that left her groggy in the morning. She'd read an article about how sleep aids were linked to dementia, so now she had to wrestle with the worry of what she was inflicting on her body long-term. She was exhausted on every level: mind, body, and soul. The coffee barely made a difference anymore.

"I need to run to the bathroom. Watch my stuff."

Roxie nodded as she picked up her phone.

On the corkboard by the restroom, a flier caught Amanda's eye.

> Let your past inform your future
>
> Past-Life Regressions - *for those who boldly dare*
>
> Are you ready to unlock your full story?
>
> Therese Montclair
>
> Transcendental Soul Guide
>
> therese@transcendence.net
>
> 323-258-LIVE

Amanda smirked. *Soul guide? Well, maybe. Maybe I could use a soul guide at this point. There has to be someone who can help me find a way through this life.*

Amanda snapped a picture of the flier on her way back to the table.

PART ONE

CHAPTER 1

They're coming. There are so many. I'm standing on the top of the tor, our lookout hill in Glastonbury, close enough to feel the heat of the stones of St. Ryan's Tower. I can see the line of them stretching for miles and miles. They're trampling the thick green grass as they force their way through the wooded narrows and out along the green rolling hills towards Glastonbury and the Abbey. I'm the fastest and the slightest. That's why I was sent to watch. It's always me.

The sun glints off the soldiers' armor, as if they were sent by God himself. It's a mesmerizing sight. I can't move, trapped by the spell of their might. Through a force of will, I release my legs and pivot quickly, too quickly, colliding with one of our sacred Thornberry trees. A thorn from a branch rips into my arm; blood trickles down the sleeve of my ripped dress. I dash for the Abbey.

On my frantic return, I see Robert sweeping the entryway outside his father's shoppe.

"You must flee. The King's army is coming!" I call out and slow my pace to deliver the warning, but Robert is stunned and doesn't respond.

"Now, dear Robert! Please! You must go. We all must go."

Robert lowers his head and answers: "Then the time has come. Like Winchester and Cleeve, they've come." His look of inevitable defeat is too much to bear. "Lord have mercy upon us."

"Please take shelter. There is no time left. I must go warn the others." I press on him to step back, off the street and towards his father's shoppe, into safety, but he doesn't move. He grabs my arms and pulls me in tight.

"Keira ... there is something I must tell you." He stares fiercely into my eyes, his hold increasing. I sense him trying to contain me forever. His warm brown eyes bear so many memories. Sweet Robert, always thoughtful and kind and there for me. His presence is like a salve, but I must go, I've already wasted precious moments.

"There's no time. The others need me." As I push Robert aside, he kisses me firmly upon the check. My first kiss. I cry as I leave him there on the dusty street, refusing to look back.

"It's the King's army!" I call, racing through the Abbey gates. My blonde hair trails behind me. My screams carry as I fly through the grounds. "There are knights on horseback everywhere! They're coming! They're coming so fast!" I scream until I choke and my voice can no longer carry my words.

As I approach the herb garden, I'm overcome by a vision. The Abbey is burning and crumbling around me. Death is everywhere. Rosemary, my pet lamb, wails before being brutally slayed, her innards yanked out and left steaming on the grass. These men are doing it — they're goblins. Goblins! I cry before collapsing into the safety of the sage. Everything goes dark.

I come to amidst the sound of the knights crashing through the Abbey gates. Monks are scattering, nursemaids and their babes wail in the orphanage. I race into the kitchen, only to find the staff still working as though nothing has happened. I yell to flee but my voice is hoarse and empty. There is nothing more I can do.

From the kitchen, I hurry towards the sanctuary of the Lady Chapel. Instinctively, I pull out my necklace. Gazing deep into the stone, I invoke a prayer:

Good Mother Earth, Goddess over all,
I pray you watch and protect me,
save me from the fall.

My body fills with a pulsing sensation that shoots directly from the ground into my feet, up my legs and spine and into my heart. I am a vessel for something so much larger than myself. Fear sparks its shivering energy through my body.

The smell of burning flesh chokes the air. Even the chapel is not safe. Fire creeps up the Abbey walls and lays waste to the wood. I remember a nursemaid telling me long ago that everything fights to live, even fire.

I crouch in the corner, shielding myself from the onslaught. A knight is quickly approaching. He's too close to where I'm hiding. I try to pull back into the shadows of the chapel but he's spotted me. Before I can react, he lifts me by the scruff of my dress and hoists me in front of him onto his steed. My muscles lock in place. Through my clutch, the pendant on my necklace embeds its outline into my palm. I know what knights do to women like me. I'm now his war prize. He'll have his way with me, and then I'll be killed. I recoil as he pulls closer.

"Hold on tight!"

"Let me go!" I attempt to free myself, but his grip is too tight.

"So long as you have the necklace, the goddess will protect us."

No one is ever supposed to see my necklace. The head monk, Father Stuart, once said that I would turn into a witch if anyone outside of the Abbey ever laid eyes upon it. I examine myself — I don't feel like a witch.

"Who are you and where are you taking me?" I yell.

The knight says nothing. We continue to gallop, past Robert's shoppe and the others along the High Street. Not until we're safely outside of Glastonbury, does the Knight speak again.

"I am Miles — and I'm taking you away."

****

A bell showered the room in a cascade of sound and a voice said, "It's time for Amanda to wake up."

Slowly, Amanda blinked her eyes open, steadying herself on the couch with her left hand, while her right wiped away the sweat dripping down her forehead. Therese was sitting across from her, as she had been a few minutes — hours, perhaps days — ago.

How long was I under? Amanda wondered. *The room smells of lavender now. Did it before? Maybe it was there and I just didn't notice.*

Therese's silver hair glistened in the soft glow of the table lamp by her desk. Her eyes were wide and inviting. She had a regal air, wearing a velvet crimson dress that fit snugly around her buxom chest and flowed effortlessly to the floor.

Therese emanates love. That's what drew me to her during our initial consultation. Yet now, after what I've just gone through – and what the hell have I just gone through? I wonder if I should have been so trusting.

"Take a moment, my dear," Therese said in a calming voice.

Amanda rubbed her eyes fully awake and pulled herself into a seated position on the soft, plush couch. Her body appeared to have made it back in one piece. Taking a mental inventory, she was still wearing the jeans and navy sweater she'd been wearing when she arrived, and her grandmother's diamond engagement ring was still on her finger. Her watch read 4:06. She'd arrived at Therese's at 3.

"I must say, your narration of your experience was so clear, I could see everything that was happening. How are you feeling?" Therese leaned forward and took Amanda's hand in her own. Hesitant at first, Amanda's need to feel comforted overtook her restraint, and she relaxed her hand in the warm palm before her. Therese's fingers were a dazzling display of silver and jeweled rings.

"I guess you didn't warn me enough," Amanda responded as she stood quickly, too quickly. Her stomach quaked; nausea moved up her body as she righted herself. "Sorry!" she called out as she flew across Therese's office, past her antique walnut desk, past the bookcases and the Norfolk pine in the corner, and straight into the bathroom, missing the toilet, and throwing up into Therese's shiny pedestal sink.

Amanda wiped her mouth and stared at herself in the mirror. Her pale skin looked whiter than usual as she wiped her face with a wet paper towel and pushed back the stray blonde locks of hair with her damp hands. Her eyes were bloodshot, dulling the vibrant green that was usually her most complimented feature.

Everything in Keira's world was so alive, so much more real than any dream I've ever had. From the smoke in the air to the grittiness between my fingers, every sensation was ... intense. Palpable. Amanda pressed her hands to her face, to her lips. *I was in that teenage body just moments ago. I felt so ... different. It was my mind, but the body was clearly someone else's. And that girl was what, sixteen, maybe? Barely?* She pressed her hands to her belly, her legs. *It's been ten years since I was in a teenage body. I'm still Amanda, yet inside me is someone else, this ... Keira.*

Amanda studied her reflection in the mirror to see if she could see the aspects of Keira in herself, in this lifetime, but all she saw was a scared twenty-five-year-old who'd had no clue what to do with her life when she arrived for her session, and now perhaps knew even less.

Her legs slightly numb and tingly, Amanda walked back to the couch wondering: *Do Therese's other clients react like this after their first time? Do they all have this intense an experience? Maybe I should have done more research before attempting such a thing. Roxie was right: I had no idea what I was getting myself into. It's so typical of me to be dumbly naïve and overly trusting.* She also had a nagging feeling she'd damaged her body in a way she'd never thought possible, and likely, was not reversible.

"Let me help you." Therese guided Amanda back down on the couch, then walked behind her desk, opened a small office-sized refrigerator, and returned with a glass bottle of apple juice that Amanda gladly took.

"Most sessions aren't this intense. I have to say," Therese began, "As I said before, I'm truly impressed by your level of recall. You were able to describe what you were experiencing so vividly, it felt like I was right there with you."

"It's like I was narrating a movie."

Therese nodded. Amanda took a long, deep breath.

"I know you have a lot to process."

Completely exhausted, Amanda nodded; yet, layered beneath the exhaustion was sheer exhilaration as her mind raced with questions. *Who is Keira? Was this truly my life once upon a time? Was the Abbey real? Does it still exist? Who was the knight and where was he taking me?* In the short amount of time she'd spent in that other world as Keira, Amanda had experienced more trauma and excitement than anything she'd ever experienced in her life.

"The first time can be very moving for people. If you're up for the journey, I'd love to guide you back again. It will get easier and feel less ... unusual ... each time you regress." Therese sipped from her ceramic mug, holding the thread of a tea bag in place with her index finger. "I believe we can do magical things together."

Magical things. Amanda thought. *I'm so ready for magic. It's like I've been given the map to a treasure hunt, and I can't walk away.*

"When can I come back?"

Therese smiled and reached for her appointment calendar.

CHAPTER 2

It was February, the height of the blues season as Amanda often referred to it. In her mind, 'there ain't nothin' but the blues' from November to April. Winter in Chicago left much to be desired. The cold wind whipped around as she pulled her new chenille scarf closer to her face. She'd smiled when she spotted it through the window of a small boutique in Andersonville a few weeks earlier. That Saturday, she'd felt particularly down about everything: Ryan, Cassie, impending winter, the state of her closet. The color reminded her of Cornflower, her favorite blue in the Crayola 64 pack. The picture of Therese's flier had been in her phone for weeks. Every few days, she'd see it as she deleted the excessive number of photos of ice on the Chicago River, the picture of the Wi-Fi code from jury duty, and the stupid selfies she'd snapped trying to get a picture of the back of her hair to explain to her hairdresser the cut she was going for.

For more than six weeks, the contact information for Therese had gone uncontacted as she waited to gather the courage to call. Then, once she'd finally done it, she'd told Roxie who'd made a few attempts to talk her out of the appointment — only relenting when Amanda agreed to meet her for coffee right after the session.

Now, although, she wasn't in the mood to meet up, and in spite of the fact that in such weather, walking just three blocks to the coffee shop felt like a trek to the other side of Antarctica, what Amanda really wanted to do was to call an Uber, go home, and soak in a deep, hot bath. But she knew Roxie was waiting for her, and it was too late to cancel.

Entering the coffee shop, she spotted Roxie's eager face, anticipation beaming in her bold brown eyes. Sporting biker boots, black leather pants, a tight black turtleneck, and dark glasses pushed up on her hair, she was a sharp contrast to the Uggs-leggings-sweater-infinity scarf set. She belonged in a café in Paris, not a Starbucks in the middle of the Loop. Roxie was like an old-school 50s Beatnik who'd joined a motorcycle gang and then stumbled into a drag show. She'd topped off her look with a feather boa, her trademark. Today's boa was red, which signaled that she was happy and energized. Roxie's boas were like mood rings: they changed colors depending on her disposition. Sometimes that called for multiple boas in one day. She carried several in her bag, just in case.

Her look matched her personality: bold, loud, and in charge. Amanda admired her confidence and candor, at least when they weren't so intense as to be off-putting. A little bit of Roxie went a long way.

Making her way toward Roxie, Amanda untangled herself from her own scarf as she reached for the tissue in her pocket to stop her runny nose. She really didn't want to be there. She should be in a steamy bath, listening to the spa channel on her satellite radio and lavishing in suds among lavender-scented candles. But ... there was Roxie.

"Nice rims," Amanda said, giving Roxie a hug.

"We finally got the new shipment of Versace. Check them out." Roxie turned her head to show off a rhinestone "R" embedded in the thick black arms of the glasses. "Custom ordered. My manager told me this was it for the year. I maxed out my allowance on these babies — and it's only February."

"You'll have to start moonlighting at Pearl Vision to get more."

"Not a bad idea," Roxie responded looking deep in thought, as though she was actually considering it. "But we didn't come here to talk about my new glasses." She patted the chair beside hers. "Sit!

Sit! Tell all! Tell all!" Her voice naturally carried, and Amanda winced noticing a couple several tables away turning to look.

"Chill!" Amanda hissed as she pressed her palms down on the table and wondered, *How does Roxie maintain such a perpetually high degree of energy? If only I could find a way to channel her spark. I could use some. She's like 28 going on 20 — and I often feel like a middle-aged woman trapped in a 25-year-old's body.*

Amanda took a deep breath to up the oxygen in her almost listless body. She remembered overhearing something at the gym about backbends being invigorating, so she arched her back slightly to see if the shift increased her energy flow. It didn't.

"I'm not sure I can go into it all, Roxie. I feel kind of wiped. I can't stay long."

"Oh no, no, no!" Roxie clutched Amanda's shoulder with her long, shiny, red nails.

Glancing at them, a thought flashed through Amanda's mind, *What was her signature color? Big Apple Attitude?*

"I was only approving this if I got the full report afterwards, remember?" Roxie protested.

"Let me at least get a drink, then," Amanda responded and headed to the counter feeling as if her legs were not quite touching the ground. Shivers coursed through her. Every image from the regression still felt so incredibly real. *Did I really see that poor lamb killed? My dreams were never that vivid.*

The barista asked for her order again. She hadn't heard him the first time. She wasn't fully back.

Returning to the table with her double soy latté, she sat down and took several big sips hoping the caffeine would activate her brain, which would then direct her tongue, and somehow, the right words would come together and all of this would make sense. "So, it worked. I had a ... vision? I guess that's what you'd call it?"

"Well, I can tell that! Were you a witch? Were you Cleopatra? Were you a guy? Is that even possible? Oh, that'd be hot. Tell me you were a guy!"

"Oh my god! Can you imagine?" Amanda laughed at the idea, then felt a touch horrified and excited, wondering how it would feel to be in a man's body. "It would be so cool, right?" Amanda tilted her head. She wasn't fully on board with the idea.

"Okay, okay, start already!" Roxie leaned forward in her chair, barely able to contain herself.

"I was in medieval England, and there was some kind of abbey. These knights came and were killing everyone." Amanda took a sip of her drink. *This is hard. Like re-telling a dream and trying to have it all make sense.*

Roxie's gaze held.

"I'd been on this hilltop, outside the town, and I saw they were coming. I tried to rush through the abbey to warn everyone ... "

"Wait," Roxie interrupted. "Who was coming? The knights?"

"Yes, but I was too late. They started killing everyone. I had a pet lamb. They like totally killed it, like pulled out its guts and then everything was lying in the grass; Rox, it was steaming!"

"Eeesh, Mandy! Enough, I get it." Roxie turned her head away in disgust.

"Right? Okay, so the next thing I know, I'm being kidnapped by this knight named Miles ... "

"Miles? You were kidnapped by a frickin' knight named ... Miles?" Roxie burst out laughing.

"Yes. I know, isn't it all ridiculous?" Amanda wiped her forehead with a napkin. It was chilly in the coffee shop, yet she suddenly felt hot. She wondered if she was getting sick.

Roxie nodded her head while her hand held back muffled laughter.

"Was he like the dude from *Outlander*? Did you see that show, where the chick slips through these stones, and suddenly she's back in Scotland where they had those tribes or whatever?"

"I don't know. I'm not into those types of shows."

"Okay, fine, doesn't matter, keep going."

"I was young, maybe sixteen? Miles was taking me away from this madness happening in the abbey. And then, as soon as he captured me, I came out of the regression. The weirdest part, though, was my name was Keira."

Roxie gave Amanda a sideways look. When Amanda thought she'd have to explain, Roxie clasped her hand over her mouth in her signature melodramatic Roxie way. "Oh! Now I remember! Did you tell the therapist?"

"No, and I'm not sure *therapist* is the right word for her. She's a soul guide or a life coach or something, I don't know."

"Jesus, Mandy, this is weird. Really, you came up with the same name from when we were kids? That was *The Dark Crystal,* right? Remember that night we watched it a couple of years ago? That was a great night. The blizzard. Poor delivery guy. Yeah, I crashed at your place. No way in hell I was leaving in that insanity. I think it was a full-on 80s movie marathon. I couldn't believe you'd never seen *The Karate Kid*. That's like, a must see. 'Wax on, wax off.'" Roxie made the circular hand movements like Mr. Miyagi.

"Yeah, didn't love that one."

"Still don't get it. It's such a classic." Roxie's voice had an I-don't-know-how-we-can-be-related-if-you-don't-like-this-movie tone. "But then again, you don't like *Amelie* and who doesn't like *Amelie*?" Roxie liked to talk with her hands. "We should do that again, have an 80s movie night. Maybe watch *The Breakfast Club* and *Pretty in Pink* or *Sixteen Candles.* It can be a Molly Ringwald film fest."

Amanda nodded, distracted by her thoughts.

"You so looked like Keira from that movie."

"My stick-straight long, blonde hair … "

"Yeah, yeah, even the spiky ears," Roxie laughed, pushing back a lock of Amanda's hair to expose her ear.

"Yes, my cute little elf ears," Amanda smirked. Although her hair was shorter now, just brushing her shoulders, she could still see the young Keira when she looked in the mirror.

"Does Uncle James still call you that?" Roxie asked.

"Who knows? He probably calls his new kid that." It was hard for Amanda to think about her dad and his new life, so usually, she didn't.

"I guess the name had more meaning than you thought," Roxie added, touching Amanda's shoulder.

Amanda nodded. "Yeah, I guess."

"So, what are you going to do next?" Roxie removed her hand. Her compassion was delivered in short bursts, but Amanda liked it when it showed up.

"I made another appointment for next Friday."

Roxie was distracted by someone coming into the coffee shop. He had thick dark hair pulled into a man bun, profiling a sharply chiseled face. His firm body was poured into tight jeans and a burnt-red silk turtleneck showed off his strong build. He was gorgeous.

Amanda saw Roxie make eye contact with him and sighed. "Did you invite a guy to meet you here?"

"Yeah," Roxie said dreamily. "His name is Kristof. He's German. I met him last night at Suzette's gallery. You remember the show she was having for that new artist from Berlin? You should have come. Lots of hot Euro guys there. Isn't he delish?"

Amanda had considered going to the gallery, but Celia, her mom, had dropped by unannounced, and by the time she left, Amanda had no inclination to leave her apartment.

Kristof waved to Roxie and got in line at the counter. Amanda didn't want to have to go into detail about her experience in front of the new flavor of the week, and anyway, the conversation had wound down, so she decided to surrender and head home. Start that bath.

"He is delish, yes, but I'm going to take off."

"Amanda, I brought him here on purpose. He has delish friends."

"And I'm sure they're all gay."

Roxie shot her a nasty look.

Amanda tried to shake it off as she gazed outside at the muted orange glow of the street lights attempting to take over for the sun.

"But he's here. Sit. You're not finished with your drink anyway."

"Sorry, I'm not in a place to be sized up."

"Don't be a bitch."

"I've been through a lot today."

Kristof arrived at their table, drink in hand. Amanda offered a quick hello as she wrapped her scarf around her neck and gathered her things to leave. Roxie glared at her when she leaned in for a goodbye hug.

Outside the café, Amanda realized that she hadn't told Roxie about Robert, the cobbler's son, or her necklace and the weird prayer she'd said. *Maybe next time. Or maybe there are some things I'll just keep to myself.*

****

At home, she went straight to her laptop without even taking off her coat. She Googled *Glastonbury* and learned that it was a sacred place in England for both pagans and Christians. Glastonbury's abbey was destroyed in 1534; it had been pillaged by King Henry VIII's knights during the dissolution of the Catholic

Church in England. She couldn't figure out why knights were attacking an abbey. She also corrected her very weak knowledge of English history; this had happened during the Renaissance, well past the medieval age.

Amanda stared at the pictures of the abbey. The images mirrored what she'd seen in her vision. She felt cold air moving around her and nearly shut off the computer, as though it was the medium channeling her past life. She Googled *Miles* and *knight*, as if she'd actually find something, but nothing useful came up.

She searched *Keira* and found results for Keira Knightley and a porn actress. Giving up, she closed the computer and walked into the bathroom, where she fully opened the tap for hot water to fill her claw-foot tub. She lit the lavender candles around the bathroom that was more spacious than any other room in her apartment. She turned on the satellite radio, already tuned to the spa channel and powered on her Bluetooth speaker.

Reincarnation. Did I truly live before? How else could I have such an intimate knowledge of that other time? I know this experience is only going to create more questions than answers in my life, and I don't need that now. It reminds me of a quote by Rilke that my freshman-year roommate pasted on the wall of our dorm room.

While the tub was filling, she returned to her computer to find the correct wording. She smiled when she found it. It truly was perfect.

> "I would like to beg you, dear Sir, as well as I can, to have patience with everything unresolved in your heart and to try to love the questions themselves, as if they were locked rooms or books written in a very foreign language.
>
> Don't search for the answers, which could not be given to you now, because you would not be able to live them.
>
> And the point is to live everything. Live the questions now. Perhaps then, someday far in the future, you will

gradually, without even noticing it, live your way into the answer."

Live into the answer. It's amazing how something can take on such a new meaning after a shockingly strange experience.

Returning to the bathroom now filled with the scent of lavender that brought back the images of England, Amanda removed her jeans and sweater. That morning she'd left for work like any other day. So much had changed in such a short time that she half-expected to see a physical change in her body. She took off her bra, underwear, and fuzzy red socks and slipped into the bath. The steaming water enveloped her as she moved her head from side to side, letting her hair float on the surface. Her muscles relaxed and a suppressed tear escaped. She watched it become one with the bathwater.

CHAPTER 3

Throughout the night, she'd wake in a semi-delirious state, uncertain as to where she was or what time period it was. Hell, she wasn't even sure *who* she was. Her dreams were still Amanda's dreams, but they had a new quality, more ... sensual. All her senses were heightened, as though she could wake up tasting the pastries from a dream of Paris.

She made her coffee on auto-pilot, and then took the steaming mug to the living room where she plopped on the couch, and lazily looked at the pictures her friends had posted on Instagram the night before. Most were selfies in bars and check-ins from after-midnight hot spots around the city. A few were of bachelorette parties and even a wedding. She hadn't posted anything online in ages. She hadn't gone out in ages, and not wanting to be dragged down by her depression, most friends had stopped texting. *Maybe I should delete my account. It's not like I want to engage with the world.*

Roxie's probably right: I'm probably messing with things on some kind of scientific, soul quantum physics level that may not be safe. Just because you can do something, doesn't mean you should, she kept telling herself, as though she'd stumbled upon some bit of cosmic wisdom. It was as if she'd unlocked a secret portal that was never meant to be exposed. But England! And the smells! Even the horse's musk seemed to linger in her Lincoln Park apartment; it was as if with the regression, she'd brought back the smells of England.

She thought about time travel: *You're not supposed to touch anything, take anything, do anything different that might alter the future. Yes! Like in Back to the Future. But did I bring the smells back with me? Is that bad in some way?* Feeling the start of a headache, Amanda went back for another cup of coffee.

****

Around 10 o'clock, Amanda finally set her phone down and peeled herself off the couch for the morning. It was Saturday and she was committed to spending the day with Celia. She could barely handle her mother on a good day, but after a restless night, and in her current state of distraction, she was bracing for a particularly challenging day.

After winning a ridiculous sum of money in the Illinois lottery ten years ago, Celia had set out to make a name for herself among the established families of Winnetka. She had reached a lifelong goal of achieving *status* in the world, but Amanda had never embraced the new lifestyle in quite the way her mother had — although, she certainly allowed it to provide a wonderful college education and a lovely apartment in a part of the city a 25-year-old had no business being able to afford.

Amanda's dad, James, had divorced Celia soon after the lottery jackpot; the money had stressed the fractures in their already-shaky marriage. James took his share of the winnings and high-tailed it out to the Santa Ynez Valley of California, quickly luring a bright young thing into marriage with his abundant wealth and charming personality.

Amanda's only regular form of communication with her father was a Christmas card. She received an occasional birthday call — or text — when he remembered, and the last she'd heard, his trophy wife was producing child number three.

"So, how's your job?" Celia asked as Amanda sank into the Rolls Royce, ducking in embarrassment as she did each time she had to ride in the car. *Why can't my mother drive something less ostentatious, like a BMW? There's wealth and then there's showiness.*

"It's fine."

"Have you given your boss that proposal yet?"

Amanda didn't respond; she just looked out the window as they wove their way through a fortunate series of green lights and out onto Lake Shore Drive. She loved this view of the city.

"You haven't even written it, have you?" Celia had been pushing Amanda for months to propose a promotion for herself to her boss, Irv.

Amanda knew Irv liked her right where she was, so a promotion was out of the question. Besides, where would she have been promoted to? "I'm not sure I want to be in marketing. I know my degree is in it, and all but … "

"I knew it. You're never going to ask for it, are you?" Celia scowled at Amanda.

Amanda kept her focus fixed outside. "Can't you just let me do my own thing?"

"Mandy, it's ridiculous that you're nothing more than a glorified secretary."

"Executive assistant."

"Exactly. This stupid new lingo for secretaries doesn't make the job any better. All I know is that I paid for four years at Northwestern, and what do you do with it? You fritter it away as a clerical maid at an insurance agency. You should have been more than this by now — and I know you think that, too. I want what's best for you, and I worry you're not doing enough to further your career. Will you look at me when I'm talking to you?"

"Mom, can we not do this today?" Amanda pleaded, turning her attention past the driver's seat and out along Lake Michigan toward Navy Pier and its towering Ferris wheel.

"You need to move on. It's been nearly a year. Maybe you need to see a different therapist?"

Amanda nodded, even though she knew Celia had her eyes on the road. She fought the tears that were still there, lingering under the surface, waiting to spill over, always. *Technically, I am seeing a new therapist,* she wanted to say, *but Therese is probably not what Celia has in mind.*

"Honey, you have to let go." Celia put her hand on Amanda's leg. "Maybe Mr. Right is around the corner, but you're not going to find him while you're pining for Mr. Wrong."

"That's cute, Mom."

Celia smiled, always strong and in control.

Amanda both admired and feared her mother. She drove her absolutely crazy most of the time, yet she also wished she had a touch of that confidence Roxie had clearly inherited from that side of the family. Celia had hardened her heart after James left and she refused to let another guy come in and steal what wasn't theirs to take. She'd dated men sporadically, but she'd never let them get close enough to lead to fulltime companionship.

Amanda always prayed for the next part of the conversation to come quickly, however hard the words ended up being.

Celia released a deep sigh, allowing the pressure to ease, before she continued: "The world doesn't get any easier when you pass thirty, hon. If you don't have a husband by then, well, then you damn well better have a good career or a lot of money. Ryan would have been a great answer, I agree, but he's also proof that you can't rely on a man. What I give you covers your rent but not much else, I'm guessing. You need a plan for your life. How are you ever going to afford to buy a condo?"

Amanda refused to make eye contact.

"I'm just trying to look out for you," Celia added.

Amanda pulled apart a split end. She was exhausted on so many levels.

"You know, maybe you need a boob job."

"Mom!"

"I'll pay for it."

"It's not about the money. For Christ sakes, I'm not getting a boob job." She had a breast-obsessed boss. She wouldn't allow him the pleasure, even if the thought had occurred to her once or twice. Okay, maybe three times.

"I'm just saying ... "

"Can we change the subject?"

"Did I tell you what Mimi Monahan's daughter is doing? She's a PR rep for the Bears."

"Isn't her uncle the general manager or something?"

"You could have a job like that. I could probably even inquire for you." Celia jerked the Rolls into the valet parking section of the Art Institute. They were there to see a traveling Van Gogh exhibit, one that Amanda had been looking forward to for weeks.

"So, did I tell you Max Harrington is back from Geneva?" Celia began as they walked in the modern art wing entrance closest to the valet drop off. She'd been trying to fix Amanda up with Max since the breakup. Max was five years older than Amanda and came from very old money. He was practically royalty by Winnetka standards, and Amanda's marriage to Max would ensure Celia's legitimacy in North Shore society forever. But Max looked like a pig, all plumped up with a tiny nose, his voice ran an octave higher than any man's should, and he had the personality of a wet dishrag. Max was the kind of boy Amanda would have been stuck with if arranged marriages still existed. In this case, they still did, and Celia was hell bent on trying to arrange one.

"Mother ... "

"He's still available."

"And you're surprised?"

"You're too picky. That's your problem. Max would be a faithful husband, unlike Ryan who was too good looking. I never trusted that boy. Max is so pleasant. And that bank account. You'd never have to go without, ever."

Amanda didn't respond.

"With this attitude of yours, you're never going to land a man. And what about children? Max would make an excellent father."

Sex with Max? Amanda shuddered at the notion. "I don't think I want kids after all." But even as she said it, she didn't think it was true. "Besides, maybe being married isn't the end all, be all. Look at how it worked out for you and Dad."

"Don't talk about your father!" Celia increased her pace to step ahead of Amanda and approach the ticket desk; then, tickets in hand, they silently entered the museum.

Celia became bored with the day soon after they'd reached the end of the exhibit. Amanda didn't protest. They'd seen the big hits: *The Starry Night, Café Terrace at Nigh*t, and *Bedroom in Arles.* She didn't need to revisit the Monets she'd seen before, or look at ancient Greek stoneware. She was ready to go home too, and was relieved when Celia took her directly back to her apartment.

"Are you sure you don't want to come tonight?" Celia asked, not ready to give up. Weeks before, she'd tried to strong-arm Amanda into joining her at some charity event.

"I'm sure. I need a chill night at home."

"Okay, sweetie. But don't hibernate so much that you miss your life."

Miss my life? If Celia only knew the half of it. Apparently, there's at least one other super-crazy life I've already lived. Maybe this life is all about chilling and recovering from past-life drama.

"Love you, Mom."

"Love you, too."

Amanda was grateful to end on a loving note. She hated it when their fights lingered on.

Closing her door behind her, Amanda called in her usual Thai delivery order and got on the couch to binge-watch Netflix. *What was that show Roxie mentioned? 'Outlander'?*

CHAPTER 4

"Late again, Miss Barnes!?" Irv bellowed for everyone in the office to hear. He loomed over Amanda, placing his thick, wide hands on her cubical desk with a thud, and looking right down her blouse. A pen hit the floor, and a towering pile of paperwork quaked. Amanda barely saved the pile from collapsing. She scanned her mess, worried about what might be visible to Irv's roaming eyes. He was known for reading emails over people's shoulders. That's how he found out about an office romance between two (now former) employees, a single mom and a married-with-children dad.

Once, Irv sat down on Amanda's desk with such force that her purse fell over and a package of Monistat, some tampons, and a pair of socks spilled out. Irv seemed to make a game of what he could shake loose during his morning rounds.

"So, where were you this morning?"

"I was sick. I left you a voicemail. Didn't you get it?"

"No, no, I didn't. Just like I didn't get the voicemail you supposedly left last Monday when you didn't come in at all. I think we have an attendance problem we need to address here, Amanda. Do you want to tell me what's going on?"

"You mean why I was sick?"

"No. I want to know why you're lying to me. If we can't resolve this, then I'm going to have to report the matter to Personnel."

In Irv's world, men were always leaders and women were always secretaries, ideally in tight pencil skirts and loosely buttoned blouses. Irv lived in a bygone era.

He casually leaned across the desk to put his hand on Amanda's shoulder and began to rub deeply. He leaned in so close that she could smell the onions from his breakfast. His touch was in that creepy place between parental figure and lover, neither of which Amanda wanted from Irv.

"There's no issue, sir." Amanda pulled away from his touch. "I was sick, and my message didn't get through. It won't happen again." *I did call him, didn't I?*

"Good. I like you Amanda, and when you're here and focused, you're very good at what you do. Let's try to keep it that way, shall we?" Irv winked as he walked away.

Amanda exhaled the ick.

On cue, Ruth's head appeared over the cubicle wall. She wore cutesy teddy bear sweatshirts, mom jeans (although she wasn't a mom), and white sneakers. Every. Day. Well, sometimes the sweatshirts had kittens or bunnies. She wore her hair parted down the middle with feathered bangs, probably the same hairstyle she had in her senior high school picture that Amanda assumed was taken sometime between 1985 and 1992.

Ruth was a *perma-temp*; she'd been brought in for a project last year and had, somehow, never left. There were a few others scattered around the company.

"Eek!" Ruth whispered over the cube wall. Others glanced over lazily then returned their attention to their work, bored with Ruth's drama.

"It's okay, Ruth."

"I don't know."

"No, really, Irv has been having a similar version of this conversation with me for a while now. Nothing's going to happen. He likes me too much."

"I don't know," Ruth repeated, shaking her head. "Irv seems really, really frustrated with you this time. Aren't you worried?"

"That's just his thing." Amanda motioned to the piles on her desk, dismissing Ruth with, "I have to get to work."

Ruth nodded and sat back down, but continued the conversation through the cube wall. "So, how was your weekend?"

Amanda slammed her head on the tallest stack of binders before her. "Fine, Ruth," she mumbled. "It was fine."

"So ... what did you do? I want to hear all about it. I need my Monday report!"

Amanda really needed to move desks. Maybe she could swap with Aaron, who sat next to Josh. She made a mental note to talk to HR and see if that was possible.

"Nothing much. I really need to get to work. I'll talk to you later, Ruth."

"Okay. Well then, remind me later to tell you about the chocolate fair I went to. It was at Navy Pier. Did you hear about it? It was only there last weekend, I think — or maybe the weekend before, too. I'm not sure. It was so yummy. I was there all afternoon Saturday with my friend, Mary, and her mom and sister. Well, not her Mom's sister, Mary's sister. Her name is Maria. Isn't that cute, Mary and Maria? Of course they're Catholic, but that's okay. So I got a belly ache from eating too much ... "

Amanda plugged in her earbuds and turned on her music. She'd gotten very good at tuning out Ruth's chatter.

The stacks of paperwork on her desk seemed to have multiplied over the weekend, leaving paperwork babies. There was never a sense of completion. The message light on her desk phone blinked at her. She parked her purse in her drawer, grabbed her Virginia is for Lovers coffee mug Roxie had given her as a gag gift, and went in search of some caffeine inspiration.

On her way to the breakroom, her mind wandered across the landscape of her office. *Is there anyone here capable of kick starting my 'real life'? A knight, perhaps, who could save me from Irv — from the tedious, mindless paperwork, from the drudgery of what I have to do in exchange for a paycheck? It certainly won't be Walter, the senior claims adjuster.*

She'd joked with Tina, the receptionist, that Walter got his title for his age more than his knowledge. Walter sat directly behind her and sniffed and huffed throughout the day, but that provided a strange comfort to her. On days he was out sick or on vacation, the silence left her feeling uneasy. Walter was sweet and non-offensive lanky and tall, but balding with no muscle and no hustle. He had been with Fine Line Insurance for many years, and would likely be there until the end; although, whether that would be the end of the company or the end of his career was hard to say. Amanda hoped she wasn't grey-haired and humpbacked by his side when that day arrived. She needed a bit of hustle herself.

Kirby sat on the other side of Walter. He was an absolute doll and funny as hell, but sadly, was the most unattractive man she'd ever met. He handled all the computer stuff; there wasn't a tech issue she'd had that he hadn't been able to fix. Kirby usually had pieces of a Snickers bar stuck in his teeth, and when any woman in the office had a bad case of PMS, he was the resource for an emergency dark chocolate fix. Amanda could tell Kirby had a thing for her and was hoping to woo her with his chocolate. There were a few times in the past year when she'd thought, *What the hell, maybe I should go for it.*

Timothy and Kayla sat beyond. They were the new hires doing data analytics stuff. They were young, attractive, and super sharp in their look and their intelligence. Amanda gave them nine months tops before they left for some uber-hip tech start-up.

Beyond the breakroom was the finance department and Josh. Even when she and Ryan were still together, she'd sometimes catch herself thinking of Josh and what it would be like to have a fling with him. Lately, Josh was her main motivation for getting dressed and out the door each day. Like all the unattainable boys she'd ever met wrapped up into one seductive package, Josh was full of angst and brooding ... and sex appeal ... and thin lips ... and sharp eyes ... and promised nothing but trouble. She knew she should give up and move on, but it was like he exuded an addictive pheromone she couldn't resist. His voice turned her on. His tall frame and long eyelashes excited her. No one should be allowed to be that hot and that unavailable.

For all that Amanda had tried — and try she did: mild flirting, dropped mentions of availability, occasional extension of offers to join her at shows — Josh had absolutely no interest in her.

Back at her cube, coffee in hand, Amanda powered on her computer. She'd set her homepage to a travel site, allowing her to search for deals first thing every morning. Today's highlights included a cruise to the Bahamas. *Nope, too confining. Besides, I'm prone to sea sickness.* There was a package deal to Acapulco, including free drinks for the entire stay. *But beaches are meant for lovers, and I'm lacking in that department at the moment. Besides, I burn so easily.* Another offered three night's hotel and round-trip airfare to Milan. *Too long a flight. Besides, what's in Milan?*

She left the site to check her frequent-flyer balance. She had enough for two free domestic tickets that had been in her account for more than a year. Still, she neurotically checked on them at least once a week, as if they'd disappear.

She was about to start some actual work when she got a text message from Roxie:

"Kristof = gay."

Amanda laughed out loud. Roxie never wanted to believe that the beautiful ones usually were — no matter how often Amanda reminded her.

The morning drifted by, and at 11:25 she took the elevator downstairs to grab her usual Cobb salad at the deli and avoid the 11:45 lunch rush. She brought her food back to her desk and ate it while texting Roxie and surfing clickbait articles about celebrity babies all grown up.

Late in the afternoon, Amanda timed a bathroom break to see if Josh was in the copy room. When she saw him there, she hustled back to her desk, gathered some papers to serve as her cover, and sauntered her way toward the copy machine.

Over the years of working at Fine Line, Amanda had created an imaginary secret identity for Josh as a hard-driving guitar player in an aggressive rock band. She could see the sweat glistening on his neck and soaked through his thin T-shirt as he wailed out *Crazy Train*. She was humming the notes that would accompany *"I'm going off the rails on a crazy train"* when Josh interrupted her.

"Is that Ozzy Osbourne?" The right side of his thin lips rose in a slight smile that made his right eye narrow.

"Maybe?" Amanda flushed.

"I didn't take you for a metalhead." He ran a hand through his long black hair, pushing it off his forehead, exposing the scar on his temple.

"I heard it on the radio this morning. Had it stuck in my head all day," Amanda lied. "So ... what did you do this weekend?" She leaned on the counter, right next to the copy machine, forcing Josh to brush her legs as he walked back and forth organizing his stacks of collated paper.

"This weekend?" Josh asked, raising an eyebrow and ignoring Amanda's body-blocking moves.

"Yeah."

"Well, let's see; last night I ordered pizza, watched *Chicago Fire* ... and that's about it. Jerked off and went to bed."

Amanda hiccupped a nervous laugh, and then blurted out, "I did the same."

"You jerked off?" Josh stopped to look directly at her, raising that damn sexy eyebrow of his again.

"No! I watched TV and ordered in."

"Yeah, that's what you do most nights, Mandy."

She melted when he called her Mandy.

His narrow, cool, blue-gray eyes focused on her. "Look, I have a stack of month's-end to finish before I can get out of here. I'd love to keep chatting about whether you do or don't masturbate ... but I have some work to do." His eyes flashed to the clock and Amanda followed them: 4:40 p.m.

"Oh crap! I have an appointment in twenty minutes!" She raced back to her cube, grabbed her purse, and ran out of the office to the elevator bank. It was only when she was out of the building and more than a block away that she realized she hadn't shut down her computer — or even logged off.

CHAPTER 5

Therese must have been in her sixties, but Amanda was amazed by the tautness of her skin, especially across her chest. It didn't show the usual ripples and sags of a woman with silver hair. *Maybe she has done some time-traveling herself.*

"Welcome."

"Thank you." Amanda's voice was muffled through the tangle of her scarf. She was grateful for the space heater in Therese's office after the six-block walk in the cold. Old buildings, like Therese's, were drafty this time of year.

"How are you today?" Therese extended her hand toward the couch, inviting Amanda to take a seat.

"I'm fine ... great ... sorry, a little flustered. I lost track of the time and had to rush to get here."

"Well, you're here now, and there's no hurry. You're my last appointment of the day. Calm down, center yourself, and we'll begin when you're ready."

"Can I use your bathroom?"

"Of course."

Amanda walked across Therese's office, remembering how the last time she was there she'd barely made it to the sink before throwing up. She stared at herself in the bathroom mirror, looking for Keira. She wasn't even sure she had to pee; she just wanted to be alone for a moment. It was a last out, of sorts, a chance to admit how crazy this was, and that maybe she should go home. Instead, she squeezed out a little pee, washed up, and pressed her wet hands against her face. She was already sweating.

"Any questions?" Therese asked as Amanda made her way back to the couch.

"Questions? ... You know, I'm not even sure what to ask. I'm overrun with questions."

Therese offered a knowing smile.

"I've been spending a lot of time on the Internet," Amanda explained while unzipping her new chocolate brown suede boots. The richness of their supple leather still gave her fingers a thrill each time she touched them.

"What have you discovered in your searching?"

"Well, Glastonbury sounds like a pretty intense place. Some think that the Holy Grail is buried there. Others say it's connected to King Arthur and some place called, I think it was called, Avon ... no, Avalon. I didn't learn anything more about Miles or Keira, though."

"I know a bit about Glastonbury," Therese offered. "It's very sacred to Christians and Pagans. Have you read *The Mists of Avalon*?"

Amanda shook her head.

"You may want to pick up a copy. It was written by Marion Zimmer Bradley. Her book *The Firebrand* is quite good, too. Much of the *Mists of Avalon* is set in Glastonbury. Not to mention that it's a wondrous, feminist story. I firmly believe that all women should read it at some point in their lives. I recommend it frequently, but I think it will have specific meaning for you, with its connection to Glastonbury."

"Maybe, but I'm not a big reader. I suffer from dyslexia and it's tough for me to get through a book. I'm more of a magazine reader."

"Well, this one might be just the right one to give a try, or maybe you can find it on audio."

Therese walked over to the mini fridge behind her desk and brought back two bottles of water. Her office glowed with a soft pink light that gave it a comforting familiarity. Amanda felt like she had been coming here her whole life.

"Are you ready to get started?"

Before nodding yes, Amanda hesitated, sank deeper into the couch, and rearranged the throw pillows to better support her neck.

"Remember, like we did last time, I'm going to relax you so you can move into a space where you can glide freely between the present and the past. Let's begin with our breath." Therese took a deep breath in and Amanda followed her lead, letting her eyes gently close as she fully exhaled.

"You're getting sleepy," Therese instructed in a soft, tone. "Your toes are relaxing, your ankles are relaxing, and your legs sink comfortably into the couch. You release the tension of your present life and let go, knowing that you are at one with the universe. You want nothing more than to relax and flow along with the cosmos. Your chest feels heavy and your arms sink beside you. Your head is firmly supported and your entire body is held in this sacred space. Your soul leaves your body and goes on its celestial walk. You see the physical space around you, as well as the other souls beside you. You are free now to explore the depths of your existence. Take us back to a time that you once lived. Amanda, what do you see?"

In a low, calm voice, Amanda began.

****

I'm holding tight to Miles, so as not to fall off the horse. We're galloping so fast through the fields; we must be near London by now. I'm grateful he's no longer wearing his armor and I don't have to continue to hug the cold steel. Miles is now clothed in soft, billowy beige pants that gather at the waist with a thick brown belt. His shirt is a mossy green that ripples around his tight torso and his feet are bound in leather boots that lace up, taking in his pants up to the knees. I would say he's handsome, as much as I wish not to think so.

I think to myself: should I try to break free? But where would I go? Am I in more danger being with him or wandering alone through the pastures of Britain?

We continue to ride and ride; my thighs are shaking, unused to gripping a horse in this manner. When it becomes unbearable, I gather the courage to ask him to stop and he obliges.

"I know you are full of questions," he says before I can speak. He helps me off the horse in the gentlest of ways. Such an odd man to have kidnapped me, and yet be so comforting.

"You needn't fear me, Keira. I am your protector," he says. His eyes bore deeply into mine, offering sincerity and importance and trust. "I am always your protector."

I pause. I'm not sure what to make of this. He's kidnapped me, yet I feel safe in his arms. How can this be? Am I under a spell?

"Then tell me who you are," I demand, "and where are you taking me? How do you know me?"

"My name is Miles, as you now know, and it's my charge to bring you home."

"Home!" I shout, "you just stole me from my home. Your army destroyed my home."

Miles is quiet and won't look at me. I pound against his chest, trying to dislodge answers from him. He grips my wrists, looks into my eyes, and starts to speak slowly. "I'm sorry that I can't share more — not yet — and some of it isn't mine to tell. I promise that soon you'll know everything. For now, please believe that you can trust me with all your heart."

Miles reaches into the side satchel on the horse and retrieves an apple and a piece of bread. "I'm sure you are hungry," he says. "Here take this; we can rest for a moment."

I nod a thank you, reach for the apple, and take a large bite. I'm starving and the sweet fruit wets my parched mouth.

"Water?" I ask.

Miles nods, opens another bag, and pulls out a bloated deerskin bladder. A charged sensation runs through my body as our hands touch.

I take the bag and mouth the words "Thank you."

The warm water soothes my body. Together we sit on the grass and eat in silence. I'm aware that he's watching me, studying me, as if he's memorizing every detail in order to recall it later. He tucks a lock of hair behind my ear and I flinch. As I pull away, I steal glances — his muscular calf, his boots nearly threadbare at the big toe. He smells like pinewood and musk. It stirs me deep inside.

"We have far to go before nightfall. It's time to press on," he says as he helps me back onto the horse. "Good boy, Maraza," he adds, lovingly slapping the horse before mounting himself. Once settled, he reaches for my arms; I shudder in a guilty delight as he gently pulls them around his torso, pressing them into his chest before we gallop away.

****

We have been traveling all day and are now much farther from Glastonbury and the Abbey than I've ever been. I'm deathly tired and oh so scared. It is all I can do to remain upright on the horse as it canters into a wooded grove that had looked like a mirage on the horizon only a few minutes earlier.

"What is this place?" I ask, a nervous catch in my voice.

"It's The Forest of Forgiveness. The Land of the Fairies," he answers.

Instinctively, I cross myself. Why isn't he crossing himself as well? The Father at the Abbey used to tell simply dreadful stories of fairy-folk and the hexes they place on Christians.

Yet, as soon as we enter, a strange peace overcomes me. My stomach stops clenching and I sit more upright. Taking in the landscape, I stare in naïve wonder. Somehow I sense a protective ring of energy. It permeates the forest. It's the same sense of calm that overcomes me in the herb garden, at the Abbey. In the garden, it often seems like the rest of the world doesn't exist, and there is only me and the plants.

The trees in this forest are not as densely spaced as they are in most wooded groves, creating an illusion that the forest had been planted rather than growing naturally. The perimeter is lifeless, but in the distance there are figures dancing and frolicking. I can't be certain if they are human, animal, or, God forbid, something entirely other.

Miles stops and dismounts from Maraza. "Let's take a rest," he says.

We are beside a small waterfall that trickles down a fern-covered hill. There is a clearing of grass beside the flowing water. How could such a luxurious patch of grass grow deep in the forest? There is clearly magic at work here.

Miles reaches for my hands and helps me down. When my feet touch the ground, he continues to hold me, gazing deeply into my eyes, enhancing my growing feeling of deep inner peace.

"The Christian world doesn't embrace the magic that exists inside the Forest of Forgiveness," he explains as he unlaces his boots, and steps into the stream. I follow his lead and am overcome with relief at the coolness of the water. When the ripples reach my ankle, my whole body is covered in refreshing chills.

"Look, here comes Maraza's horn," Miles says, directing my attention to his horse. I watch in awe as a single horn sprouts from the horse's head, then rub my eyes in disbelief and cross myself once again, thinking, this is definitely a dangerous place.

"Unicorns are not real. This horse has a magical hex upon it!" I exclaim.

"Ah, but Keira, they are only imaginary to those who do not know how to see."

"But that's not true at all," I protest.

"The unicorn threatens the Christian world because they don't understand magic. You have so much to learn, beautiful one."

Miles pushes my hair from my eyes. I know I should pull away, run away, but instead I find it impossible not to be drawn further to him. The way he refers to me as 'beautiful one' makes me feel feminine and important, in the same way that I often do when Robert, the cobbler's son from the market, gazes upon me and smiles. I want to find a way to keep Miles's eyes upon me too. There must truly be a spell on these woods. How else could I possibly feel such warmth and compassion for the man who, just hours earlier, kidnapped me?

"Christians, like the ones you lived with in the Abbey, believe a unicorn's power stems from evil rather than from the same God and truth that we believe." Miles is kind in his explanation, and I find myself wanting to believe what he's saying, even though it goes against all reason. "Perhaps Queen Isolde can explain it better."

"Queen Isolde? There's a queen here?" I ask.

"The most powerful queen in England lives in these woods," Miles tells me.

"But the queen is in London." Unless Queen Isolde is the queen of the fairy-folk, I think, and cross myself for continued protection.

Miles is patient with my lack of understanding. "Queen Isolde is a different kind of queen," he says. "The unicorn has become a pawn in the war between their world and ours."

"I don't know about any war," I answer, dismissing the wearisome part of the conversation and thinking: I'm so utterly tired of men and their endless wars. "Please tell me more about this queen. What is she like? Is she beautiful and intelligent? Do her people adore or fear her?"

"You shall meet her soon," Miles replies and smiles at me.

"But who am I to meet a queen?"

Miles takes my hand in his. The translucent blue of his eyes is like a portal into his soul as he says, "We must be on our way. She's expecting us."

"Us? I don't understand."

"You will in time, Keira."

As he helps me back onto his horse — now a unicorn — I want to press him further for answers, but I sense that it is futile. Soon, we are at full gallop, travelling deeper and deeper into the forest.

Some time has passed and it's late in the day. Maraza, this magical creature, has brought us to a cottage that's shaped like a miniature castle. It has spires and turrets and glitters in brilliant dust. So much of the stone walls are missing that I wonder what keeps it from collapsing. Covering the house are brilliant flowers that bloom from each crevice; they have an uncanny resemblance to those on my necklace, spectacularly huge in bright and vivid pinks and purples. It's like the house is aflame in flowers. And the smell! The aroma is dizzying: sweet and strong. When we reach the cottage, Miles dismounts and again helps me down from Maraza.

I turn to look at the house, and a dwarf-like woman pops out from the lower portion of the front door. I nearly fall backward in surprise as she comes bounding towards us with an odd sense of knowing. When she smiles, I am consumed by an uncanny feeling that this woman is not a stranger — yet she is no one I have ever met.

"Miles!" she cries, throwing her arms open for an embrace. "You succeeded!" She smiles at me. It seems I am the reason for the success.

"Did you have any doubt that I would?" Miles asks as they hold each other tight. Everything feels familiar, yet it leaves me flustered and scared. I know better than to trust strangers. I fear I've fallen into a trap. I think I should hate him for what his people did to the Abbey, yet the harder I try to hate, the harder it is to feel anything, but ... love. There's no doubt, they have put a spell on me. A lovely, lovely spell.

The small woman greets me saying, "Hello, my dear one. I've been waiting so very long to see you."

"What do you mean?" I ask, but my heart already anticipates the answer.

"You know the emptiness that fills you," she begins, "I am the piece to make you whole."

"No," I whisper as the puzzle pieces fall together. I'm feeling dizzy and confused. Can this be true?

"Yes," the woman answers. "I am your mother."

Everything turns hazy and just like in the herb garden, I can no longer focus. My knees give way and I drop to the forest floor.

****

"Thank you, Keira," Therese concluded, ending the session.

Amanda opened her eyes slowly, but to avoid the nausea she'd experienced the last time, she did not sit up. She felt for her grandmother's ring. Everything was still in place. *It happened again. Just like before. The same story! What does this all mean?* These questions and more raced through her mind. *This whole other life has been hidden inside me all this time. What else is hidden in there? How many lives have I lived?*

"It's like the story was put on pause, and was waiting there for me to continue it," Amanda said, sharing her bewilderment with Therese. "And I see everything so clearly. It's literally like I'm narrating a movie when I explain what I'm seeing."

"And I can see it too," Therese responded. "You regressed right to where the story left off last time. This is rare; I'll admit, I haven't come across it very often."

"How do I know if I had other past lives? Was this other life it? It was so long ago; surely I've lived between then and now, right?"

"We will discover that in time." Therese smiled broadly, "Maybe there are lessons you need to learn from this life, so your soul is directing you to a very specific story."

Amanda wondered *what can the lesson be from this long-ago life? But then there's the unicorn and that weird, magical forest. That can't be real, can it? It's probably my imagination, embellishing things.*

"My dear, you are so open. It's truly beautiful!" Therese clasped her hands together with childlike joy.

Amanda felt as if she were Therese's long-awaited prize, the way Keira was to the woman in the regression. She was feeling rather vulnerable and naïve as she hoped the prize wasn't merely a toy to be played with.

"This time things were clearer, Therese."

"How so?"

"Well ... there was an incredible amount of emotion and love pouring out of Miles." Amanda was surprised when a teardrop landed on her hand. "Do you believe in the concept of soul mates?" She slowly pushed herself into a seated position, as she became a little more alert with each passing moment.

"I do."

"Well, I think Miles is my soul mate. I've never felt that kind of love before, and I don't think Keira had either. And that feeling ... that feeling I had in his arms. It was Keira, but it was me. It was incredible." Amanda hugged herself tightly, trying to recapture the sensation. "That sounds so weird, doesn't it? I don't even know how to really articulate it."

"Not at all."

"Sometimes I think it's crazy and I'm going to spend my entire life searching for the perfect guy. I thought I had him, but then ... well, then I didn't. Maybe he really is out there. Maybe he's even searching for me too?" Amanda reached for the box of Kleenex.

"I'm sorry you were hurt; but often, yes, we say goodbye to invite in what we truly need." Therese leaned forward to touch Amanda's arm.

Amanda smiled a thank you in return. "What's really strange for me — I guess what I'm processing, is that I'm beginning to think it was all okay. Cassie and Ryan and the whole mess, maybe it was meant to be. Maybe there's someone else out there who's my ***true*** soul mate, and it wasn't Ryan. I certainly never felt anything like that, ever, with him. We were good. Comfortable. We weren't in love like that. Not even in the beginning. I've never felt like that with anyone."

"Perhaps you're right," Therese assured her.

Amanda chuckled and thought *how happy Roxie will be to hear this, so relentless she is about insisting I finally get over Ryan.*

"Isn't love why we're all here?" Therese proposed and Amanda smiled. She supposed it was true, but she'd never heard it said so succinctly before. "Our time has ended for today."

Amanda looked at the clock. It was more than an hour since she arrived. *How did the time go by so quickly?*

Pulling on her boots, she zipped them and wobbled a bit, trying to stand. Therese helped ease her to her feet. She was grateful she could take the "L" home and not have to get into a car and drive. *I wouldn't trust myself behind the wheel in this state,* she thought.

"Looking forward to our next session," Therese said as she pressed Amanda's hands inside hers, as if praying, and bowed goodbye. Amanda threw her arms around Therese in a hug and whispered a thank you in her ear before opening the door to leave.

CHAPTER 6

Amanda cursed her alarm clock for the hundredth time that morning. She frantically pressed the button for the elevator inside her office building. *Why is it always so slow when I'm running late?* Her phone read 8:55 a.m. *Damn middle-of-the-night power outage. I can't win even when I'm legitimately trying. I really, really need to find a new job. A new career. Basically, a new life.*

Amanda tore down the hallway to the hidden employee entrance, twisting her ankle in the process.

"Oh, Barnes, how I wait with baited-breath to see your smiling face each morning," Josh taunted, as she hobbled through the door. "And I see you had time to stop for Starbucks. You didn't even see if I wanted any."

"Good morning to you, too," Amanda shot back, throwing her empty cup into a nearby trashcan.

"Irv's been talking about you to the other admins."

Amanda shook her head at Josh. She hadn't even thought of him until she got to work. Normally, the notion of flirting with him was what got her motivated to get out the door each day. Lately, her mind was too preoccupied with Miles.

"Hope you make it to the end of the day without getting fired," Josh called after her, as she hobbled to her cube.

****

By 10 o'clock, Amanda had responded to a dozen e-mails and finished a two-page spreadsheet that was at least a week overdue. Once she hit Save, she declared it coffee time and left her desk for the breakroom. She had just filled up her mug when Ruth walked in behind her. Nine times out of ten, Ruth followed her when she took a break.

Ruth hummed *Me and My Shadow* while reaching for a packet of raspberry tea, her favorite, which Amanda knew because Ruth threw pathetic mock tantrums when it was out of stock, which it was from time to time. Amanda nodded toward Ruth, but her eye was on Josh, whose cube was within view.

Josh's back was to her and his head was tilted to the side, cradling the phone between his shoulder and ear. Amanda stared at the exposed skin on the side of his neck, distracted by the idea of placing small kisses up and down it, stopping at his ear for a little nibble. *Damn it, he's so hot. It isn't fair.*

"I'm really scared for you," Ruth said, tipping the contents of a packet of sweetener into her tea. "Sounds like one more late show and you might get fired."

Amanda looked back at Josh and they made eye contact. She motioned for him to come over, but he shrugged his shoulders as if to say "Sorry" and turned back to his computer. *How could I think of leaving and never seeing him again? It's one of the only sources of joy in my life. Besides, Irv would probably replace me with a younger, cuter girl, and Josh would start flirting with her. What if he asked her out instead? And what if she said yes? And what if they really hit it off and started dating? And then he'd propose at someplace like The Signature Room on top of the Hancock Building, at night, with the lights of the city painting the skyline. Then they'd get married at someplace amazing like the top floor of the Harold Washington Library. After the wedding they'd honeymoon in Hawaii .... Ugh.*

If anyone's going to flirt with Josh, it's going to be me. It's probably a stupid reason to stay at a job I don't like, but life is full of stupid reasons for doing just about everything.

"You're right. I should look," Amanda gave in to Ruth, hoping she would go back to her desk.

"I'm so worried. Irv really seems like he has it in for you. Are you heading back to the desk?" she asked, implying that their back-to-back cubes were one shared work environment. Amanda nodded, but didn't move. She was waiting for Josh.

****

Roxie texted about meeting for lunch. She was finally ready to show off her latest conquest, Andre, the restaurateur. Andre owned *Dolce Amado,* a trendy restaurant in River North. Amanda usually preferred a salad or sandwich to-go, but Roxie had been talking about the restaurant — and Andre — for weeks. Amanda knew she would have to give in and go eventually, and today seemed as good a day as any.

"Prime corner window seat. Nice." Amanda smiled. The table she was shown to was big enough to seat twelve. As she sat down in the very hip, very uncomfortable metal chair, she thought *they must want to turn tables fast.*

"You can get any seat in the house if you sleep with the owner," Roxie smiled.

"He's not the one with the souped-up El Camino who lives above the record store, is he?"

"No, no, that was Tony the Tiger. He and I are so over. This is Andre the ... " Roxie stopped talking when a slender, dark-haired man approached their table in a sleek Italian suit.

"Roxie," he moaned with a smile.

Amanda knew that it hadn't been many hours since Andre had been in Roxie's bed. There was a certain sigh men exuded around Roxie, and Andre was exuding it to the Nth degree.

"Andre, you adorable thing, you." She tugged on her red curls and batted her heavily mascaraed lashes. "Meet my cousin, Amanda. She's the one I was telling you about." Roxie stroked Andre's forearm as he leaned in so close to Amanda she could feel his breath on her neck. It made her cringe. She inched her chair in the opposite direction.

"Hellooo, Amanda," Andre was clearly sizing her up, like he might a nice cut of steak. The hair on the back of her neck stood on end. *How does Roxie like guys like this?*

"Hi," she mustered, putting her gaze to her menu. Roxie kicked Amanda in the shin, apologizing to Andre as she scooted her chair closer to where he stood. Amanda pictured her and Roxie eventually scooting fully around the table.

"Roxie did not adequately describe your beauty," Andre oozed, as he pulled out a chair and sat down next to Amanda. He let the words roll off his tongue in the most sensual of ways. For a moment, Amanda wondered what it would be like to have sex with someone so exotic. She'd never veered too far off the all- American frat boy track. Once in college, pre-Ryan, she'd had a night of dirty dancing with a Brazilian exchange student, but when he walked her back to her dorm, she kissed him goodbye and sent him on his way. Casual sex was always something for others. She marveled at Roxie's endless ability to get naked with someone new.

Amanda's eyes bore into Roxie.

"Have you two ordered? I recommend the salmon special today. It's phenomenal," Andre said, picking up on the tension, and switching to his upscale restaurant tone.

All Amanda wanted was a bottomless glass of Cabernet. After her little morning chats with Josh and Ruth, though, she knew alcohol on her breath would give Irv an excuse to get rid of her immediately. So far, it had been a battle of who could outmaneuver whom.

Roxie and Amanda agreed to have the salmon.

"Would you cooperate a little more for me?" Roxie snapped as soon as Andre was out of earshot. "He has front-row tickets to

Madonna!" The words exploded from her as though a balloon had been trapped in her trachea.

"So you're screwing him for concert tickets?"

"Hey, I will trade sex any day and any way for those concert tickets. They are *front-row* seats."

"It's not free, Roxie, if you have to pay with your body." Amanda thought back to how little the morality lesson worked. "You know, they have a word for that. Besides, I think it's me he wants to go to bed with now."

"Yeah, I noticed that too. Would a threesome work for you?" Roxie snickered. "I gotta get those tickets."

Amanda wouldn't dignify her comment with a response.

"Hey, did I ever tell you that Rick guy I dated once asked me if you'd be up for that?"

"Eww!"

"Right? Anyway, what's going on? You seem all pissed off today, so I'm assuming it's work. Again." Roxie switched gears, pouring olive oil onto her bread plate and soaking it up with a piece of nut-encrusted rustic bread.

"Josh and Ruth told me today that Irv's been bragging to everyone: One more late show and it's the wonderful world of unemployment for me."

"Maybe you should see that as a blessing. You hate your job and you're not even using your degree at all."

"You sound like Celia."

"Well, maybe your mom is right. What do I know? I gave up on college. Look, I want to have a nice lunch. I haven't seen you in weeks. Let's not get into this. It's always the same when we talk about your job. So what are your plans for Easter? Meeting up with the ever-eligible Max Harrington at the country club?" Roxie dragged another piece of bread through the olive oil on her bread plate. It looked good, but Amanda wasn't very hungry.

"Probably? You joining?"

"Hell no. I plan to be in bed that morning."

"With Andre?"

Roxie shrugged her shoulders, and tore off another piece of bread.

"I don't know how you do it."

"Have some bread. It's really good." Roxie pushed the basket closer to Amanda, but she shook her head. "More for me." Roxie ripped off another chunk. "I think that dating would really help you feel better. Andre has lots of friends."

"I'm fine."

"But you're not working through your shit; you're avoiding it. What's good in your life? You hate your job. Your apartment reminds you of Ryan. You're looking for answers in some past life for fuck's sake?"

"I'm working through my shit, Rox. Please don't play parent with me. I don't need it."

Amanda thought about her regression in the woods with Miles. *I DO have a man. A strong, handsome, loyal, swoon-worthy man. He's just, inconveniently, several hundred years in my past. I can't tell that to Roxie, though. And if I can't tell her, then I really am all alone.*

"But you're not working through anything," Roxie insisted as the salad course arrived. Amanda turned on the silent treatment and let her eyes drift toward the back of the restaurant and into the kitchen.

"I see the salad is to your liking," Andre said as he returned to the table a few minutes later.

"It's great, babe, thanks."

Roxie pulled Andre in for a kiss and stabbed her endive and watercress salad with a fork to feed him a bite. He pulled it off the fork with his teeth and drew the greens into his mouth.

Amanda lowered her head and picked at her plate.

CHAPTER 7

Amanda braved the Chicago winter to arrive on time for her third regression. She anxiously awaited the seasonal change that was imminent. It was now early March, and Daylight Saving Time and Easter were right around the corner. Soon the birds would be chirping, parks would be full of couples strolling, and life would sprout back from the Midwest deep freeze. Everyone anticipated the thaw.

"Welcome," Therese said, as Amanda uncoiled her scarf and let the stressful day fall from her shoulders. Irv had been exceptionally annoying — relentlessly in her face all day about some client deliverable he said wasn't typed up properly. Even Ruth agreed his expectations didn't match what he'd originally asked for in the meeting last week. Amanda was beginning to wonder if he was messing with her on purpose. She had enough of her own mistakes to own up to; she didn't need him baiting her with traps.

"Thank you." Amanda responded, settling into her usual spot on the couch, and allowing herself to fall into the comfort of Therese's warm, inviting office.

"How have you been since our last session?" Therese asked.

"Good, I guess." Amanda hesitated, "Maybe I've been a little anxious. Work has been stressful."

"Well, these sessions will remind you of the hiccup in time this job presents in your life."

Amanda smiled and nodded. This was quite a large hiccup.

"Is there anything you'd like to discuss before we begin?"

"No, I'm good."

"Okay. Sit back and relax," Therese instructed, pouring lavender oil into her scent diffuser. She lowered the lights in the room to a near twilight state, and Amanda's energy quieted. Therese took her seat in the high-backed bronze velvet chair, and as she began her script, it wasn't long before Amanda was once again transported to another time.

****

I'm in the Forest of Forgiveness, lying on the ground. Miles is beside me, caressing my forehead. We're outside the odd cottage that's covered in blossoms of pinks and purples and intoxicating smells surround the house. The same strange woman is here with us. My mother? But how?

I have a terrible headache. She hovers above me, placing a lavender-scented, warm, damp cloth on my forehead. Her efforts are maternal, but too late. I am nearly a woman myself, likely soon a mother too.

The cloth helps to diminish the ache. Lavender is my favorite herb. I cannot possibly be unhappy when I smell lavender. For a moment, I allow the scent to carry me away from this land of confusion and uncertainty and back to the old peace and safety of my herb garden at the Abbey.

"You fainted, dear child," she explains. "I'm sorry to have shared such a heavy weight with you after all you've been through today. We never expected your return to be so ... dramatic."

Miles motions to take me in his arms, cradling me like a baby. I accept and put an arm around his neck, anchoring myself against his warm body. The crystal blue of his eyes sparkles with a sweetness that's real. He truly cares for me, but in a way, I know it's more than that. He loves me. And that is what I can't understand or make sense of. Where is this love coming from? And why? Gripping me tight, he carries me into the cottage as the woman trails behind us.

"She often has guests of unusual sizes," Miles explains before gently setting me down on a fluffy red pillow. "She can't really accommodate furniture."

The woman returns with a tray, balancing a teapot, three teacups, a platter of scones, and a crystal jar of clotted cream. My mouth waters at the sight of the pastries. Staring, I try to discover any trace of connection, to see a family resemblance, to understand how this person could possibly be my mother. The unanswered questions add to my headache.

"Thank you," I say as I devour the scone. The food tempers my headache. I look at Miles and wonder what kind of spell he's placed on me. I'm utterly captivated in his presence. "How did you know who I was?" I ask him, the first of many questions.

"It was the necklace," he says, reaching forward and cupping the pendant in his palm. Again, he pierces me with his eyes and teases me with a smile.

"But how could you see my necklace from so far away?"

"I felt it." Miles holds a fist to his heart, and I explode in gooseflesh. I'm feeling something too.

The woman pulls out a necklace hidden under the layers of her dress. It's identical to mine with its deep grey, mirror-like brilliance. Her pendant is covered in pink and purple flowers, identical to the blooms that cover the cottage.

Gazing into it, a power overtakes me. I have only felt that from mine on the rarest of occasions.

She tells me, "When you invoked the protective goddess prayer, 'Good Mother Earth, Goddess over all. I pray you watch and protect me. Save me from the fall,' it told me you were there. It told me you had been spared."

Hearing this, I wonder, is this woman, my mother, a witch? If so, would that then make me a witch, too? Do they burn witches here, as they do in Glastonbury?

"If you are my mother, then who is my father? And why did you leave me at the Abbey? And how could you be my mother when you're such a tiny creature? And ... "

"So many questions, dear child, there are so many questions. I understand your thirst for knowledge, but the answers will come when you are ready for them. What you need to know now is that I am Queen Isolde, guardian of our people."

"You're Queen Isolde?!" I asked. She is not what I had imagined when Miles described a queen.

"Now is a dangerous time for us. The nature and the timing of your return have occurred as predicted, and we have great work to accomplish in a short amount of time."

"Great work?" I look to Miles, but his eyes are fixed on Queen Isolde.

"I cannot share more with you right now, child. I fear I have already told you too much. It is now time for rest."

"Oh, I'm not certain I can rest now, as tired as I am. And if you're a queen, that would make me a princess."

Queen Isolde nods. So then, I'm a princess. How can this be? What does this mean?

"Keira," Miles says, "I fear I must return, or the other knights will search for me."

"No! You can't leave me. What is happening? Are you simply to deliver me and then leave?"

"I must, but this is not goodbye." Miles's eyes convey a promise of return. He delicately touches my cheek with his hand. "Trust that."

Reluctantly, perhaps for us both, he guides me outside to say goodbye. He gets on his knees to hug Queen Isolde, and then stands up and pulls me towards him.

"We will see each other again soon, beautiful one," he whispers in my ear and kisses my temple before mounting Maraza and cantering away.

****

"Thank you, Keira," Therese was gentle as she brought Amanda out of her trance state.

Amanda opened her eyes slowly, respecting the wooziness that accompanied re-entry. She was finally getting the hang of transitioning between worlds. If she allowed herself stillness, the nausea quickly passed.

Reflecting for a moment on Keira's world, Amanda realized it was so much more alive, more vivid, and beautiful than her stale life of endless days: Coffee. Work. Take-out. Netflix. Repeat. *How has my soul progressed to this point in contemporary Chicago where I'm floundering at love and clueless to any sense of purpose? Shouldn't I know more by now? Shouldn't I have evolved further than this? What the hell is wrong with me?*

"How many lives do people usually have?"

"That's a great question, my dear. We are all old souls who've experienced a grand series of adventures. I once guided a man through ten different time periods, and likely, that was not his complete collection. Stories that remain in the same era, continuing on, the way yours have, are rare. We've stumbled onto something special here."

Amanda smiled as her mind reflected: *It's nice to feel special. Inspiring, actually. Maybe the stagnation in my life is my own fault. Can I use the regressions as motivation to change? But change toward what? A new corporate job will have the same issues. Just because I change the window dressing, a life of purpose won't magically result. Besides, it's not like I could conjure up Miles to suddenly appear in this life.*

"I'm delighted that we've started this journey," Therese said. "I'm so curious to see where the universe takes us. I truly enjoy your visits and look forward to each one."

"Thank you," Amanda took a drink of water before continuing, "and really, thank you for opening a world of possibility I never would have known had it not been for you. What kismet it was to have found your number that day in Starbucks. Truly, thank you."

Amanda gathered her things and left Therese's office, heading into the cool Chicago air, now slightly brighter at 5:00 p.m. than it had been a few weeks earlier.

CHAPTER 8

Easter came early, along with a bitter cold front full of dusty lake-effect snow. Amanda entered the bowels of her apartment building's garage to retrieve her rusty old Saab from its cozy parking space tucked in the farthest corner of the lowest level. Living in the city, she could usually get around by train, taxis, ride shares, or walking, but getting to the 'burbs was a whole other adventure. She slid her chilled pantyhose-exposed legs into the car and cranked up the heat. How she daydreamed of a newer model, with heated seats. Of course, that reality could probably happen if she had a better paying job. Maybe it was time to start looking.

The drive to the North Shore always took longer than she planned, so when she finally made it to the church, she had to search for a spot. After her third time around the lot full of shiny new Teslas, Mercedes, and BMWs, she gave up and parked across the street.

On her way into the building, she noted the parade of women entering First Hope Episcopalian Church. They looked a bit out of place, sporting wide-brimmed, flouncy, pastel Easter hats with full-length furs. She was supposed to meet Celia in the lobby, but watching the endless flow of people entering the church, she wasn't sure she'd be able to find her. *At least,* Amanda thought, *I'll stick out in my wool pea coat.*

As Amanda entered the church, she noticed a black streak along the outside of her cream-colored pump. *I must have brushed it along the edge of the car while getting out.* Kneeling, she tried to rub it off, but that only spread the stain and turned her fingers black. Cursing under her breath, she stood up and found herself face to face with the one and only Max Harrington, the most eligible bachelor of the North Shore.

"Hi, Amanda! Your mom said you'd be here." The cold made his plump, rosy, pockmarked cheeks even redder.

"Hi Max."

"What happened to your shoe?"

"Not sure. Would you excuse me? I need to find a restroom." Amanda displayed her dirty fingers like a hall pass and walked away without waiting for a reply.

"Oh, there's my angel!" Celia's exclamation caused everyone in the general vicinity to turn. Amanda gave a fake runway smile, and made her way to her mother who immediately asked, "Where's Roxie? I thought she was coming with you."

"You know Roxie."

"Oh that girl!" Celia dramatically sighed.

"Hey Mom, I need to use the restroom. I smudged my shoe on my way in. I'll meet you right back here."

"I had a nice man I wanted her to meet," Celia called after her.

"Maybe you should start a matchmaking business," Amanda countered.

Celia smirked, unamused by Amanda's sass. Amanda pointed to her shoes and made her way to the bathroom. When she came out a few minutes later, the entire lobby was empty and Celia was nowhere to be found. Amanda searched the aisles, but couldn't spot her amongst the sea of Easter hats. Was she wearing the lilac with ribbon and tulle or the pale green, broad-rimmed number with white polka dots? Amanda was so focused on her search that she didn't notice Max sidle up beside her.

"I saved a spot for you." He gestured to the empty seat beside him. The pastor had already begun, and it was either bench buddies with Max or standing in the back of the church.

"Um, thanks."

Now everyone would assume she was sitting with Max by choice. If it weren't for the blister already forming from her too-tight pumps, she probably would have chosen to stand.

Amanda studied the church. Her eyes walked the walls, taking in the massive cross with the bloody body of Jesus hanging in subdued agony. It was like an out-of-body experience; she felt very much a stranger in this church she'd been going to with Celia for years. She'd spent plenty of teenage hours staring at those walls, day-dreaming of boys. Amanda closed her eyes, trying to concentrate on what the pastor was saying, but instead, Queen Isolde's voice filled her head.

"Child, I am with you, even here. The love of the Goddess is strong and protects you. Picture the pendant on your necklace. See its beautiful blooms. Notice the ridges and shadows in the purple and pink blossoms. Meditate on the hematite below. It is this rock that gives life structure. The rock supports the beauty and allows it to exist and thrive. Be at peace with the beauty of the rock as much as with that of the flowers. Clasp the pendant in your palm. Do you see it, my child?"

"I do." Amanda spoke the words softly, like answering a prayer, her hand enclosed the pendant. The smooth cadence of Queen Isolde's voice moved over her, inviting peace and re-assurance.

"What did you say?" Max asked, startling her back to the present.

Amanda's eyes opened as she thought, i*t was only a vision — but it felt so real. I could hear Queen Isolde's voice. How did it find me here, outside of Therese's office?*

"Nothing," Amanda whispered to Max. She shook her head indicating he should forget it.

"Are you sure you're okay?" He placed a palm on her leg as if it would be welcome.

"I'm fine!" she snapped, shooing his hand away. The people in the pew in front of them turned and glared. Max inched away.

Amanda finally spotted Celia at the far end of the same side of the church, several rows ahead. Her mother beamed when she saw Amanda sitting next to Max, and while Amanda quickly shook her head no in defense, Celia had turned around before she could see her protest.

Returning to her reverie, Amanda only caught an occasional word about Christ and redemption. Queen Isolde had dropped a veiled version of the forest around her and instead of hearing the pastor's words, she saw Maraza's horn emerging from his head. She tried to recreate the sensation of being in Queen Isolde's presence. When the pastor raised his voice, bellowing words about salvation, she saw the abbey burning and that poor lamb being killed. Tears welled in her eyes. Silently, she opened her clutch for a tissue.

The noise level in the room shook Amanda out of her haze. The priest must have concluded the mass because people were exiting the pews.

"Good service, huh?" Max remarked, offering Amanda his handkerchief.

How very chivalrous. Why can't the cute ones have such polished manners? she thought as she replied: "Oh, uh, yeah," and nodded in thanks as she turned away to blow her nose and wipe the tears from the corner of her eyes.

"Well, I mean, you look like it really spoke to you." Max placed his doughy hand on her shoulder and gently rubbed her back. Amanda immediately noticed the difference between Max's limp palm and Miles's confident grasp when holding her. Max was very touchy; Miles was too; but with Miles, she ached for it.

"It was a good one," she smiled, politely pulling away from Max. "I'm going to catch up with my mom now. Nice to see you."

"I'll see you at the club!"

Yes, he probably will. Unfortunately. His hopefulness is depressing, she thought as she spotted Celia in the crowded vestibule of the church and moved quickly in her direction..

"Isn't that Max just the nicest thing?" Celia cooed, linking arms with her daughter.

"Yes, very ... nice." *If only nice were enough to light a fire.*

"Oh, Amanda," Celia's friend Charlotte chimed in, echoing Celia. "He's quite a catch."

"So, lunch is at the North Shore Country Club. Do you remember how to get there, sweetie?" Celia overused words like 'sweetie' and 'honey' in front of other people to give them the impression of a kind of super-loving, adoration-filled relationship, rather than their weird co-dependent arrangement.

"I know where the club is. I'll see you there," Amanda assured her.

The snow had slowed to a faint dusting, but the clouds still hung low and dark. Amanda got in her car and cranked up Lizzo on Kiss FM. Listening to the music, she imagined she was a dirty Catholic school girl who wore a thong and push-up bra under her uniform and smoked behind the gym during her lunch break. *The kind of girl Josh probably dated in high school. The kind of girl I'd like to be next time around.*

****

North Shore Country Club was in desperate need of an extreme club makeover. Maybe it could be a reality TV show: *Makeovers of Ultra-Pretentious but Thoroughly Outdated Country Clubs.* The walls were a combo of bleached wood wainscoting with an upper half papered in faded pastel blue and green brushstrokes with bursts of yellow. The ceiling fans sported shiny gold hardware and accents of wicker lattice. The décor was top-of-the-line, circa 1989. Amanda entered the dining room and spotted Celia at the only table of all women.

"Well, there's our angel!" Charlotte sang out.

Amanda wondered, *Is it my cream dress and blonde hair that defines me as an angel or my compliant nature?*

"Did you get lost? You should have made it here fifteen minutes ago," Celia asked.

"I hit some construction," Amanda lied. She'd dawdled in her car for a long while, debating about driving home instead of going to the club.

"Where? I didn't see any construction. You must have come the wrong way." Celia's parental tone, a hangover from her teens, still triggered Amanda. Those hadn't been their best years together.

Celia signaled the waiter saying, "Our table is finally all here. You may start the first course."

"What are we having?" Amanda asked, taking the empty seat.

"Today, I believe it's the Cornish hen. Is that right, Louise?"

"I do believe you're right," Louise replied to Celia.

"So, how is our sweetie, Max?" Charlotte practically sang, angling into Amanda's personal space. "I saw you sitting with him at church. Your mom is so excited to see the two of you together."

"It was the only available seat." Amanda knew her snarky tone was probably over the top, but every ounce of her didn't want to be stuck at this table having Easter lunch. She was jealous of Roxie's way of always getting out of these things — and with no consequence.

"He's such an eligible bachelor, if you know what I mean," Charlotte completely ignored Amanda's tone, nudging her in the side, nearly bruising her rib in the process.

"Amanda, your mom said you're considering getting breast-enhancement surgery!" Louise exclaimed from across the table.

"Mom!"

"What, darling?"

"I brought Dr. Ricter's business card," Louise continued. "I simply adore what he did for me." Louise drew her hands around her breasts like the *Price Is Right* girl might show off a designer living room set saying, 'You too can own this, if the price is right!' "I told him you'd be calling."

"I'm not getting a boob job!" she said emphatically.

"Oh, darling." *The excessive endearments again.* "I do think it would go a long way towards helping to win over Max — or any other boy for that matter. You ***are*** a little on the underdeveloped side." At that, everyone at the table stared at Amanda's chest.

"That's it!" Amanda felt a surge of Keira's energy bolt through her. An awareness, maybe for the first time, of the role she was playing in her own story. "I'm leaving!" She pushed her chair away from the table with a force that sent it flying behind her, a bit more forcefully than she'd intended.

"What are you doing? Sit down!" Celia scolded. "You're making a scene!"

"No. I'm leaving." Amanda righted the chair and pushed it in to the table, then she reached down again to pick up her purse.

"The first course hasn't even been served," Celia protested.

"I'm not hungry," Amanda fired back, and then pivoted to the table, "If you all have so much good relationship advice, how come you're all single?"

As the women's jaws dropped, Amanda held her head high, buttoned her plain pea coat, and walked out of the club.

CHAPTER 9

The handwritten note, thumbtacked to Therese's office door read, "Stepped out for a minute. Come in and make yourself at home. Be back shortly." Amanda was surprised that Therese would leave her office unlocked. *Doesn't she worry about someone stealing stuff?* she wondered and paused before entering, feeling a bit like an intruder herself. Stepping inside cautiously, she kicked off her boots. *The weather's finally beginning to change,* she thought. *Soon, I'll treat myself to a pedicure, dig out my sandals, and welcome the sun.*

As Amanda took her seat on the couch, her phone buzzed with a new voicemail. *Odd, I didn't even hear it ring.*

It was Celia. Amanda knew her mom was still bent out of shape over her scene at the country club, but she didn't want to deal with a conversation with her before a regression; the last thing she needed was that negative energy. *Whatever she's calling about will have to wait.* Amanda powered off her phone and buried it in her purse.

She had always wanted to inspect the Zen fountain in Therese's office so she walked over to it and let her fingers play in the trickling water. Feeling like a naughty child, she kept looking over her shoulder as if Therese would scold her if she found her there.

She let her eyes wander around the room. Hidden atop the bookcase, she noticed a crystal wand. With an amethyst handle, the wand was one solid crystal about the length of Amanda's forearm and half as wide. She carefully retrieved it from the shelf, studying the colored gems placed around the section where the amethyst connected with the crystal. It was heavier than she expected, and an odd power surged through her body, entering through her heart and spidering up and down her. She heard Miles and then Queen Isolde calling to her, inviting her to join them. Amanda put the wand back and retreated to the couch. *Has the crystal opened a path for direct entry? Maybe I can do this on my own, like I did in church last weekend. I don't want to though — it's scary if I'm not tethered to the security of Therese. What if I get lost? What if I can't come back?*

A book called *The Crystal Bible* called to Amanda from the coffee table. She laughed, imagining that her burgeoning psychic powers had mysteriously lifted the book and dropped it on the table for her to find. She intended to look up amethyst - her favorite gem and the one on the wand – but when she saw *hematite* in the table of contents, she knew that was the section she needed to read. The sensation of Keira's hematite necklace pulsed through the book. Amanda settled deeper into the comfort of the familiar couch, turned to page forty, and read the description:

"Hematite is particularly effective at grounding and protecting. It harmonizes mind, body, and spirit. Used during out-of-body journeying, it protects the soul and guides it back to the body."

Protects the soul and grounds the body. Of all the stones that could appear in my regressions, how have I chosen this one? Amanda paused to let the weight of what she had read sink in. *It's as if I'm playing with black magic, opening up some other dimension, and my window of time to get out is quickly shrinking. Or maybe it's already closed. I should leave. Enough with these coincidences and talking voices and obsessions with imaginary people.* She stood up from the couch to leave just as Therese walked in.

"Sorry to keep you waiting, Keira," Therese sang, floating into the room and placing her overstuffed Whole Foods canvas bag on her desk. Out tumbled mushrooms, radishes, and tomatoes. "I've had a very, very busy week and I never made it to the store. I'm supposed to take a salad to a dinner party tonight, and oh, well I guess you don't need to hear the whole story." Therese gathered the rolling vegetables and stuffed them back into the bag.

"Did you call me Keira?" Amanda sat down on the couch. She wasn't going anywhere.

"Did I? You know, it's such a pretty name, I may have. Does that bother you?"

"No, in fact, it felt ... natural."

"Well, it was your name at one time. Perhaps it's your soul name."

"Soul name? I've never heard of such a thing." Suddenly feeling chilly, she pulled Therese's ruby chenille throw from the back of the couch and wrapped it around her legs. She ran her hands up and down across the soft fabric, her palms pressing reassuringly into her legs.

"It's sort of the name that trumps all others," Therese explained. "Perhaps it was the name you had in the life you were happiest in, or maybe it has the perfect pitch to blend with the universe. Or, perhaps it's the name you had in the life that was your starting point as a soul."

"My starting point as a soul?" *Here we are again, back into trippy quantum weirdness.*

"Souls have to be created like everything else. Perhaps Keira was your first incarnation, and thus in a way, your most pleasant: devoid of legacy negativity, and full of hope. Hope is the first and most true of all sensations. As we continue to incarnate, we build up karma, not all of which is positive."

"This is some heavy stuff, Therese."

"Yes, I suppose it is if you're hearing it for the first time."

"So, if what you're saying is true, then we spend the rest of eternity trying to fix the mistakes we made from our first life. That's too depressing. You don't honestly believe that, do you?"

"Life is all about re-learning what we already know. When we are in our spirit form, the truths return. It's our job to integrate that spirit knowledge into the physical plane of existence. Not many of us get there. It's quite the celestial challenge."

"Whoa. Did you learn this from all these books you have?"

"That, and my own intuition. You can learn a lot if you stop thinking and quiet your mind."

Is this woman a witch, a psychic, or a loon? Or, all of the above? What is it about her presence that makes me take everything she says as truth?

"So many of the answers lay inside us, but we are often too frightened to trust what we know. I think that's what Queen Isolde is trying to teach Keira." Therese glanced at her watch, ready to move on. "I want to be sensitive to our time together; shall we begin?"

Amanda nodded.

"All right then, lie down on the couch, get comfortable, and take a few deep breaths."

****

I'm in Glastonbury, on the High Street. I see Robert, the cobbler's son. He always makes me happy. Even though he's dressed in tatters and his face is smudged with grease, he looks regal, like he might really be a prince in hiding and pretending to be a merchant. I want to take him to the Chalice Well and wash away the dirt.

His hair is a thick, sandy blonde that juts into his eyes, and he constantly brushes it away with his forearm. He hasn't reached his growth spurt yet, so he only comes up to my shoulder. His father, the cobbler, is quite tall, so it's likely Robert will be too — and probably soon. For now, though, he has to strain his neck to make eye contact with me, even though we're the same age. I feel a giddy excitement each time I see him.

"Good day, Keira!" Robert says as he leaves his mending to join me. His cheeks glow in my presence.

"Good day to you as well, Robert!" I reply.

"Here to purchase wool?" he asks and nods towards my basket.

"I'm a kitchen maid," I remind him. "The weavers purchase the wool."

"Ah, yes, of course I remember," he says.

Robert's father is busy repairing a sole. He doesn't notice Robert is dawdling.

It's my job to gather food needed to prepare the meals. I tend the garden and also have to pick herbs for the Abbey doctor. I know all the herbs. Lavender is my favorite. I always have a sprig of it under my pillow. I've found flowers and plants in the fields that are edible and can heal you. I don't share these with the monks, though, or they'll call me a witch. Witches get burned in the town square.

"Have you ever seen a witch?" I ask Robert.

"No! Have you?" Robert shifts his voice to a whisper, as though the mere mention of a witch will bring one out from the shadows. We move away from the stall and start walking along the High Street. When we reach the baker's stand, Robert purchases a piece of sugared bread for us to share. We find a grassy spot to sit and enjoy the treat.

"I've seen them burned," I continue, "they make a dreadful cry as the fire climbs up their gowns and eats at their faces. I refuse to go anymore. Sometimes they make me do extra chores because I won't go. I don't care. I'll do the work of all the cooks so that I never have to go. It's not because they're witches. It's simply a dreadful sight to see."

"I don't ever want to see a witch burned," Robert says, ripping apart the bread with his teeth. He hands half to me and I savor the sensation of the sugar melting on my tongue. The Abbey doesn't keep sugar.

"Are you apprenticing to become a cook?" he asks me.

"Girls don't become cooks!" I answer. "I'll always be a kitchen maid. It's fine, though. I love the garden. I couldn't ever bear to leave it. I can become a nun if I want to, but that's a dreadful, boring life. You have to pray at least six times a day!"

"Do kitchen maids get married?" he asks.

"Why?" I answer. "Do you want to marry me?"

Robert flushes red again.

"Well, some can get married," I continue, "but it's very, very rare, and not usually pleasant. The priest decides which maids get to leave, and they can only go when a replacement maid has been fully trained. Then, there are those like Helena. She was forced to marry the butcher because her belly swelled with child. Helena told me that a monk actually caused the swelling, and although she cried and cried, the priest told her she was lucky that she was going to have a husband and be allowed to keep her child."

"That doesn't seem right," Robert mutters.

"I've never seen Helena since. The butcher keeps her locked in that house," I say, pointing to the house at the end of the row. "He's afraid she's going to run away."

"What about her child?" Robert asks.

"It died right after it was born."

"Oh that's terrible! But if it died, then why does she still have to live with him?" he asks.

"Because he bought her," I explain.

Robert's glow fades as he adds, "A lot of things that happen to girls don't seem right."

Robert is so naïve to the ways of our world. He'll be a good man to his wife someday. Maybe that wife will be me. "So Robert, have you heard any more scuttle about what we spoke of last time?" I ask him.

Robert's eyes lower and turn away, "Yes. Yes, I fear I have."

"Well, tell me!"

"The crier said that Cleeve has already burned, and the knights are on their way to Wells. The Abbott in Winchester was hung, drawn, and quartered, all right there in Winchester's town square. They want to destroy everything Catholic. He said it's only a matter of time before they will arrive in Glastonbury."

I absorb all that Robert says, and then realizing the time, know I'm running late. The kitchen will expect me to be back with the day's purchases. "I'm sorry Robert, I must go." Yet instead of running towards the Abbey, I run toward the Glastonbury Tor, and I keep running and running until I reach the top.

****

"What are you doing?" Amanda demanded as she came awake, to the sound of a miniature gong. It was not more than six inches wide and still vibrating.

"I was having some difficulty bringing you out of the regression. I use this for emergencies."

"Emergencies?"

"Oh, *emergency* isn't really the right word. I've seen this before. A client who regressed to colonial times in the Caribbean was a slave on a boat just landing from Africa. After his arduous sea voyage, he was faced with severe and brutal beatings. In the regression, he kept running away. I tried to bring him back, but he simply vanished into the mangroves. So, I began to tap on my Nepalese gong, merely a decorative piece in my office at that time. It eventually drew him out of the regression. So now I bring it out when I feel like things may be heading out of my control. When you ran for the Tor, I was worried you might keep running and I wouldn't be able to find you."

Out of her range of control? Amanda thought. *Everything needs to be in Therese's control or the regressions shouldn't happen.*

"Have you ever not been able to bring someone back?" Amanda asked nervously, not really wanting to know. "Someone couldn't end up lost in time, could they?"

"No, my child, everyone comes back ... eventually. Don't be alarmed. Clients simply have their own way and time, and sometimes they need help."

There was something about Therese's tone that sounded exactly like Glinda the Good Witch in *The Wizard of Oz.* It brought a wave of relief to Amanda's jangled nerves.

"Amanda, tell me why you think you went back to an earlier time in Keira's life?" Therese asked, placing the gong back on the wall.

"I don't know."

"Well, how did it make you feel?" Therese's voice shifted into a parental tone.

"Different." Amanda rubbed her hands and curled into herself like a nervous child. She couldn't understand why, but she didn't want to talk about Robert.

"Is this difficult for you?"

"What do you mean?" Amanda tightened her body. She ached for Robert in a way that was different from her feelings for Miles. She missed him deeply and didn't want to trivialize him with an analytical discussion.

"Well, your mannerisms and tone are reminiscent of Keira. It appears that you're not able to analyze this, perhaps, because you're still being Keira."

"No, I'm not. I'm awake. I'm Amanda!" *What's happening to me? Why do I sound like a petulant child, even to myself?*

"Calm down." Therese lowered her voice and continued in a reassuring tone. "Do you know the significance of the cobbler's son?"

"I miss him!" Amanda burst into tears.

"Do you remember mentioning the name 'Robert' in your first session?"

Amanda stared at Therese.

"You ran into him in the market, coming back from the Tor during your first regression. You were warning him about the King's army, and he wanted to say something to you. Do you recall?"

"Yes. Yes! That was Robert!" Amanda felt like she had finally re-entered her body. The fuzziness was gone. The intensity of the sensation she felt for Robert, though, lingered on.

"Is Robert someone that Keira sees again in her life?" Therese asked.

"Robert was very special to Keira." Amanda felt like she was in a trance state as she went on to describe her feelings. "She loved him dearly."

"Would you like to end here, my dear? This has been an intense session, and it seems like you need to absorb this on your own."

Amanda nodded. She wanted desperately to get out of there. She needed to be alone.

Therese pulled Amanda to her feet and brought her close in a hug. While she held her in her arms, she whispered in her ear, "Be well, child. This will all make sense someday. It's therapeutic to let it out. Crying is one of the best ways to heal."

CHAPTER 10

It was another fine day at Fine Line. Amanda pulled up her bookmarked travel site to check out the day's deals. *A week in Disney World with the family, airfare included. Uh, what family? My parents never took me to either Disney World or Disneyland.*

What child is perpetually denied a trip to the Magic Kingdom? she wondered. *My parents never saw the world though kids' eyes. More often than not, I ended up in the kids' club of a resort while they toured a winery or got drunk by the pool. Dad probably takes his new kids to Disney. They probably have annual passes.*

The rest of the travel deals were filled with vacation packages to Mexico and the Caribbean. Nothing looked especially inspiring, different, or new. She opened her Mileage Plus account. *I have enough miles to fly free to Santa Barbara. Maybe it's time to see Dad.* She pictured Carli, his Barbie doll wife, in their pretentious model-home kitchen. *No, that wouldn't be a vacation.* She closed out of the website and her phone beeped. Roxie had texted: 'Lunch today? Deli? Noon?'

"Sure," Amanda replied.

At 10:00 a.m., she made her way to the break room for her mid-morning coffee refill. She was delighted to see Josh there, reading a newspaper.

"Morning," Amanda said, reaching for a Styrofoam coffee cup, too lazy to go back to her desk and get her mug. *I've lobbied the facilities guy, on multiple occasions, to exchange the Styrofoam for a more environmentally friendly product, but nothing changes. I wonder if I'm the only person in the office who even cares.*

"Well, aren't we looking rather dapper today?" Josh said, lifting his eyes from his paper only long enough to acknowledge that Amanda had entered the room.

"Mr. Hitchens is here," Amanda said as she poured her coffee.

"That's a nice color on you."

She looked down at the new pale violet suit her mother had bought her. Celia insisted she get it, using that stupid line *Look the part, be the part.* Amanda was quite certain a suit wasn't going to magically convert her into a career-climbing exec, but if it brought out a compliment from Josh, then it wasn't a total loss. And she did feel good, wearing a suit. It was like she was playing dress up. Adulting.

"Thanks," she muttered, shaking powdered creamer into her coffee.

"What's Mr. Hitchens in for today?" Josh asked. His mug had a picture of a group of people stacking their hands on top of one another in a 'Go-Team-Go' maneuver. The caption read ***Meetings: None of us is as dumb as all of us.***

"I think there's more paperwork to sign for the Monument deal closing."

"Gotcha." Before leaving the break room, he walked over and placed a hand on Amanda's shoulder. "Good look, Mandy. You should dress up more often."

Amanda studied his gait, thinking, *the way he walks, the way he carries himself, could he be? No. For sure, no. Yet he showed up in my vision at church on Easter. I can't start thinking that every guy I'm attracted to is Miles. That would be insane.*

Amanda eyed the donuts, but nothing looked appealing. *I'm overthinking all this soul stuff,* she told herself, *Josh is a dude who isn't even into me. Well, maybe slightly, but honestly, probably not at all.*

****

Amanda had her coat on, her purse on her shoulder, and her computer in standby mode when Irv came looking for her right before noon.

"Oh, there you are!" He walked over with Mr. Hitchens. "Amanda, you remember Mr. Hitchens."

"Hello." Amanda extended her hand and nodded her head.

"Good day to you." He took Amanda's hand and kissed it.

Although she hated when he did that, he was such a sweet old man, she felt bad pulling away. *Mr. Hitchens has more money than he knows what to do with. He goes around buying private museums and galleries, following his passion for the finer things in life. Fine Line insures them all. Billionaires are good for business. His soft blue eyes, long silver hair, and distinguished frame carry an air of wealth. I wonder what he looked like when he was in his prime,* Amanda mused.

"Can you pull those reports I requested yesterday?" Irv asked.

Caught off-guard, Amanda didn't respond. *I delivered them, didn't I? I hope there's nothing else I've forgotten.*

Irv continued. "We need it in time for our review meeting after lunch. We're on our way out. Set them on my desk when you get them printed."

"Or perhaps Amanda would like to join us for lunch?" Mr. Hitchens winked at her.

"I have an appointment. Thank you though," she replied. *Thank goodness I have an out.*

As they walked away, she checked the time. She had ten minutes. Opening Excel took forever to load, but she finally found the documents Irv wanted. *I never completed a final column of data entry; so that's why I didn't give him the reports. If I do it now, I'll really be late for lunch. I'll have to come back early to finish.* She turned off her monitor and left.

When she arrived at the deli, Roxie was in line talking on her phone. "You look extra nice today. What's up?" Roxie asked. She was wearing a yellow boa. Yellow was her uninspired color. It signified that everything was steady and easy: not great, not bad. You didn't want to see Roxie in green.

"Big client in town," Amanda explained. "In fact, I'll need to cut out early. I have a bunch of reports to print before they get back."

"I'm so glad I don't work in an office."

Amanda thought about the annoying hipsters who were regulars at Roxie's eyewear store, and she was glad she didn't work there.

"So, how was Easter at the club?"

"I don't know. I walked out before the meal was served."

"You did what?!"

"It was a table full of my mom's friends and they were ... they were annoying me, so I left."

"You just walked out?" Roxie exclaimed, and then it was their turn in line. They each ordered turkey sandwiches and a San Pellegrino. "Where do you want to sit?" Roxie asked, scanning the busy restaurant.

Amanda pointed to a table, near the window.

"So, seriously, you just left?" Roxie continued their conversation as she wiped away the crumbs of the last customer's lunch before they sat down.

"Pretty much."

"I bet your mom freaked! What were they doing?"

"They were all talking to me about how I needed to get a boob job to attract Max," Amanda laughed, which made Roxie laugh. And they couldn't stop.

"So how's Andre?" Amanda asked after they finally caught their breath.

"Over."

"Already?"

"Yeah."

"Did you make it to the Madonna concert?"

"No. That lame-ass took someone else. Can you believe it? He called me the next day to see if I wanted to get together and I told him to shove his skinny dick where the sun don't shine."

Amanda cringed at Roxie's volume. She was sure that others could hear.

"Sorry." It amazed Amanda how emotionally cold Roxie remained after every breakup. Amanda was always devastated by breakups, even when she was the one doing the breaking.

"Apart from missing Madonna, it's for the best. It freed me up to pursue Wendell."

"Wendell? What kind of name is that?" She picked up her pickle and placed it on Roxie's plate. "Is he a concert pianist?" Amanda joked.

"Actually, he is!"

Amanda nearly spat out her water.

"He's a master pianist. You know what they say about the fingers of piano players ... " Roxie wiggled her fingers and a wicked grin spread across her face.

Amanda rolled her eyes.

Roxie took too big a bite out of her turkey sandwich, and said around it, "You need to get laid." Roxie chewed with her mouth open.

Amanda looked away. "And how do you propose I do that, since my fiancée slept with my best friend?"

"Oh, dear lord! When the hell are you going to move on? Ryan's not the only man in the city who can take you to bed."

"Sorry, I'm distracted today." Amanda watched the flow of customers entering the deli. *It seems the more time I spend in the regressions, the less I have to contribute to conversations with Roxie.*

Who's sleeping with who and the minutiae of working feel dumb and unimportant. Isn't there a grand scheme of things bigger than all of this? She wondered. *But for now, here I sit in the deli with my cousin.* "So, where did you find the master pianist?"

"He came into my store one day last week. Needed glasses, the usual. I hooked him up with a sharp pair of wire rims. God, he's hot. And he has the sexist, deepest voice, with a little bit of a gravel pitch to it ... " Roxie continued to talk, but Amanda had checked out; she was lost in the Forest of Forgiveness, in the sensation of Miles' fingertips on her skin.

"Earth to Mandy!"

"Oh, jeez," Amanda looked at her watch. "I need to run. I have to get those reports done before Irv gets back."

"It's only quarter 'til. You can stay a few more minutes," Roxie insisted, but then her phone rang.

Amanda slipped an arm into her coat sleeve.

"I'm at lunch. I can't talk. Yes. We're still on. Tonight."

Amanda put the other arm in its sleeve.

Roxie patted the table, signaling Amanda to stay. "Yes. Okay, I have to run. Bye!" Roxie sang the last word. "Wendell must have heard us," she smiled.

Amanda put her purse on her shoulder.

"Aren't you hungry?" Roxie asked, pointing to her empty plate. Amanda's was still full of food.

"I had a big breakfast," Amanda lied.

"You haven't touched your sandwich at all."

"I have a protein bar at the office."

"I'm not letting you go until you tell me what the hell is wrong. I can tell something's up. It's me, Roxie; I know you better than you know yourself. And don't tell me it's Ryan. This is different. Josh maybe? Did you find out he has a girlfriend?"

"It's not Josh."

"Then what is it?"

"I'm not sure I can explain." Amanda began to get up from the booth again but Roxie grabbed her arm.

"Try me."

"I don't know ... "

"Bullshit. Tell me what the hell is going on."

Amanda desperately wanted to talk to someone, but she didn't trust Roxie. Not with this. It was too big. "I've taken a total of five baths since Friday night. This morning, I was late for work again. I ... I feel like ... "

"You feel like a loser," Roxie finished her thought for her.

"No! I feel like I'm losing my grip on my life. All I think about is what happens in the regression sessions with Therese."

"So stop going. It's all stupid anyway."

Amanda couldn't have pegged Roxie's reaction better. The thought of never seeing Miles, the Forest of Forgiveness, or Queen Isolde was so unbearable that it brought tears to her eyes. The more she regressed, the less she wanted to come back. It wasn't ***that*** life she wanted to give up.

"I have to go."

"Nice having lunch with you," Roxie said in the snide tone that she used when she lost a battle.

"Don't be a bitch."

"Why don't you let me know when you decide to be Amanda again? Maybe then we can have a nice meal together."

But that's exactly it; I don't ever want to be Amanda again, she thought as she rushed away.

CHAPTER 11

I'm collecting St. John's Wort when suddenly my special necklace begins to feel warm and glow. It's the necklace the monks found on me when I was left at the gates of the Abbey. I gaze into the dark spaces between the flowers and a voice calls to me: "Look into the stone, find the betwixt and between the flowers and the rock. Enter the stone and enter your house." Someone comes into focus. She's in a field of wildflowers; her smile covers her face, her eyes beam with joy. She's waving to me, sending her happiness like a lightning bolt into my chest where it hugs my heart. I desperately want to climb into the stone. Suddenly, I feel a hand on my shoulder and I jump at the surprise of it. When I look up, I see Father Francis eying me sternly. He towers over me like a giant, blocking the sun and causing a chill to spread across my shoulders.

"You must never gaze into the stone, my child," he warns.

But why, I wonder. The stone feels so good and warming in my hand, it warms hotter in my palm as his voice grows cooler down my neck.

"The stone is an evil place that captures little children."

I shudder. How can that be so?

"Others have tried entering their stones, but the place between the rock and the flower will seize you like quicksand and swallow you alive."

The image shakes me. I try to rip the necklace from my neck but it won't break. It's as if the leather string is metal.

"I should take it from you," he says. But he doesn't.

Does the necklace ... scare him? I wonder.

He takes a step back, now appearing fearful of even me, as if I had any power over him. As if I have any power at all.

"If others know that you have it, you will turn into a witch and be burned in the town square," he cautions.

I've been forced to watch the witch burnings more times than I care to, and nothing terrifies me more. The sound of enthusiastic chants from the crowd while a woman is enveloped in flames haunts me.

The necklace clasp falls open and the necklace tumbles into my hand. I scratch at the earth, burying the pendant and chain, yet after the Father walks away, I find myself digging at the loose soil. The stone calls again, its faint music emanating from the soil. The necklace glows as I retrieve it. I look around and confirm that I am alone. A fog has rolled in. I return my gaze to the stone, which continues to hum a soothing melody. I tuck the necklace safely into a pocket of my dress and run away.

****

Amanda's alarm startled her awake. *It was all a dream. I wasn't in the herb garden. Did I regress on my own, without Therese? Is that even possible? Something is off. I don't feel well. Like, really I don't feel well.* It took her a moment to realize how chilled she was, although her skin felt warm to the touch. She extracted herself from the tangle of covers, and ambled the short distance to her bathroom. Pulling a thermometer from the medicine cabinet, she headed back to bed and a minute later saw it register 101.8 degrees. *There's nothing left to do but go back to sleep and hope I can continue the dream. I'll have to miss my weekly session with Therese,* she thought with regret.

Now, I'll have to spend another week in misery: waiting, wondering, insistently curious about what Keira is up to in England. Every moment I spend in Chicago, in this life now, is beginning to feel like torture.

I know I should feel more concerned about work, but Irv can't fire me for legitimately being sick. I'll get a doctor's note this time, if I can somehow make it to the doctor. Can I phone in to a doctor's office for a note? I sure hope so because there's no way in hell I'm leaving my apartment anytime soon.

****

Later that morning, Amanda powered on her phone, having turned it off in an effort to sleep. There was a voicemail from Celia.

"Hi, hon, it's me, Mom. Listen, I tried you at the office, but I guess you didn't leave an out-of-office message because I had to call the front desk to find out that you called in sick. I hope you're not really sick because I need you to go to the botanical gardens with me tomorrow. There's a showing of this season's orchids and Louisa called to say that she can't make it. She cancelled on me last time. In fact, I think it was the same damn show, the orchids, now that I think of it. What is wrong with that woman? Doesn't she ... well ... okay, now, if you really are sick, I hope you don't have that thing that's going around. If you had taken Airborne like I told you, you wouldn't be in this mess. So wherever you are, call me."

Amanda pressed Delete. *I'll deal with Celia later, when I feel a little better.* She looked at the clock. It was 11 a.m. *I'm due to be at Therese's office at 4 p.m. I really need to call and cancel, but I don't want to.*

"Welcome, Therese Montclair is here to assist you. Let me be your soul guide as you manage the murky waters of your past and find your true being," Therese's voicemail message began. "I'm sorry I cannot personally take your call. I must be guiding another soul. Please leave your name and the best way to reach you, and I will come find you upon my return to the here and now. Bless you."

"Hi, Therese, it's Amanda. I'm sorry, but I have to cancel my appointment. I'm home in bed with a fever. Will you let me know if you have any availability and can get me in before our usual time next week? Thanks." Amanda hung up and started crying.

She dragged herself to the bathroom and drew a eucalyptus-infused bath, hoping the warm water would comfort her. She thought she'd remembered something about how you weren't supposed to take a bath with a fever, but she didn't care. After sprinkling in her favorite lavender salts and lighting the candles around the perimeter of the tub, she slid into the water and let the steam envelop her. Amanda's vision clouded and her head felt heavy. The scented oils overtook her senses. The water was so hot it gave her goose bumps, in the way temperatures can sometimes reverse outcomes. She closed her eyes and thought of Miles, Keira, and her life that was, literally, once upon a time.

****

I'm kneeling in the garden behind Queen Isolde's house. The sun falls lower on the horizon. The day is starting its close. I long for the warmth of summer. As the season turns to winter, the forest is getting more chilled every day. I shear lavender, tying stems into bundles with a muted gold ribbon. The scent makes me teary-eyed at the memory of my garden in the Abbey. Had anyone survived? The monks, the kitchen workers, the Abbot? What's become of my people, of my home? And Robert. The guilt of leaving Robert and the others behind overwhelms me. He'll never know what happened to me, nor will I know about him.

Miles has been gone for weeks, although thoughts of him fill much of my waking moments. He unlocked an aching passion that I never knew I possessed. My body physically yearns for him; my arms long to hold his chest and broad shoulders.

As the sun dips below the horizon, I move inside, placing the lavender in an earthenware vase. Queen Isolde's lessons about how the stories from the Bible, the stories of Mary and Jesus and others, might not even be true, fill my head, and confuse me. The Bible has always been a safe place, and I love its stories. Queen Isolde contends that Adam and Eve are merely allegorical characters. In Glastonbury, Queen Isolde would be declared a witch and burned at the stake. A headache creeps across my scalp, so I make a cup of tea. While I am waiting for the water to warm, I explore Queen Isolde's kitchen.

This is the first time I've been alone in the house. I discover odd measuring containers and large pots that remind me of drawings of witches' cauldrons. I investigate the clear jars full of pickling vegetables, imagining this is what a witch's kitchen would look like. When I open one of the jars, the smell overpowers me: it is the smell of vinegar and something else.

****

Amanda erupted from the water, gasping for breath. All of the candles washed out with a hiss, as a surge of water crested the ridge of the tub, flooding the floor. She jumped from the tub, frantically mopping up the water, but the towels quickly became heavy and drenched. There was still so much water. In desperation, she threw down her robe to soak up more, but then stood there naked and wet, realizing that all the towels she owned — and now her robe — were on the floor, sopping wet.

Amanda let out a primal scream and collapsed to the wet floor. Pulling her body into a tight ball, she half-cried, half-laughed as she shivered on the cold tile floor.

CHAPTER 12

Amanda had every intention of making it in to work on time. She was at Starbucks at 7:45 a.m., a record-early arrival. As she approached her office building, she spotted a gargoyle perched high on a rafter above the entryway. His mad mouth, crazed eyes, and striking claws felt like they were warning her not to enter. She looked away for a moment, wondering if it was simply an apparition, but when she looked back, the gargoyle was still there. Heeding it's warning, she quickly hurried past, continuing down Monroe Street.

After having been cooped up in her apartment for the entire weekend, the cool morning air felt heavenly. Amanda wandered east on Monroe until she reached the Art Institute; from there, she continued along Michigan Avenue, and past Grant Park. Overcome with a memory of dancing barefoot in the thick grass at Lollapalloza, years before, she frolicked a little, the music running through her as if it were still playing, trapped in the trees, waiting for her after all these years.

Amanda veered toward the lake. Buckingham Fountain wasn't yet open for the season. She took a moment to watch the city workers performing their annual maintenance. Spring was on its way.

Strolling past the Chicago Yacht Club, she walked along the embankment of Lake Michigan loving the view of the skyline — especially how the Shedd Aquarium capped the southern edge of the looping shoreline. The lake and everything around it had a placid feel. Amanda sat down on the pavement to feel closer to the water. The light played on the swells.

It was a nice day by April standards. The temperature was in the low 60s, and the sun provided just enough warmth to maintain a subtle glow around Amanda. She dropped a hand down the easement and let her fingers glide along the top of the water. The sensation of her fingers touching the lake caused her to shake from head to toe. Unexpectedly, strangely, the smell of salt water filled her senses. She closed her eyes to take it in. Removing a black pump and trouser sock, she rolled up her linen pant leg, and slid a toe into the icy water. As she did, she heard Miles call.

"Come in, Keira. It's not too cold. I want to float with you on the waves of the sea. Join me."

She could see his head and his toes. The waves supported his floating body. He beamed at her, beckoning her with his lips, mouthing 'Keira, Keira, Keira.'

The embankment was now a cliff with a rocky shore. Entranced by the waves tumbling, she longed for the painful sharpness of the water. The more she let her foot sink in, the stronger Miles' voice became. The chill made her whole body writhe in an odd form of pleasure. She pushed forward, allowing her entire foot to slip into the water.

"You're almost there, my love," Miles encouraged. His voice was so much clearer now.

She reached for her other shoe, removed it and her sock, and slid both her feet into the water.

"Yes! Come join me. The water feels so wonderful. Let's drift away, my love."

Someone reached down and grabbed Amanda's shoulder. "Are you okay?" he asked.

Amanda's eyes moved up the man's Spandex-covered legs to his torso and finally to his face. Wraparound black sunglasses hid his eyes. Amanda averted her gaze, searching the lake for Miles.

"Do you need help?" He still had not removed his hand from her shoulder.

Miles was gone.

"You made him leave! Go away! You made him leave!"

"Ma'am, there's no one there."

"He was there! He was there. You made him leave!" Amanda pushed the man away. He shook his sunglassed head and jogged off. Overcome with hiccupping tears, Amanda forced her foot back into the water.

Miles, I'm still here. Where are you? Please come back! Miles, don't leave me. Look, I can go in more, Amanda begged, letting the frigid water surround her leg. She was shaking from the intensity of the cold, but he was gone. Her repeated cries weren't bringing him back. She pulled her leg out of the water, pulled both knees to her chest, and hugged herself as she rocked back and forth.

****

Amanda snuck in the back door of her office and made a beeline for the bathroom. Her mascara had smudged into raccoon eyes. With a wet paper towel, she wiped away the black rings. Still, her eyes were puffy and bloodshot. Without eye makeup, her blonde lashes simply vanished into her face. *Well, at least everyone will believe that I've been sick,* she thought before leaving the bathroom.

"You're back! Oh, yay!" Ruth squealed. "You look horrible though, hon."

"I've been sick," Amanda answered as she powered on her computer. *Ruth needs to get out of my personal space and go back to her side of the cube wall.*

"Let me feel your forehead. Oh my gosh, Mandy, you're burning up! I'll go get Irv." Ruth ran to Irv's office, nearly knocking Josh over on her way.

"You look like shit." Josh leaned on Amanda's cube wall.

"You really know how to make a girl feel special."

"Are you still sick or something?"

"I'm fine, Josh. Leave me alone."

Josh moved out of the way to allow Irv to enter her cube.

"Wow, Amanda, you don't look good." Irv pressed the back of his hand to her forehead, like a parent would for a child. Everyone in the nearby vicinity stared. "I was going to ask you for a doctor's note, but it's clear you're ill. Get your things and go home."

"But I have a doctor's note," Amanda protested, digging through her oversized purse. *It was so much effort to get it.* "I don't want to get fired. I have to work."

"Amanda, you're sick. Go home. We can live without you. Ruth's already finished the Hobart report you never got to. She can help me out with anything you would have done."

"But, but, wait," Amanda gestured as she searched for the note in her mess of a purse. "Found it!" she pulled out the tattered slip of paper.

Irv glanced at it disapprovingly. "Did your mother write this?" He wrinkled his nose at the frayed piece of paper before tossing it in the trash. "I really don't care, Amanda. We'll see you here tomorrow, but only if you're well."

Amanda was relieved. She really didn't want to be there. She never wanted to be there. She collected her things and shut down her computer. Ruth popped around the cube wall and essentially vomited a Walgreen's load of cold medicine, pain relievers, and Lord knew what else directly into Amanda's open purse.

"You keep all of this on you at work?" Amanda asked amazed.

"You never know when you're going to need things. I keep my eyes out for sales. Take this first." Ruth held up a florescent orange bottle and opened the top. It reeked like baby puke. "It will make you feel so much better."

"You're mad, woman. You know that, don't you?"

“Oh hush.” Ruth waved her off. “Here, you need a scarf.” Ruth pulled a bright pink scarf that had been dangling from her back pocket and wound it around Amanda’s neck. “Someone as sick as you shouldn’t be walking around without being properly bundled.”

Amanda’s pumpkin-colored poet blouse was now accented by a fluorescent pink fluffy scarf. She left the building, feeling equally relieved to be headed home and worried about not having a job to return to.

****

Amanda picked up her mail before taking the elevator to her apartment. Flipping through the junk, she noticed a brochure for condominiums in Florida. The pictures were so warm and inviting, full of lush green lawns, translucent blue pools, and white shimmering buildings. She flipped it over and saw it was addressed to someone else. *Looks like fate put it in my box. Is it a sign? I could walk straight into that ad and start a new life. I’d sink my toes into the soft, warm Florida sand. I’d frolic in the surf with someone who looked like Josh or Miles. I’d hug palm trees and live on Cuban food.*

I could do Florida, she said to herself, tossing all the other junk mail into the lobby mailroom trash can.

CHAPTER 13

It had been a week since her vivid dream and regression in the bathtub. She was anxious to tell Therese about her experiences. Tapping into Keira's world had become a daily routine. Besides the bathtub, the dream, and Lake Michigan, she'd had a very strong vision that very morning. While staring out the apartment window, she'd seen blooming flowers crawl up the building. They were the same flowers that surrounded Queen Isolde's cottage. Opening the window had infused her entire living room with the smell of the sweet blossoms. But a moment later, the flowers were gone, leaving her dizzy and disoriented. The city was back to smelling dirty and smoggy, thick with the humidity of early spring.

Amanda had planned to walk to Therese's office, but a thunderstorm had rolled in from the lake. It was raining as if the sky hadn't cried for months. She opted to hop in a cab. Even so, by the time she made it from the cab to Therese's building, she was drenched.

"Look how wet you are! Oh dear, let me find you a towel."

"Thank you," Amanda called, not budging from the entryway mat, embarrassed by the pool of water under her feet. A moment later, Therese emerged from the bathroom with a soft, lilac-hued bath towel.

"I keep these on hand, just in case."

"Thank you." Amanda toweled herself dry. "Oh Therese, you're not going to believe this, but I regressed on my own! I'm so thrilled. I've been waiting to see you all week!"

"Did you? Well, that doesn't really surprise me. This experience has been quite intense for you, maybe a little too real.

My dear, you *should* be able to access Keira's world on your own. We all have the power. Most of us simply haven't unlocked the door."

"I guess." Amanda tried to imagine others in her life – Roxie or her Mom or heck, even Irv – regressing back to a past life. She just couldn't see it.

"You must be careful, though. You're not trained to handle these complexities. You don't want to let yourself do this too often. Here in my office, I maintain a controlled environment. I know how to take you in safely, and more importantly, how to bring you back. When you're on your own, there's no one grounding you. You need someone to make sure you make it back."

Amanda dismissed the warning. That was for others, less capable. Not her.

Therese sighed, "Also, it can have ... well, it can have an addictive quality, I suppose. Getting used to the past can make it harder to exist in the present."

"I'm so excited! There was a strong lavender scent in Keira's world, too. I need to get some lavender perfume."

"Amanda, have you been losing weight?"

"I was sick recently. Remember?"

Therese paused.

"I'm ready," Amanda said. "I'm ready to begin. Isn't that what you asked? I'm fine. Please, I'm fine. Can we just get started?" Amanda hadn't come to be analyzed.

Therese nodded her head and they began.

****

We're in the Forest of Forgiveness, the Queen and I sit in a clearing, deep within a grove. It must be mid-day, as the sun streams through the pine needles, warming our wool picnic blanket. We're sharing a brothy soup of root vegetables and meat, filled with spices I've never tasted before, rich and dense and full of complexities. Queen Isolde passes the clay tureen with tenderness and compassion. We each enjoy a pewter mug of mead, the bottle sits half empty between us on the table.

I blow on my soup, having already burned the roof of my mouth. I ask what I should call her.

"Queen Isolde, Priestess of the Lighted Ones is my name and title, but if you wish, you may call me Mother. I would like that very much. But that is your decision."

"Mother ... " The word feels warm and comforting rolling off my tongue. "I will call you Mother."

Every day, I'm feeling more at ease with this new life. The Abbey drifts into the recesses of my mind.

"I have more questions, if I may ... Mother."

Queen Isolde nods approval.

"Why did you leave me at the Abbey? How could a mother who shows so much warmth and devotion leave a newborn infant there in the middle of nowhere?"

"Oh, my darling, leaving you was the hardest decision I ever had to make." Isolde seems to drift off to that place people go when they're reliving a difficult time yet want to shield those around them from the truth, then she speaks again, "If I felt I had a choice, I would have chosen anything else."

I take Queen Isolde's hand in mine, hoping to absorb some of the memory's pain.

"As I've mentioned a little to you, it was such a time of danger for us. We were being hunted and I needed to flee to preserve our people, to try to hold onto our way of life. At the time, Christians were not our enemy. I knew they would take good care of you."

Queen Isolde's eyes fill with tears. "If only I could wipe away the memories and re-write the story." She takes a long deep cleansing breath to calm herself before continuing. "We were under siege by an enemy, a warrior people from the north. They thought they could attain our natural healing ways by conquering us. I suppose it's the age-old lesson of trying to take with force that which was given through peace and love. Not only would the monks feed and protect you, but they would train you in a skill and educate you. It was more than I could offer, hiding in caves, living in hollows, trying to lay low until we could re-build in a more secure space. We are forced to live with the choices we make. We took a chance on bringing you here, now. You were brought up as a Catholic, my child."

The hesitation is thick in her voice. "It didn't seem realistic to bring you back. It still may not be," she adds

I want to believe that I can adjust to this new world. "Can you tell me who my father is? Will I get a chance to meet him?"

Queen Isolde shakes her head.

"You cannot tell me if I will meet him?" I ask in confusion. "Or you cannot tell me who he is?" Having asked the question, I am unsure that I want to learn the answer.

Queen Isolde takes a deep breath before she replies, "Each spring we have rites. The Christians have turned this into May Day. These events are held at night and everyone is costumed in elaborate masks. We all mate in the dark, then part ways. I conceived you during the rites. I'm sorry, child," Queen Isolde pauses to take a drink of mead. "I don't know who your father is."

Words I learned at the Abbey come to mind: harlot, wench. The impropriety conflicts with Queen Isolde's regal role. I stare into my bowl, lost in confusion.

"I'm sorry, Queen Isolde continues, our land lies under the nose of the Christian empire, yet it is far apart and hidden. We are creatures who only exist in fairy tales in your world. Understand, though, that we are real. We have rituals. We thrive. Everything fights to survive, child. Even as it is being devoured, it fights. You know this."

****

Tears streamed down Amanda's face as she tried to speak to Therese, but the words caught in her throat. "I miss her. I know that feeling of motherly love. I remember it, but it's been so long since I've felt it. That's not what my mom and I have." Amanda reached for a tissue. "It hurts to leave Keira's world. I want to go back under."

"I know you do," Therese whispered, leaning across the couch and tenderly rubbing Amanda's arm. "I know." She paused, "Tell me about the relationship you have with your mother."

Amanda coughed a sarcastic laugh. "It's not great. My mother can be superficial and fake. Sometimes I feel I'm merely a pawn in her world. She won the lottery and has all this money she doesn't need. She uses it to make up for the emptiness inside her; at least, that's what a shrink told me a few years back." Amanda felt slightly embarrassed. *Maybe I shouldn't have said shrink to Therese; perhaps that was offensive? She didn't seem to notice.*

"Are your parents still married?"

"Their divorce happened soon after the lottery. The money helped them part ways and still have comfortable lives. He's as bad as she is. They were a perfect pair. There wasn't a lot of *active* parenting happening in my childhood."

"I see. How old were you when they divorced?"

"Nine."

Therese's head nodded, knowingly. She sipped her water and continued, "What was life with your mother like before the divorce ... and the money?"

"She was unhappy. I remember her drinking a lot. She still drinks a lot but the depression isn't as intense. I think my dad was the root of most of the unhappiness."

"You're an only child?"

"Yes. My mom wasn't sure she wanted kids and then one day, oops! I don't think either of them were super happy to be parents."

"I'm so sorry." Therese's empathy felt healing in a magical, Queen Isolde kind of way.

Amanda moved awkwardly on the couch, bearing the heavy words of the conversation. Once again she wondered what to make of her story, especially now with the added complexity of her deeper story — her story over time and through the ages.

"Shall we call it a day?" Therese sighed and Amanda noticed the time. It was ten minutes past when they normally stopped.

"The time really flies when I'm in here with you."

Therese smiled.

"Thank you, Therese. Thank you for everything."

CHAPTER 14

It was Celia's birthday, and since Amanda had outgrown childhood birthday celebrations, they'd typically celebrated their birthdays together, seeing as they were merely 10 days apart in May. But the last thing Amanda wanted now was to celebrate her birthday, to be reminded of that horrible night, one year before, when her world had fallen apart.

Amanda had requested no birthday attention, and suggested instead that they celebrate on Celia's actual birthday rather than a date between both. That way, all the focus could be placed on her mom. Thus, Amanda found herself staring into her closet, feeling overwhelmed by the simple act of choosing an outfit. Thoughts of that night wouldn't stop racing through her head. She saw the outfit she'd worn, still hanging in her closet. Without hesitation, Amanda took it off the hanger and stuffed it in the kitchen trash.

The last time she'd gone to the theater ended up being her final date with Ryan, a week before Roxie's party. He'd caught her snoring through the second half of *Les Miserables* and was pissy all through dinner. She couldn't help it. It was a miserably boring play. *He and Cassie probably go to the theater all the time.*

Amanda finally willed herself into putting on the red cocktail dress, the one with the plunging back. She had lost a lot of weight over the last few months and felt disgusted at her image in the mirror. Her shoulder blades stuck out like angel wings ready to carry her away. But that image brought a smile to her face. *If only they could really take me away.* She put on the simple black dress next. The flirty bottom skirting with matching three-quarter-length sleeves made her feel like a child. She tossed it into a bag for Goodwill that she'd been slowly filling for months. She settled on her black, flowing gypsy pants and a wraparound cinnamon-colored blouse with a low-cut neckline. When she put on the gold chain necklace that Celia had bought her last Christmas, she felt complete.

The next step was to practice the bomb she was planning to drop at dinner. *There's no reason I have to stay in Chicago. I detest the cold. Starting over will be healthy. Surely Celia will understand. Roxie's growing more and more tiresome, and Mom, well, what was to miss with her? Maybe moving will help me stop obsessing over Josh too. Therese has freed me, and now that I'm able to regress on my own, perhaps I don't need her anymore. Everyone should agree that a fresh start will be healthy.*

"Mom, I've decided to move," she said into the mirror. *No, too direct.*

"Mom, have you ever been to Florida? I hear it's lovely down there. I was thinking of going for a long visit." *Softer, but misleading.*

"Don't you get sick of these cold, dreary winters? I think I have that seasonal reaction to weather, where you get depressed in the winter. Wouldn't it be nice to live someplace where it's warm all the time?"

Amanda's phone rang. It was Celia. No more time to practice. She would have to see what happened at the restaurant. Phone in hand, she walked to her front window and could see the Rolls double-parked outside her building. *Why does Celia always have to be so early?*

"I know you're here, but I haven't put on my makeup. I just got dressed, and my hair is still wet," Amanda said before her mom could even say hello.

"We're going to be late. Why aren't you ready?"

"You're early. Besides, yelling at me on the phone isn't going to make me get ready any faster. Either park and come up, or wait. I'll be down as soon as I can."

"I'll come up, or I'll never get you out of there."

Amanda watched as Celia turned on the hazards, left the car double-parked, and started walking toward the building's entrance.

"You're just going to park there and leave your hazards on?" Amanda was still staring out the window. Of course Celia would do such a thing.

"Hush up and buzz me in."

"But Mom ... "

A minute later, Amanda opened the door for Celia. Wearing a floor-length fur, Celia looked like a living legend, a remembrance of the past. Amanda's mascara wand jutted out between her fingers like a fancy cigarette, as she held the door open.

"Why are you wearing a fur coat in May?"

"It's chilly tonight." Celia pushed Amanda out of the way. Amanda shook her head and walked back to the bathroom.

"I'll be out as soon as I can."

"Is this my birthday present?" Celia must have spotted the gift on the coffee table.

"Yes, Miss Nosey."

"It's so small. But it's in a Tiffany's box. You know how I love that place!"

Amanda put on her lipstick, rushing the application. If Celia was alone in her living room, Lord knew what she would find.

****

Amanda kept nodding off during the performance. She wanted to like opera. The sets were gorgeous. The blonde's voice sent shivers through her, but ultimately it was dull. She knew that it wasn't opera that Celia enjoyed, but rather being seen at the opera or, at the very least, being able to reference having attended. One of these years, she had to talk her mom into doing something different.

Two hours and a cat nap later, the opera was over. Amanda had made reservations at *Ambria*, a quaint French restaurant that her mother adored, and one that had become a special place to celebrate life's events. She and Ryan had discussed having their rehearsal dinner there, and Amanda was momentarily lost, imagining his family and hers sitting together, toasting the happy couple. How fragile life plans were.

In the private corner they usually requested, Celia and Amanda discussed the performance, as though they actually knew what they were talking about. When that conversation ran out of steam, Celia turned to picking apart Amanda, the usual topic. Fortunately, Amanda had already had two very large glasses of Chardonnay, and was loosened up enough to hold her own.

"You're losing a lot of weight."

"How kind of you to notice, Mom." Amanda took another big gulp. *Perhaps it's time to order a third glass?*

"I know you've been sick a lot lately. You need to start eating more. You barely picked at your meal tonight."

"I'm fine. Dieting for summer, you know."

"Well, stop it. You look like a refugee."

"Open your present now." She reached for the Tiffany's box and handed it to Celia as the wait staff cleared the entrée plates to prepare for dessert and coffee.

Celia pulled at the bow and lifted the top of the box. Inside was a small dragonfly brooch, sparkling in blues and greens.

"It's nice," Celia said in a tone that people use when doing a poor job of faking sincerity.

Amanda quickly offered her prepared response. "I thought it would be good for spring."

"Yes, it will be." Celia put it back in the box.

"The gift receipt is taped inside the lid."

"Oh, no, I like it, honey," Celia insisted politely and buried the present in her purse. The colors would have nicely accented Celia's outfit. The simple act of rejection was the perfect impetus for the conversation shift that needed to come next. Amanda didn't stall any longer.

"So, Mom, I have something to talk to you about," she said as the French press coffee arrived.

"You're not pregnant, are you?"

"No! Jeez." *This is going to be harder than I thought.*

"Well, you never know these days."

Amanda decided not to explain that you had to be having sex in order to get pregnant. That would probably only invite another horrible chat about Max.

"Are you sick?" Celia had that look of deep concern that people have when they're bracing for something big, like cancer. "Is that why you've lost so much weight?"

"No!" She added, quickly, "Actually, I'm thinking about moving away."

Celia stared.

"Did you hear me?" She knew Celia heard.

"So now you're going to leave me like your father? Are you going to California to be with him?"

"That's not what this is about."

"Oh, then enlighten me." Celia violently pressed on the plunger of the coffee pot.

"I've never lived anywhere but Chicago. My job sucks. My life sucks. Maybe it's time for a change?"

"What about me? It's okay to leave your mother behind?"

Ugh! Why does Celia have to be so ... Celia?! "I'll move somewhere warm and you can come visit me. I'm thinking Florida."

"Don't be ridiculous. That's where old people go. You're not going to find Mr. Right there. I might, but you won't."

"There are a lot of places for young people in Florida, like Miami."

"I can't believe you're bringing this up now, on my birthday, for heaven's sake! You waited all through dinner until my cake arrived." At that moment, the entire wait staff showed up at their table. The waiter held a small plate with a slice of chocolate cake and one lone, brightly burning candle.

The staff sang "Happy Birthday." Amanda sang along with them, grateful to have the pressure lifted for a minute.

"Happy birthday, Mom." She toasted with her coffee cup as the singing waiters left the table. "Here's to another year."

Celia glared at Amanda and blew out her candle.

CHAPTER 15

Amanda finally got around to calling Roxie on Sunday afternoon. She braced herself before making the call. She knew it wasn't going to go well. It had been more than two weeks since they last spoke. Six rings, then voicemail. "Hey girl, it's Mandy. Sorry I've been out of it lately. I had a nasty cold — then my mom's birthday. It seems like it's been one thing after another. I'm free today if you can get together. Maybe an early dinner at Café Bangkok? I think the *tom kha ghi* would be great for my throat. Call me."

Roxie called back two minutes later, and Amanda knew that she had been screening her call. Roxie could be vindictive, apparently a trait that goes with being a Scorpio.

"Sorry about not calling," Amanda apologized.

Roxie didn't reply.

"Are you free for dinner?"

"Sure," Roxie spat the word into the phone.

"I said I'm sorry. I've been really sick."

"I heard what you said."

Amanda regretted calling.

"I'll need to cancel my plans with Rick," Roxie huffed.

"If you have plans tonight, we can go another time. I'm free tomorrow, too. Is Rick the guy from Dolce Amado?" Amanda tried for an uncharacteristically sweet tone, suddenly feeling guilty for hurting Roxie. Really though, she was torn. She didn't want to go to dinner but she knew that she needed a chance, in person, to explain the upcoming Florida move. Today would be as good a day to do it as any.

"No, that was Andre. You knew we broke up. He went to Madonna without me. Jeez, Mandy. Rick's a new guy. You haven't heard about him because you haven't been around. I've been trying to get rid of him for a few days now. This will give me a good excuse."

"Wait, Rick's the pianist, right?" Amanda asked, ignoring the insult.

"No, that was Wendell. That never went anywhere. I'll see you at Bangkok at six."

Amanda eyed her watch: four hours until dinner. She looked around her apartment. Her place had plummeted into a sad state of neglect. The stench of garbage and sickness could no longer be masked by scented candles. She pulled the vacuum out of the front closet and got to work.

****

Café Bangkok was a dive, replete with cafeteria-style tables and stained linoleum floors. The dingy bulbs of the fluorescent lighting were in serious need of an upgrade. The food, on the other hand, was to die for. By 6 p.m. nearly any night of the week, there was a line halfway around the building. It was also a BYOB joint. Amanda's brown paper bag of beer doubled as a peace offering.

Amanda saw Roxie, already seated, at a window seat. She was wearing a green boa. Amanda considered making a run for it.

"Chinese beer in a Thai restaurant? That should be illegal," Roxie joked as Amanda pulled out a bottle of Tsingtao beer from the paper bag.

"Can you name any Thai beers?"

"Yeah, Singha."

"Okay, I didn't think of that."

Amanda settled into the seat across from Roxie. The green boa screamed at her.

"I ordered some spring rolls." Roxie slid a Betty Boop bottle opener across the table. Amanda recognized it as the one that lived in Roxie's purse, always ready for BYOB or unexpected stopovers late at night at someone's apartment. She also had a travel wine opener in there. She was like a traveling party.

"Thanks." Amanda applied Betty's wide mouth to the cap of her bottle and popped it off.

"So, Miss Disappearance, what's going on in your world?"

"I was sick and really out of it. I tried to go into work one day and even Irv sent me home. I think he's grooming Ruth to take over for me and what's weird is I don't even care. I need the job, but I can't make myself work hard enough to keep it."

"Because you hate it."

"No, it's more than that."

"Let me guess!" Roxie exclaimed with ample sarcasm. "You're pregnant with Josh's baby, and you're going to elope to Vegas."

"What is up with everyone thinking I'm pregnant?"

"Are you? It would describe your weird moods lately. Although when you're pregnant, you're supposed to eat more, not less. You look like shit. You're all pasty and scrawny. You look like some kind of refugee."

"That's what my mom said."

"Well, you do. What's really wrong? Don't feed me this bullshit that it's all on account of a bad cold."

Amanda took in a deep breath and went for it. "I'm thinking about moving away, like out of state."

"What?!" Roxie boomed, causing their waiter to nearly drop the spring rolls. "That's possibly more shocking than you being pregnant with Josh's baby. Where would you go? Why?"

"Maybe Florida." Amanda dipped a spring roll into the peanut sauce, trying to play the whole thing off as casual.

"Florida? Since when?"

"Since I got a brochure in the mail last week. Everyone's smiling in the pictures, and no one is wearing a fur coat or shivering."

"Wait, you got some junk mail and now you're moving? Do you even know anyone there?"

Amanda shook her head.

"This is ridiculous. You're too introverted to make it out there. Is this because of that Therese nutcase?"

Amanda didn't let on how much the comment stung. She didn't want to defend Therese to Roxie or anyone. Therese was the only good thing in her life.

"I need to get out. I hate the cold winters. My life is a freaking failure. Look at me. My only prospect on the dating front is a guy who couldn't care less about me … "

"Don't forget about Max."

"Oh, yes, of course. How could I forget Max?"

"Well honestly, Mandy, you won't leave your apartment and come out with me. If your dating prospects are slim, you've got no one to blame but yourself."

"Fair enough. But seriously, my mother acts like I'm still a pre-teen. We've already covered my job more than necessary. If I don't take charge of my life soon, I'm going to be a bitter old secretary, freezing my ass off alone, caring for an aging witch." She could see Roxie's mental wheels turning.

"Celia's not a witch."

"Okay, maybe I got a bit out of control."

"So, if you move to LA, I'd consider going with you."

Los Angeles with Roxie? No way! Amanda could totally picture wild parties filled with fake, struggling actors. Everyone would be out for themselves. Roxie would assume her theater persona as a new permanent personality on steroids. LA. wasn't happening.

"I'm not going to California. I'm terrified of earthquakes. And even if I wanted to, my dad's there. Celia would disown me."

"True." Roxie reached for a spring roll. "But I still don't get it. You get sick and suddenly you want to move?"

"I need to travel, see what's out there. Roxie, I need to get out and live a little."

"Hawaii's warm."

"People don't move to Hawaii."

"Sure they do."

"At some level, I don't even care where I go, as long as I get out of here. I've only been to Mexico, and I wouldn't call that trip to Cancun adventurous."

"We had fun," Roxie said, the memory twinkling brightly in her eyes.

"We never left the all-inclusive resort. No side trips to Mayan ruins or visits to local jungles – hell, we barely even made it to the beach."

"But that poolside bar was incredible. Remember those guys from Brazil?"

"Rox, I know this is going to sound weird, but I feel like I've outgrown Amanda. I need to see who I'm going to be next."

"You need to stop seeing this Therese chick. That's what you need to do. She's messed you up good, girlfriend. You never said freaky things like this before. You also weren't bone thin. Look at you. You could melt away."

"I'm eating the spring rolls." Amanda defended herself by holding up a half-eaten roll.

"I'll put money on the table that you don't eat more than three bites of the curry you're going to order."

"Whatever."

At that moment, the waiter came by to take their order. Amanda ordered the green curry with shrimp. Roxie glared at her the entire time.

"Do you offer kid-size portions?" Roxie asked the waiter.

"Roxie, don't," Amanda begged. The waiter stared.

"Yes, we do."

"Can you make my friend's curry a kid's size?"

"No sir, I'm fine with my entrée," Amanda interrupted, staring Roxie down. The waiter shook his head as Roxie ordered.

"You're such a jerk," Amanda said to Roxie when he was out of earshot.

"Sometimes. So let me tell you how horrible this guy Rick was."

CHAPTER 16

With May came warmer days and more skin. Everywhere, you could see people in flimsy tops and short skirts, anxious to have the sun warm them after their long hibernation. Amanda was no exception in her cream-colored, ruffled linen skirt that tickled the space above her knees and her peach silk tank top that rippled loosely around her chest. If the wind caught it just right, a passerby could get a glimpse of her cleavage. The image gave her a unique sense of adventure and daring. There was more to her than met the eye.

But as Amanda entered the office, her spirits sank the way they always did — depressed at the thought of being holed up all day in a windowless cube. She was so very tired of her days spent staring at a computer monitor, typing in mindless data that had no relevance to her life. *How do people find those jobs where they're doing something good for the world? I won't get a desk job in Florida, that's for sure. Maybe I'll work for a non-profit. Save the turtles or something.*

Irv hovered by her cube. Amanda sighed, dropping her overstuffed purse on the desk. She was hoping for a bit of time to settle in first. It was 8:18 a.m. She wasn't *that* late.

"Good morning!" Amanda's voice was as bright and cheery as she could muster.

"We're continuing to find errors in your data entry, Amanda. We need to talk about this."

"Right now?"

"Don't give me attitude, little girl. I sign your paychecks."

"Little girl?" Amanda looked at Irv in disgust. "Did you just call me 'little girl'?"

"Amanda!" Irv's cheeks puffed into red balloons and she pictured them floating above her cube and carrying him away.

"Fine, what do we need to talk about?" Amanda took a long swig of coffee and leaned against her desk. Irv stared at her legs. "Irv!" Amanda barked, reminding him that her legs didn't talk.

"Accounting's been finding a lot of errors in your analysis reports. From now on, I want to review them first. I'll need time to do that, so have the reports to me by two instead of four."

"Since I don't get the data until 11 o'clock some days, I won't even be able to start until late morning. The only way I could be done by two, is if I don't take a lunch break."

"Well, that sounds like a small price to pay to keep your job."

Amanda fell dejectedly into her stiff office chair. She hated her job, her cubicle, and Irv most of all. Irv, with his thinning gray hair and thick double chin. Irv, who needed suspenders to hold up his pants. Irv, who had probably been wearing Old Spice from Walgreen's since he first learned to shave. Amanda shivered. *Is the air conditioning actually on? It isn't that warm outside yet.*

She logged onto the travel site before she opened her email. A pop-up ad for the Colorado Renaissance Festival caught her eye. It featured knights on horseback jousting, a king eating a turkey leg and sporting a jovial grin, and a lady adorned in Renaissance attire. It was the lady who caught Amanda's attention. This woman looked a bit like Keira. She was waving in the picture. Amanda could almost hear her calling.

She clicked through to the festival's main website and her mouth fell open. In full color, from the thick head of black hair to the crystal-clear blue eyes, there was Miles. *How can he be staring at me through my monitor? Right here, in this life*?

Amanda looked into his eyes and felt as if she could see straight through to his soul. It was him. Every aching molecule of her knew it. Clicking through the pictures on the website, looking for more of Miles, led her to the header: "Colorado Renaissance Festival - *Now Hiring."*

Amanda's heart raced with anticipation. She checked the amount in her United account and played with some dates in the booking calendar. *I could leave this weekend. Destiny has presented itself — through a pop-up ad! I'm not going to wait!*

A raw energy surged through her. She powered off her computer, tossed her personal items into a grocery bag, grabbed her purse, and walked over to Irv's office. Through the glass window in the door, she could see he was on the phone. He looked up, saw her, and shooed her away. She didn't leave.

He put his hand over the mouthpiece of the receiver. "What is so goddamned important ... "

"I'm quitting, Irv. Write the fucking reports yourself." Amanda's grin radiated throughout her entire being. This was the moment she'd been waiting for. She was finally free.

Irv's mouth hung open. The phone receiver dangled from his hand like a dead appendage. Out of the corner of her eye, Amanda saw Josh and Ruth hurrying toward him.

"What's going on?" Ruth asked, with genuine concern directed toward Irv.

"Amanda just quit. Without notice." Irv placed extra emphasis on the last part as he slammed the receiver down on the console.

"No way!" Josh yelled. "I never thought she'd have the balls."

Amanda walked up to Josh, ran a finger across his shocked face and said, "More balls than you'll ever know, File Boy." She kissed him on the check, before waltzing past all of them and out the front door.

CHAPTER 17

Today's the day — my last regression with Therese. How can I end this? If it wasn't for Therese and her hoodoo-voodoo magic, none of this would be happening. I wonder how many other patients of hers have changed their lives.

"Hello, my child." Therese greeted Amanda with open arms.

"Hi," she managed, falling into Therese's hug and shedding her first tears since making the decision to move earlier that week.

"Sit down. I want to hear all about your new adventure." Therese beckoned Amanda to take her usual spot on the couch.

"I'm going to Colorado. I'm going to get a job at the Renaissance Festival."

"The Renaissance Festival?"

"I've finally figured out what I want to do."

"Or what Keira wants to do?"

Amanda was surprised. *I thought Therese would be thrilled for me, for making such a bold move.*

"My dear, it sounds as though you are pursuing Keira's path. I don't know if that means you've found Amanda's."

"But nothing has filled me with such happiness and energy. I've never felt so sure of anything in my life. Besides, we're one in the same, right?"

"You are, but I guess I wasn't successful in helping you build a sense of separation between this world and your past. While I wish you a wonderful journey as you search for your life purpose, let me remind you that you've already lived Keira's life. There is nothing that you can do to live that life again. It is my wish for you that you fall in love with who you are now, in this incarnation, and find a new identity you can embrace. We incarnate to grow."

Growth had gotten Amanda nowhere. *This life is crap compared to my past. It's simply time to course correct.*

"For the first time in my life, I actually know what I'm doing," she explained to Therese, hoping for more understanding, more empathy than she was likely going to get. *If only Therese could see the website. If she saw Miles, then she would agree. Should I pull it up on my phone? But what if Therese still doesn't approve? Then what? There's no turning back now. I've quit my job, sold my crappy car, sublet my apartment, and bought a one-way plane ticket. I'm Colorado-bound. I don't need any more reassurance.*

"I hope you're right, my child." Therese looked at the clock. "Are you ready for your last session?"

"Yes," Amanda said, with a firm air of conviction. *This session has to be special,* she thought before she went under.

****

I sit perched on a chair in the middle of Queen Isolde's kitchen. There are a flurry of women bustling around me, braiding flowers into my hair, and applying colored pastes from jars onto my eyelashes, cheeks, and lips. The women look like fairies, thin and light and glowing. All of them have hair in sparkling hues of cinnamon, auburn, honey, and white, and their flowing hair nearly sweeps the floor as they work. I savor everything that is happening. I never want to forget a moment of this glorious day.

Today, Miles and I are to be married in the herb garden, behind Queen Isolde's house. She was so delighted when we asked her to bless our union.

"She's ready," one of the fairy women announces to Queen Isolde, and the queen comes over to admire me.

"You truly are an angel! Most definitely, a princess." Queen Isolde smiles, handing me a mirror. I cannot believe the reflection. The women have transformed me into a vision so beautiful, it's as if they painted their glow around me, and I too have become fairy-like. My eyes sparkle with green, glimmering brilliance and my lips shine with the color of a fresh peach.

"You enter London like this, my child, and people will cry 'Helen of Troy is reborn and lives and walks the earth again!'" Queen Isolde cries and everyone breaks into laughter.

"Thank you all," I say, feeling a deep gratitude to each of the women. "You have transformed me."

Queen Isolde helps me to my feet and walks me outside to the garden. Miles is standing under a canopy of ivy. He too has been transformed, glowing as if the fairy people have touched him the same way. Wearing a wreath of ivy around his head that matches the ivy dripping from the canopy, he is adorned in a loose-fitting, dark-green tunic with matching pants. He is like Pan of the Forest, come to woo me away. A place deep inside of me tingles. It's the same sensation that I have been feeling since meeting Miles months ago. I cannot wait to hold him in my arms.

Queen Isolde walks me to Miles, placing my hand in his. It is only the three of us in the garden, yet I can feel the presence of the others watching through the windows.

Miles' smile runs wide and bright, steady and unwavering.

"Welcome to this sacred space, Keira and Miles. We are here to reunite your souls," Queen Isolde begins. My knees start to shake. I wish I could remember the other lives Miles and I have shared. I wonder if I will ever be able to see the way he can.

Then Queen Isolde says, "Miles, please reaffirm your devotion to Keira."

And he responds, "I, Miles, reaffirm my love and devotion to Keira. I have pledged to be her soulmate through this life and others. I pledge to learn from her, to support her, and to adore her in every way I can. I pledge to right all wrongs I have done towards her and to push her towards soul growth. For it is through love that we grow. I promise you all this in this life and beyond."

Queen Isolde turns to me and says, "Keira, please reaffirm your devotion to Miles."

Without hesitation, I respond, "I, Keira, reaffirm my love and devotion for you, Miles. I pledge to support you, care for you, and learn from you. I pledge never to knowingly harm you and to always push for your soul growth, for it is through that, that I grow, too. I promise you all this in this life and beyond."

Queen Isolde faces both of us and then speaks, "I ask that you always love, honor, and cherish one another through all phases of your life, that you seek the divine within you and between you. In the presence of the divine, I confirm that you two are wed. Please kiss to seal your commitment."

She takes a step back, and Miles and I gaze upon one another — the first time as man and wife. Miles passionately presses his lips to mine, and I become dizzy at his touch. His tongue slides into my mouth and the sensation of it touching mine causes me to lose my balance. I feel as if I might fall, but his strength holds me.

Queen Isolde concludes by saying, "In the eyes of the divine, you have been officially reunited. Your marriage in London will make you husband and wife under the law of England, but in the spiritual sense, take comfort in the knowledge that you have always been one."

The three of us move together for an embrace. The supportive love and energy of our circle is strong. I close my eyes and privately thank God for delivering me into this new life, a life so full of warmth and love. A stray thought of Robert flutters in, but I quickly shoo it away. Miles is my destiny.

When the ceremony is done, Miles takes me on a walk to the lake. We stroll around the mossy edges to the far side. The sun is warm and radiates off my skin.

"We're almost there," he says, and directs my gaze to a clearing. When we reach the spot, it's soft and mossy, and tucked under a secluded hill. Miles smiles into my eyes and I feel his gaze penetrate me. "I feel you shaking," he says. "You're not scared, are you?"

I tell him I am not, even though I'm terrified. I remember feeling the same nervousness when Robert stole me away for a kiss behind the market stands in Glastonbury. It was nothing, though, compared to this. Miles' eyes take in my body, and I feel modest even though I'm fully dressed. He runs his fingers through my fine hair. I love the space just by his temples, and lean forward to touch it with my lips. The warmth of his skin soothes my nervous lips.

"You have such beautiful, golden hair," Miles whispers, lifting it up and kissing the back of my neck. Goosebumps trail down the left side of my body.

"I need to sit down," I say, knowing my legs are about to give way. Together, we lie on the soft, warm ground; Miles tucks his cloak under my head and then straddles me with his legs across my hips. He doesn't break eye contact while he unbuttons my blouse. I begin to wiggle nervously. He presses on, massaging my breasts and leaning over to touch his lips to them. The goosebumps now blanket my entire body. He traces kisses from one shoulder to the other, and then he kisses in circles where my neck meets my breast-bone. He stops at my heart, pauses a moment, and gently leans on it with his cheek. He leaves a trail of kisses down my abdomen. An intense pulsing awakens inside me. I desperately need his touch. I am firmly aware that I have just crossed the line from child to adult.

Miles deftly unlaces my ruffled peasant skirt and pulls it off my hips and then down my legs, tossing it beside us. He removes his shirt. I've never felt more grounded, lying pressed directly into the Earth. The warm sun on my skin drapes me like a blanket dropped from God. We press our bodies together. Lips locked, tongues frantically exploring one another's mouths, we further seal our commitment and devotion. Together. Forever.

****

Amanda came to in a state of extreme embarrassment. She looked at Therese, who appeared to have just had an orgasm herself. Her face was beaded lightly in sweat and her cheeks flushed a deep pink. Amanda wished she could crawl under the couch and sneak out the door.

"It's okay," Therese assured her. "Sex isn't anything to be embarrassed about. And it was an important piece of Miles' and Keira's story."

Amanda appreciated her peaceful, logical manner, and nodded, glancing down to be sure her shirt was buttoned. She wanted to remove herself from Keira, knowing full well that that was no longer an option. She noticed the throbbing sensation between her legs. *Unbelievable! I never had sex so good in my present life. Does sex like this really exist outside of romance novels?*

"Well, my dear, I have to say, you regressed to an ideal ending," Therese concluded.

"But I want to find out what happens to Keira and Miles. What does the rest of their life look like? Do they have kids? Grow old together and die? How does their story end? Can I call you? We can do this remotely, right? Maybe Skype? FaceTime?"

"Amanda, you can do this on your own. You no longer need me. You haven't needed me for a while." Therese stepped behind her desk and retrieved something from her drawer. When she returned, she opened her palm to reveal a hematite bracelet.

"Hematite is grounding. Take this bracelet as a reminder that your place is in the present, no matter where your visions take you. Let me also leave you with a quote that has always moved me. It's by Omar Khayyam, a Persian poet who lived in the ninth century:

'Tis all a chequer-board of nights and days
where destiny with men for pieces plays:
hither and thither moves, and mates, and slays,
and one by one, back in the closet lays.'

"Wow." Amanda took in the words, knowing she would need to look them up again.

Therese nodded. "I've enjoyed our time together tremendously. I wish you all the beauty and joy in the world."

Therese placed her hands on Amanda's head, pulled it closer, and kissed her forehead. Amanda felt as if a magical piece of Therese had been passed to her through the kiss. *I wonder if Therese is part of my past. Maybe she was Queen Isolde? And are these sessions merely fate bringing us together again?* She touched the bracelet ... *hematite, like in the crystal book ... just like in Keira's world ... the grounding connection between my lives.*

"I don't know how to say goodbye to you," Amanda said through her tears. Therese pulled her into an embrace and they cried together. "Thank you, thank you, thank you," Amanda whispered. "How can I ever thank you enough?"

"Be well, my child, be well," Therese said, as Amanda left her office for the last time.

CHAPTER 18

There was only Roxie and Celia left to say goodbye to, and then an airplane ride to her new life.

"Colorado?" Roxie asked for the hundredth time since they sat down. She twirled her blue boa. Blue. Detached. Apropos. No matter how many times Amanda had explained about Colorado, Roxie couldn't wrap her head around it.

"Yes, Colorado."

"What happened to Florida and warmth? It's not exactly warm in Colorado."

"Actually, you're wrong. I did some research; it's very hot and dry in the summer. In fact, they don't have humidity, so it's even better than Florida. Besides, I'm only going for the summer. The festival ends in August. I can always go to Florida after that. Maybe I'll find a Renaissance festival there. They have these fairs everywhere, you know."

"No, I don't know anything about them," Roxie declared in a snide tone. "Anyway, have you ever even been to Colorado?"

"Roxie!" Amanda took a big sip of her latté, exasperated by Roxie's relentless lack of support.

"No, I'm serious. It's the Wild West. You know, cowboys and Indians. You don't even like Westerns."

"Have you ever been there?" Amanda shot back in frustration. She was this close to tossing her latté on Roxie.

"I've been to Idaho, so I get the 'west,'" Roxie snapped, air quotes and all. "I really think this is a bit rash. Just because you've been having these encounters and all, and you saw some guy in an ad that looks like 'Lancelot'…" she said, with more air quotes.

"Miles, not Lancelot."

"Whatever. I mean ... jeez ... I seriously think it's time for an intervention!"

They had been at Starbucks for nearly an hour and Amanda was running out of patience and time. Her mother would be at her place soon. "I have to go. I don't have a choice."

"Of course you do."

"It's fate. I have to heed my calling."

Roxie choked on her drink and shook her head at Amanda.

"Listen to yourself. Heed your calling. What the fuck, Mandy?"

"Seriously, it's pulling me. You don't understand. This part of my life is over. I've known that for a while. It's time for me to move on. Ryan moved on and moved west. My dad moved on and moved west. I need to do the same."

Roxie lifted a critical eyebrow. "So, there's no way I'm going to be able to talk you out of this?"

Amanda shook her head. "They're hiring now. I can't waste any more time. Who knows what positions are even left."

"What are you going to do with all of your stuff?"

"I'm taking most of it to Goodwill. I don't want to hold onto anything that reminds me of my life here in Chicago."

"This is ludicrous."

Amanda had had enough. She was wasting precious packing time. "I have a lot to do. I need to get going."

"Is this goodbye then?"

"For now, yes. I'll be back. It's not like I'm moving to Mars."

They hugged tightly before going their separate ways. They were family. Bound together forever. For better or worse. Like sisters.

****

"Where have you been?" Celia greeted Amanda when she opened her apartment door.

Amanda jumped in surprise. *Why did I give her a key?* she thought before answering, "I was saying goodbye to Roxie. Besides, you're early. I thought you weren't coming for another half hour."

"I still don't understand why you're doing this to us. Roxie must be beside herself."

"Mom, we've talked about this every night this week. What more can I say?"

"It's very mean, what you're doing. I thought I raised you to be more considerate."

Cartoon images of gigantic mallets descending from the sky and smashing Celia into the floor filled Amanda's mind. She went into the kitchen for a LaCroix and a cool down. Soon. Soon she'd have space, real physical space, between Celia and herself.

"You can't leave me. Who's going to go to my events with me? Who am I going to go out to dinner with when I'm in the city? Amanda won't you reconsider this nonsense?"

"Why does this have to be about you? Why does everything always have to be about you?" Amanda slammed the can down so hard, La Croix sprayed all over the countertop. "This is about me! This is about my life!"

"But ... you're my baby!" Celia burst through her anger and exploded in tears. Amanda put her arms around her mother. She was nervous to leave her life too, to walk away from the known world of Roxie and Celia, always there. The intensity of her need to explore, though, to be on her own, to find her purpose, it all fueled her more than she'd ever thought possible. She needed to leave to find herself.

"Why are you going to Colorado? I thought you and Max were starting something."

"See? That's the whole point, Mom. You don't know a goddamn thing about me or my life." Amanda walked away from the embrace and began packing. She had to get out of Illinois, or Celia would truly smother any last flicker of flame inside of her.

"Watch your language, young lady. I don't like this new tone of yours."

"Mom, I hate my life here. I hated my job. I don't have a boyfriend, and if I did, it would never in a million years be Max. I want to start over. It's that simple." Amanda took a deep breath to try to calm down. She sipped her water. She was beginning to worry that she would give Celia a heart attack.

"I'm going to work at the Renaissance Festival for the summer. I'm not giving up my lease here. I'm subletting the place. I may only be gone for a few months. Maybe I'll come back to Chicago at the end of the summer."

Without knowledge of the regressions, Celia would never understand. Amanda couldn't explain that she had seen Miles in an ad and heard his voice calling her, and that if she didn't go, she would risk losing her one chance at true happiness in this life. Hell, Celia didn't even believe in reincarnation, so how was Amanda supposed to explain anything? She also doubted very much that Celia believed in true love.

"All I know is that I have to go." Amanda walked into her bedroom and transferred her energy into frantically sorting sweaters into Keep and Goodwill piles.

"Since when are you interested in Renaissance festivals?" Celia asked, walking into her room. It was creepy, the way Celia was tracking Amanda's thoughts.

"I told you, a friend from college invited me to come. She's a manager there and says she'll get me a good position."

"Which friend?"

"Janice. You never met her. Her family is from Denver. I think she's the marketing director for the festival."

"You're lying." Celia tried to make eye contact but Amanda kept her gaze focused on the pile of sweaters.

"Whatever you want to believe."

"Fine. I can see I won't be able to talk you out of this."

Amanda ignored her. Celia was trying her favorite strategy, reverse-logic guilt. Amanda wasn't going to fall for it.

"What would be nice is if you could help me pack."

Celia huffed, looking around Amanda's room. "What do you intend to do with all of this ... stuff?"

"Whatever doesn't fit in my storage locker goes to Goodwill. Those four suitcases," Amanda said, pointing to the corner of her living room, "are what are going on the plane. Oh, and I need to cash that CD you started for me at the bank. Do you think you could go help with that?"

Celia threw her arms up in defeat. "I'll go get your money. Then, maybe, when I get back I can talk some sense into you. You know, I asked my friend if you could stay at their winter home in Scottsdale for a little while. I told her that you were having a bit of a breakdown and needed some time away. The house is in a gated community and has wonderful amenities like a pool and hot tub in the back yard and a community golf course. In fact, I could go down with you for a few weeks. I could use a vacation. She said we're welcome any time."

"Mom, I have zero interest in Arizona."

"You need a break, Amanda. This would be the perfect retreat."

"Could you *please* stop trying to run my life? *Please?*"

"You're turning into quite a little bitch, I hope you know. I don't know how you think that attitude is going to get you a man."

"Takes one to know one," Amanda whispered under her breath while Celia went to get her purse and keys.

"What was that?" Celia asked, poking her head back in the bedroom.

"Nothing."

****

Amanda sped through her remaining sorting. By the time Celia returned, she had the bedroom and bathroom entirely packed. All that was left was her kitchen and a utility closet.

"You're rather efficient, aren't you?" Celia commented, handing Amanda the cashier's check for thirty thousand dollars.

"Thank you," Amanda replied, taking the check and folding it into her wallet.

"You'll still have your phone, right?"

"I'm going to another state, not another country."

"Okay. Well, I need to get back. I have a dinner in Evanston that starts soon."

Celia opened her arms for a hug. Amanda noticed the difference between Celia's hug and Queen Isolde's. Celia really didn't know how to love. Amanda's anger turned to pity. She shed a tear and hugged her mom goodbye.

PART TWO

CHAPTER 19

The sky, which had been darkening during her drive from the Denver airport, worsened once she exited the highway at Larkspur. Rain fell in sheets, then quickly turned to quarter-size hail that slammed into her rental car. *What the hell, Colorado? Wasn't it over 90 degrees when I left the airport just an hour ago?*

Amanda pulled over. *Is the damage covered under the rental agreement? Did I say no to extra coverage?* she wondered. *I was in such a rush to get out of the rental agency that I didn't bother to read over the details. This is all starting to feel like a really bad idea. I should have never come to Colorado. Amanda isn't a risk-taker. Keira was the risk-taker.*

Amanda sat trapped in the rental car on the side of the highway, shaking. The pounding rain reached every nerve in her body. Between her tearful eyes and the deluge outside of the car, she couldn't see a thing. She covered her face, said a prayer, and asked God for reassurance.

Right then, the hail tapered off and the sky cleared. A ray of sun beamed down through the dark clouds, directly onto her economy car. Amanda felt renewed in the warm glow that comforted her like a safety blanket, telling her everything was going to be okay. *I have to believe. I have to have faith. Maybe I'm not a risk-taker, but I do want to live life more fully. I want to be Keira.*

She followed the back road, immediately feeling at home. The drive reminded her of the wooded groves of the Forest of Forgiveness, towering pines in carefully constructed patterns created a filter for the sifted sunlight. The entrance to the park was a castle front with turrets and spires, like a movie lot. The castle had an enormous sign welcoming visitors. Parking her car, Amanda imagined the world inside, and her feet couldn't take her there fast enough. At the main gate was a man in full Renaissance garb, dressed like a jester in red tights under bulbous blue shorts and a matching blue button-up tunic. A hat adorned with dangly bells balanced perfectly atop his head.

"Good day, ye lass! Welcome to the Renaissance Festival and the most excellent land of our King Henry!" As the man spoke, the bells jingled on his hat.

"Thank you." Amanda curtsied on instinct, probably the first time doing so since grade school. "I would like to apply for a job. Where do I go?"

"But of course!" The jester came up to Amanda and put his arm around her. "Follow me and I'll take you to the Tower! The Tower of Applications, that is. I am Baldwin the Fool. I am the Walmart greeter of our fine Faire." Amanda couldn't help but chuckle. *This is going to be fun.*

Baldwin led Amanda to a building directly inside the front gate. It appeared to be a gift shop selling magic broomsticks. To the right of the store, she noticed a tucked-away staircase with a sign that read APPLY WITHIN. Amanda thought back to some of the Harry Potter she had read before she got bored with the series. It was like she'd stepped into Diagon Alley, the secret shopping area in London for witches and warlocks. She made her way up the staircase to an office where a man, probably in his early twenties, with blonde hair and soft eyes sat behind a folding table that held a laptop, stacks of paper applications, and a bottle of water.

"I was told to come up here to apply. Do I talk with you?"

"Heck yeah!" The blonde man wore a faded T-shirt that read *Venice Beach Surf Shop* and cut-off Army green pants that served as shorts. Obviously, he hadn't gotten the Renaissance memo. "Have you worked here before?"

"No." Amanda was nervous. "Is that going to be a problem?"

"Of course not! Hey, I'm P.J. What's your name?"

Amanda hesitated for a second. "Keira." *Everyone's so over-the-top nice. I wonder if this is simply the Renaissance Festival causing people to act out roles, or if this is truly how people are in Colorado. Or maybe it's the legalized pot.*

"Cool name. What are you interested in, Keira?"

Wherever Miles works, Amanda thought, *but how can I say so without sounding like a stalker. That's tricky.* "I'm not sure. Can you tell me what you have available?"

"Most definitely!" P.J.'s heavy surfer cadence provided a sharp contrast to Baldwin's authentic period accent. Amanda was curious why a surfer would choose to spend his summer in landlocked Colorado. "Up there on the wall is a listing of what jobs are left. Scan it over, then come back here and I'll get you an application. The Faire opens next week. Orientation is this coming Tuesday. We'll be done by the end of this weekend."

Amanda walked over to the listings. The top read **Hark, ye merry lads and lasses!** Welcome to the Renaissance Festival of Colorado. King Henry needs to fill the following positions to support his most glorious kingdom of England!

The jobs ranged from concession stand workers to gift shop clerks to ride attendants to people who simply walked around the grounds in costume. Amanda knew she wasn't outgoing enough for the last job. There were still plenty of postings and her fears were allayed.

"I'm interested in the retail jobs," she told P.J. "I worked at The Gap in high school, Pottery Barn in college — you know, over summer and Christmas breaks. So I have experience."

"Right on." He smiled as he put an application on a clipboard. "Head over there and fill this out. Bring it back to me when you're done."

Amanda walked over to a different folding table to complete the application. When she was through, P.J. directed her to a room at the end of a long hallway where a pudgy, red-headed man with a goatee sat in royal Renaissance-era garb behind an ostentatious looking walnut desk with elaborate etchings in the legs. *He looks like he's posing for a glamour shot. He has to be King Henry,* she guessed.

"Welcome!" he bellowed as he sprang to life. She could picture invisible strings holding him from above and moving him like a puppet. The King reminded her of a cartoon, a caricature of the real thing.

"Thank you," Amanda curtsied for the second time that day.

"What brings ye to the merry ol' land of England?" The King beckoned her closer to the table.

She hadn't thought to practice her pitch. *I can't very well say I saw my soul mate in a pop-up ad. Or maybe I could? This seems to be an anything-goes sort of place.* "I'm looking for a life change," she started, deciding that sounded best. "I want to be part of the Renaissance Festival." She took a seat on the folding chair directly in front of King Henry.

"Ah! A pilgrimage. Perhaps a coming home?" *Yes,* she thought, *I'm definitely home.* "Welcome, welcome! What's your sweet lass's name?"

"My name is Ama ... I mean Keira. My name is Keira."

"You sound a bit unsure of that." King Henry raised his eyebrows at Amanda and she felt like a school girl in line for punishment.

"Please call me Keira."

"Well then, Keira it is. You may call me Henry, as in King Henry VIII. I rule over this realm and make all the hiring decisions. Now, Keira, what life do you see yourself having behind our castle moat?"

That may have been the most profound question ever asked of her. *I want a life new and fresh, one filled with adventure and romance, but how can I communicate all of that to King Henry?* "I see my life getting a major overhaul. I want to be Keira of the Forest and spread my fairy dust. I want to bring magic into the world!"

"A fairy! How glorious!" King Henry opened a binder full of three-hole punched paper. "Your application requests retail. How does Faerytale Fynery sound? They sell flowered tiaras, angel wings, magic wands, things of that nature."

"That sounds terrific!"

He closed the binder and clasped his hands. A broad grin spread across his face. "Splendid, just splendid! You're hired!"

"Really? You don't need to ask me any more questions?"

"No, no, no. I can see the fairy spirit lives brightly inside you. You belong here. Now run along back down the hall to P.J. Tell him you'll be working at Faerytale Fynery with Melinda. Such a truly wonderful woman. She is mother to all the lost souls who come for solace. P.J. will instruct you from there." King Henry stood up, handed Amanda her application, and reached his hand out to shake hers.

"Thank you!" Amanda gathered her purse and clipboard and went back down the hall in search of P.J.

"Well, that was easy," she said. "I got the job."

"Right on." P.J. took Amanda's clipboard and placed it on top of a precarious stack of paperwork that left Amanda feeling a little less confident about the Faire. Irv would have a heart attack on the spot if he saw P.J.'s desk.

"King Henry told me that you would fill me in on what I need to do next."

"Yep, yep," P.J. mumbled, searching his desk for something. Finally, he located a gold pen. "Ah! Can't work without me lucky pen." He winked, like the leprechaun from Lucky Charms. "So, where did Henry place you?"

"I believe it's called Faerytale Fynery. I'll be working with someone named Melinda."

"Ah, Melinda! She's a crack-up. You'll love her. She's like the mother of the Faire."

"That's what Henry was saying."

"Yeah, she's great. So here's the deal. Orientation is this Tuesday. The festival opens the next day. Show up at 10:00 a.m. for orientation. You'll be here most of the day. On Wednesday, you have to be ready to go by 9:00 a.m. We have an on-site wardrobe and makeup department that opens at 7:30. It's kind of a madhouse, so we usually recommend getting there early. They'll give you a tour of the Costumery during orientation. The place closes at six each night. We're open Thursday through Sunday so everyone gets Monday through Wednesday off. You *have* to agree to work all weeks. So if you have any trips or weddings or anything like that, you need to let me know now because this may not work. We let you have one 'free day' in case you're sick, but beyond that, it gets serious. All sound good so far?"

Amanda nodded. She had nothing on her plate ... no commitments with Celia, no art gallery shows with Roxie. For the first time, she was utterly free. At that moment, a lanky high-school-aged boy wearing a reverse baseball cap and black Converse with loose laces entered the office.

"Hey there," P.J. called.

"I worked at the food court last year."

"Cool. Go ahead and grab a clipboard, fill out the application, and I'll have you talk to King Henry."

The boy nodded, and P.J. turned back to Amanda. "I think that covers it."

"One more thing, I just got in from Chicago. Do you have any suggestions on housing? I was planning to get a hotel room for the next few nights, but I have to find a place to live, too."

"Sure. For hotels, I would recommend the *Hampton Inn* or *Holiday Inn*. They're both on the main drag, right off the highway outside of Castle Rock. If you can't afford those, there's a youth hostel in downtown Castle Rock. It's only twenty bucks a night, but you know, it's a hostel."

Amanda immediately ruled out the hostel. She had never stayed in one, and the idea of communal housing sounded particularly unappealing.

"As you can see," P.J. continued. "Larkspur's a rather tiny place. No real amenities here. For something more long-term, check out Housing Finders in Castle Rock. They're totally cool chicks. We send all of our out-of-area employees to them. They'll find you a sweet month-to-month lease."

"Perfect." Amanda gathered her new-hire packet and went back to the folding table to complete the paperwork. *Looks like my journey is underway,* she thought with satisfaction. *Maybe I really am becoming Keira. I've made it to Colorado and landed a job at the festival. Now all I have to do is find Miles.*

CHAPTER 20

The clock on the bedside table read 10:05 a.m. Amanda got up to open the blinds to an overcast day, thankful for a reprieve from the heat and sun. Through her window of the *Hampton Inn* she could see a warehouse parking lot and the highway. The clouds had blocked the mountains, making the area seemingly no different than anywhere, even Illinois. After dragging herself out of bed, she pulled on her rayon gauchos and slipped on a tank top. She had to make the bow extra big on the pants to keep them from sliding down her slender hips. Amanda checked herself in the mirror and wiped away the sleep in the corners of her eyes. She brushed her teeth, rolled on some deodorant, threw her hair into a ponytail, and slipped on her flip-flops. It was time to find coffee and definitely not hotel lobby coffee.

Downtown Castle Rock was still waking up. She plugged 'coffee shop' into her GPS and followed the directions to a brightly painted building. The Grounds. Perfect. She parked her car, grabbed her purse, and nearly floated into the cafe. The aroma overpowered her senses, leaving Amanda with confidence that they knew what they were doing. She approached the counter and a buff-looking woman with spiky hair and overalls approached her.

"Whatcha havin'?" the woman asked, looking past Amanda and out the door. Amanda turned, but no one else was there. The overhead music was playing something loud and grinding.

"I'm sorry. Are you asking me?"

"You're the only one waiting." The woman head-banged along to the music.

Amanda quietly let out an annoyed sigh and then read the menu board that hung above the espresso machines. The board was too jumbled to read, and Amanda felt pressured by the woman's incessant movement, so she went with her usual. "Can I have a double soy latté?"

The woman nodded her head, and Amanda wasn't sure if she was still moving to the music, or if she was acknowledging her order. Amanda looked around at the funky artwork, old beat-up couches, and broken chairs. It was definitely a bit more on the bohemian side, maybe something she'd find in Wicker Park or Ukrainian Village back in Chicago. Her anxiety grew as a couple of guys with Mohawks, clad in black leather and layered in piercings, stormed in.

"Yo chief, my main man!" the barista called to one of the Mohawked guys. He high-fived her across the counter, and Amanda had to step out of the way quickly to avoid getting smashed between them. They continued to talk in a language that certainly wasn't English. She wasn't sure she was ready for this new version of the Wild West.

She'd have to keep looking for other coffee shops. This wasn't a place where she could relax and hang out. Grabbing her latté and a handful of napkins, she nearly ran out the door. Tomorrow's goal would be to find a normal, comfortable coffee shop, then deal with housing.

Back in the comparative safety of her hotel room, she started the hot water and swirled it about the tub with her fingers. Even though it was summer, she longed to be submerged in the comfort of a bath. Perhaps she could even make herself regress and maybe see Miles. The pre-fabricated plastic tub made her homesick for the claw-footed cast-iron one she'd left behind in Chicago.

As the tub filled, she dug through her luggage until she found her lavender oil. She tapped a few drops into the water, and inhaled the soothing aroma. Sitting on the narrow ledge of the tub, her feet and ankles submerged, she remembered the guided meditations on a new app she'd downloaded. She quickly turned, and with wet feet went to locate her portable speaker. *If I play it while I'm in the bath, perhaps I can trigger a regression.* Finding the speaker buried in the bottom of her duffel bag, she synched the devices, and then opened the app. The first meditation she saw was *Journey of the Soul.* That looked perfect although it had a cheesy-looking image of pastel-colored angels. *I can handle the cheese factor if it works,* she thought. With everything ready, she went back to the tub and slid into the warm and soothing water.

"You will now join me on a journey of the soul," the resonant, throaty male voice began. "We will relax as we explore the depths of your consciousness. Let's begin with some active breathing. On the count of three, breathe in deeply, allowing the breath to fill your body completely. You should feel it in the back of your lungs, your chest, your pelvis."

Amanda giggled uncontrollably. This isn't like Therese at all. This is silly and there's no way I'm going to feel breath in my pelvis. She scolded herself to get serious and begin to breathe properly.

"In ... and out. In ... and out. Honor the breath and let it clear out the stagnation. Let it remove the toxic negative energy that is draining your core. With your next breath in, imagine you are a being filled with light and love. The universe is channeling its wonderful, supportive energy through you."

Amanda began to relax and concentrate on the Forest of Forgiveness. She could see the trees and Queen Isolde's house. With each breath, she relaxed deeper into the tub.

She had no idea how much time had passed, but nothing had happened. Amanda was still Amanda and her image of the Forest was only a memory of past regressions. It wasn't happening. The water was cooling and the meditation was over. She had gone into a deep state, had maybe even fallen asleep, but there had been no regression. A few tears ran down her face. She climbed out of the tub and wrapped her shivering body in a stiff hotel towel.

CHAPTER 21

First she couldn't regress, and now she'd lost Therese's hematite bracelet, the one she'd been instructed to always wear. She didn't want to believe that losing the bracelet was a sign she'd made a big mistake in coming to Colorado. She continued to search the room for more than an hour, completely gutting all four suitcases and her purse at least three times. She kept telling herself to calm down, that it would turn up, but she wasn't able to stay calm. Looking under the hotel bed, behind the nightstand, and beneath the bathroom sink, she searched everywhere. She went through her rental car, the glove compartment, under the seats, the trunk. The bracelet had vanished. Amanda swore she wouldn't leave the room until she found it, but after another half-hour of searching, there was no place she hadn't scoured thoroughly. She left a note for the cleaning staff describing the bracelet, and promised a huge reward if it was found.

****

Amanda had to find a place to live before Thursday. At $179 a night, she didn't want to stay at the hotel any longer than absolutely necessary. The Housing Finder's website said they opened at 9:00 a.m., so she decided to do another pass through downtown Castle Rock in search of a Starbucks, and be at Housing Finder's door ready and waiting when they opened.

She cruised around the vicinity of Housing Finders and was delighted to see a place called Jumpin' Java Beans. As she walked inside, her face lit up. The coffee shop was full of business people on their way to work. Swing music piped through the speakers, and the chairs and tables looked clean. She got her drink, grabbed a free local paper, and sat at an empty table to enjoy the normality of it all. *I've never lived anywhere other than Chicago. How long will it take before I feel like a local?*

At ten minutes before nine, she started walking down the block toward Housing Finders. Right next door to their office, she noticed the County Clerk building. A large sign in the window read "Marriage Licenses, License Plates, Name Changes." *Did fate direct me here?* Amanda stood in front of the building, feeling as though her legs wouldn't take her in, but neither would they let her walk away. After mustering her courage, she stepped inside the 1950s-era building and was pleased to discover there was no line at the counter.

"Yes?" a clerk inquired from behind metal bars. Amanda wondered, *was this place once a jail? The metal bars feel like a bit of overkill for a government administrative office. Maybe it was an old-time bank like in the movies.*

"I wanted to find out what I need to do to change my name."

"Grab a form 24-0192, fill it out, and give it to me."

"Really? It's that easy?"

The clerk nodded, "Sometimes you have to go before a judge, but it's not that complicated.

Amanda took the form and stared. It was full of legal mumbo jumbo and looked very official. *Could becoming Keira be as simple as completing a government form and paying a fee? What does it mean to become Keira legally? Will Amanda simply disappear?*

It was all too weighty to figure out while standing in a sterile government building. She thanked the clerk, took the form, and left for Housing Finders.

****

Amanda stepped inside the office and groaned. Housing Finders looked like a sorority's social hour. Every desk housed a perky, young, blonde female who was animatedly talking to the woman next to her. No one had even heard her enter.

"Hello?"

"Hi!" exclaimed one of the women. "Welcome to Housing Finders." In unison, five faces fell upon Amanda.

"I'm looking for a furnished apartment," she said, sounding more unsure of herself than she actually was.

"Well, you came to the right place," another said, generating a flurry of giggles from the others. "Come on over. We don't bite!"

Amanda approached the desk and the others went back to gabbing.

"I'm Amanda," the bobbed blonde said, extending her hand to Amanda. *I've entered a nightmare,* Amanda laughed to herself. *That's it. I most definitely am becoming Keira.*

"My name is Keira," Amanda answered.

"Keira's a cool name — so much more interesting than Amanda."

Amanda smiled.

"So what kind of an apartment are you looking for, Keira?"

"I'm here for the Renaissance Festival. P.J. at the Faire sent me to talk to you. He said that you could find me temporary housing."

Suddenly the other girls broke into another round of giggles. Amanda felt self-conscious. What could they possibly be laughing at?

"P.J.," two of the blondes sang at their Amanda and kept laughing.

"How is P.J.?" a fourth asked the Housing Finders Amanda.

"Stop it, guys!" she squealed, her face flushed red. Amanda quietly watched. She hoped none of them knew Miles.

"Oh, for sure we can help!" Housing Finders Amanda exclaimed, ignoring the others. "We still have a few spots open in

The Enclave." Amanda audibly gasped at the name of the development. It sounded a bit over the top.

"So, it's an apartment building that sets aside a block of units for people who work at the Faire. I have a studio and a two-bedroom left. Sorry, but the one-bedrooms go fast. They're the best ones."

"How much do they run?"

"The studio is $1,400 a month and the two-bedroom is $2,100. They both require one month's rent as a security deposit. Oh, and you can't have pets in any of the units. Well, when I say pets, I mean cats and dogs. Like if you have fish or a cute little lizard or something it might be okay. I know one person ... "

Amanda did the math in her head. At those rates, she would go through her savings faster than she'd hoped, and she had no idea how long this career sabbatical of hers was going to last. The Faire wasn't paying much more than minimum wage, which after gas and food wouldn't cover even a quarter of her living expenses. "Is that the going rate for all apartments?"

"Pretty much, and especially if you want a month-to-month lease. I should also let you know that the complex comes with an outdoor pool, a hot tub, and covered parking, not that that matters so much in the summer, but we do get a lot of hail sometimes, so that can be a big deal."

"Yes, I experienced that already. Do you have any pictures?"

"Of course!" The girl reached behind the desk for a brochure and gave it to Amanda. "If you're interested, I can call the property manager and see if he's available to give you a tour. Like I said, this place is really popular with Festival employees, so the units go fast."

Amanda glanced at the brochure. It looked perfect.

"I'll take a look," she said, handing back the pamphlet. "Please give him a call."

****

Amanda toured The Enclave after lunch and found the site manager to be friendly enough. The apartment was actually quite clean and bright. The furniture was rather dingy, though, and full of nicks and scratches. It was particle-board assemble-yourself furniture. *I'm only going to be there for the summer,* she told herself. *How nice a place do I really need? Besides, it has a nearly Olympic-sized swimming pool right in the center of the complex.*

She returned to Amanda at Housing Finders and signed the lease for the studio. By that evening, she had keys to an apartment in hand. She returned to the hotel excited to check out, but more than that, anxious to see if the cleaning staff had found her hematite bracelet from Therese.

All they'd left was an apologetic note saying they hadn't seen a bracelet. She crumpled the note and threw it in the trash.

****

Amanda had never rented a furnished apartment. Laying on the futon that converted into a bed, she wondered how many other people had lived there. *It's no different than a hotel,* she told herself, *although no one really thinks of staying in a hotel for more than a few nights. The place reminds me of my freshman year in the dorms. I never imagined that someone could live in such a tiny space for real.* From the futon, she could see the small kitchen with a two- burner stove but no oven, and a refrigerator that came up to her thigh. The one closet would somehow have to hold all of the contents she'd need to store: towels, clothes, coats, everything. The only interior door was to the bathroom, and that only housed the toilet and the tub. The vanity and sink sat to the right of the kitchen, in plain view of the front door. It was cozy, she told herself, and truly all she needed for the summer. She'd just expected Colorado to be cheaper.

Amanda went down to her car to bring up the last of her bags. Looking up toward her apartment, she noticed a man standing at the window of a unit directly below hers. Walking back from her car with her duffel bag and bottled water, she realized he was tracking her. He was only in silhouette so it was hard to make out details, and besides, Amanda didn't want him to know she saw him.

Her phone began to play *Shut up and Let Me Go* by The Ting Tings, a song she'd loved in high school. She had finally taken the time to program ringtones for each phone number, and it was now a feature she didn't know how she'd lived without.

"Hi, Mom."

"I've been trying to find you!" Celia barked. "Are you okay? You don't sound well."

"I'm fine. I just ran up some stairs, I'm out of breath." Amanda thought about commenting on the altitude, but that would probably only freak her out. "What's up?" Amanda asked, refusing to acknowledge the multiple missed calls from Celia she'd noticed in the last two days.

"Why haven't you called? I get one 'I landed' phone call and then nothing for days. Do you know how worried I've been? If you had children, you would know what it's like."

"I've been busy. Sorry. I just found an apartment today. I'm moving in right now."

"Is it nice?"

Amanda thought about what would constitute nice to her mother and knew that her new apartment was not it. "It will do."

"Does it have a guest room? I want to come out for a visit."

Amanda's face turned white. The thought of Celia visiting had never occurred to her. *No. There's absolutely no way that could happen.*

"It's a studio. You know, basically one big room. There's definitely not enough room for two. There may not even be room enough for me. Besides, I'm going to be working all the time."

"I can stay at a hotel."

Amanda laughed to herself trying to picture Celia in a *Hampton Inn*. *Westins* were about as low as she would go when traveling, and that even seemed too swanky for Castle Rock.

"Listen, I was talking to Marguerite … "

"Your cleaning lady?"

"No, my friend in Scottsdale, you remember her? She's from France. Well, she offered her place in Arizona again. I was thinking that I could come out next weekend, and then we could fly to Phoenix together from Denver."

"Mom, I have to go. I ordered some food, and the delivery driver's here," Amanda lied.

"Are you eating? There's no one there to keep an eye on you and make sure that you're taking care of yourself."

"My doorbell is ringing. I have to go."

"Okay but call me about Phoenix."

"Bye, Mom." Amanda hung up, powered off her phone, and collapsed on the futon. *I've made it,* she realized. *I'm now officially living in Colorado. I have a mailing address. I'm a thousand miles away from Celia. No pop-in visits. My first taste of true freedom. And Miles. He's here, somewhere in this town. The rest of my life is about to begin.*

CHAPTER 22

Amanda wasn't sure how to dress for orientation. The weather was unbearably hot, so she opted for shorts, a tank top, and Tevas. She was beginning to panic at the thought of wearing weighty Renaissance garb day after day in the oppressive Colorado heat, and also glad she hadn't chosen to work at a Faire in Florida, where humidity would have added its own problems.

In choosing her clothes, she had to think through the very real possibility that today could be the day she would finally meet up with Miles. *I want to wow him, but not look out of place among the other Faire employees.* She played out their reunion over and over in her mind. She thought she saw him at Jumpin' Java Beans one afternoon and even at Safeway when she was shopping for food to fill up her baby fridge.

****

On her drive to work, Amanda also began to wonder about Melinda. *What will she be like? Will she be motherly, like King Henry suggested? Motherly in a Queen Isolde way or a Celia way?* She'd never had a female boss and the thought excited her. *Surely, a woman would be better than any of the men I've worked for. Irv, of course, was the epitome of a horrible male boss.* Amanda laughed, thinking back to some of the other male highlights of her brief working life.

There was Gus, the residence hall manager, from when I worked the front desk of my dorm my freshman and sophomore years. He preened himself in the office mirror, reeking of cheap cologne. Car keys in hand, he'd always cite how I was in charge, because he had important errands to attend to for the dorm. He always made it sound like a badge of honor. A huge responsibility. His errands were always dates and he frequently left me low on cash, so I could never exchange five dollar bills for quarters, leaving my fellow dorm mates stuck with dirty laundry.

Jose at The Gap was a piece of work. He thought it was appropriate to start his day by yelling at the staff in military form to get them 'properly pumped for action!' Considering the staff consisted of female teens, and action meant folding clothes, the tactic rarely worked. Amanda wracked her brain but couldn't think of any good experiences with bosses. *No wonder I've hated work. Work obviously hated me.*

****

Amanda parked her car and practically pranced across the dusty parking lot to the entrance of the Faire. There were signs pointing her to orientation; she followed them, brimming with enthusiasm as she walked down the cobblestone lane, looking at the store names like Dragon Wingery, Ye Olde Blacksmith, and Crystal Encounters. A crystal store! Why had she not thought to tell King Henry that she wanted to work in a crystal store? That would have been perfect.

She continued along the market way. The stores were so authentic and vividly real that she felt as if she were walking in downtown Glastonbury with Robert; that reminded her, *I've never gotten closure as to why he appeared in my regressions; I wonder what his purpose was in Keira's life. Unless I can regress again, I'll never know.*

Dismissing this thought, Amanda followed the other walkers, assuming everyone was also on their way to the King's Stage. She laughed out loud when she saw a sign for the bathroom marked The Royal Flush. At the King's Stage Amphitheater, she took a seat next to a woman her age. The wooden seats were old and warped, and she got a splinter in her hand. There had to be more than a hundred people in the crowd; Amanda was surprised to see that the Faire employed so many people. It was also a more diverse group than she'd expected — from old hippies to some who didn't even look like they were out of their teen years. Of course, there was only one face in the crowd she was searching for, but so far, he was nowhere to be found.

"Welcome, lads and lasses!" bellowed a boisterous male voice. Through the crowds milling about looking for seats, Amanda couldn't see who was on the stage as the booming voice called out, "Welcome to the Renaissance Festival of Colorado and the opening of our twenty-first season of this most splendid event!"

When she finally could see the stage, she recognized King Henry. His potbelly tested the seams of his outfit, and his nose had the glow of an alcoholic. Amanda wondered what he did in the off-season. She pictured him in a bar in northern Wisconsin in the middle of January, layered in fleece, his face deep in a large lager. *He would probably be drooling over a dye-job blonde at the jukebox.* She shuddered at the image.

"Today, we will cover what you need to know about being a personage in this mighty land. You will understand the rules of our kingdom and shall be able to navigate your way through our realm."

A stout woman with rosy cheeks and curly brown hair, seated at Amanda's right, leaned over and whispered, "Sometimes you just wish he'd say, 'You'll get the tour of the place and learn the rules,' you know?" The woman sat upright and continued staring straight ahead with a broad plastic smile. Amanda wanted to believe that all these people were gypsies who traveled from festival to festival, like circus folk. *I've run away to join the gypsies! That's it.* She knew they were probably schoolteachers trying to supplement their income and have a little fun along the way. Either that or they were out-of-work actors, happy for any gig they could get. She pictured herself in a gypsy caravan, her head in a babushka, and her clothes in tatters wrapped around her with scarves. Her face would be smudged, her eyes wild like a werewolf. The picture was so clear in her mind that she wondered if that had been another past life. She let herself dwell on that idea, completely missing the rest of King Henry's talk. The next thing she knew, he was dismissing the group for a tour of the Faire grounds.

Startled by a hand on her shoulder, Amanda turned to see a woman with mousy, straight, brown hair and kind, hazel eyes. She had a soft smile and thin lips, and Amanda liked her instantly.

"You were smart," she said, pointing to Amanda's water bottle.

"I've quickly learned the importance of staying hydrated here." Amanda responded holding up her bottle. "Between the altitude and the dryness, I nearly fainted my first day in Colorado. I've had a water bottle with me ever since."

"Yeah, I always forget. Then I end up forgetting bug spray when I go to the one in Minnesota. I'm a mess," she giggled, tossing a lock of hair away from her eyes. "My name's Claire. Although, at the Faire, I'm Lady Jane. Plain Jane," she snickered. "What's your name?"

"Keira."

"Your Faire name?"

"Both." Amanda was nervous that if she made eye contact, she'd have to tell Claire the truth. She'd decided that morning that everyone at the Faire was to know her only as Keira. She was bound to be rid of Amanda, one way or another. "So what do you do at the Faire?"

"I'm in the court. I'm one of the Queen's ladies-in-waiting. Waiting for what? Who knows!" She broke into wild laughter. "Sorry, bad joke. This is my fifth summer here, but only my second in the court. I'm a Faire junkie. I go from one to another from March until November every year. I find it a great way to avoid figuring out what to do with my life."

"I was wondering if people actually did that. I think this life could get very addictive, very fast. Who wants to go back to reality?"

"Precisely! So tell me what you're going to be doing in our mighty kingdom? From the looks of you, I'm guessing you're a virgin."

"Excuse me?"

"Oh come on! Virgin Faire employee." Claire fist-bumped Amanda's shoulder, her hearty laugh rolling over them both. "It's your first year. Am I right?"

"Ah, yes, you are," Amanda laughed in a guarded way. Claire seemed so free and sure of herself. She could use a friend like Claire on this new adventure. "I'm going to work at Faerytale Fynery. You know, fitting young girls with flowered tiaras. Every girl needs to be a princess."

"I like that. You're going to fit in rather nicely here."

As the crowd of employees started their tour, Amanda kept a watchful eye out for Miles. *Where is he? He had to be at orientation, right? Maybe he's such a regular he got to skip orientation? What if the picture on the website was from a previous year and he hasn't returned? Or worse, what if it was a stock photo and he's never even been here – just a random dude dressing up for a photo shoot?*

Amanda tried not to panic. She didn't want to admit how half-baked her plan actually was. The tour moved deeper into the Faire grounds with everyone eventually making their way through Market Cross Lane where Amanda found her shop. She looked in awe at the colorful storefront covered in painted fairies. The wood support beams sparkled with layers of gold paint. She couldn't wait until tomorrow when all this really began. The group passed the Celestial Stage and Amanda was captured by the suns and moons that hung suspended from the trees above where the audience would sit. The floor was painted in the same glittering gold that covered the beams on the storefront. Everything was so completely over-the-top magical, like the Renaissance version of Disney World.

"The Celestial Stage is my favorite," Claire said, noticing Amanda's captivation.

"It's incredible."

"You definitely have to come here on one of your lunch breaks and check out Zora, the fortune teller. She'll hypnotize a member of the audience and take them back to other lives. It's amazing to watch. I once saw a Korean woman start talking in some Native American language. It was way freaky! I've never had the guts to have her try it out on me."

Amanda smiled. She had definitely found her home.

Next, the group came upon Princess Elizabeth's Splendid Swing. The swing hung from tall pine trees and looked like it could sit five adults at one time. Ribbons flew from the back end, giving it such a playful feel that Amanda wanted to jump out of the group and hop on for a ride.

"Do you see that pulley?"

Amanda nodded.

"Well the operator turns the pulley system and the swing pulls back into the trees until you feel like you will slide right off and then, just at that moment, they release it and you go flying through those two pines over there. The best part," Claire leaned in closer, "is Chris and Dwayne. They hang out in the back and give you extra pushes to keep it going. On real warm days, they wear loose fitting vests with no shirts. They both have long ponytails and are built, if you know what I mean. If you've ever had fantasies of doing it with a carny, they'll fulfill them."

Amanda was pretty sure that carnies never entered into her fantasies. She only wanted one person to fulfill her fantasies, and so far, he was nowhere to be found.

****

The sun was really beating down and Amanda's water bottle was empty. The place was much larger than she ever would have guessed, and she figured they must have walked several miles already.

"So, what did you do before you came out here?" Claire asked.

"Nothing special. I was a secretary to a womanizing jerk at an insurance company."

"Ooh, sounds like all kinds of stereotypes wrapped up into one."

"For sure."

"Where did you say you're from?"

"Chicago."

"This must be a big change from there."

"Tell me about it. My job and Chicago feel like another lifetime. It's hard to believe that I just quit last week." Amanda briefly thought back to Fine Line. No more sitting at a cube, under air-conditioning vents that never stopped running, spending her days preparing meaningless reports filled with data she didn't understand. No more wearing suits when Mr. Hitchens was in town, or listening to light rock through the cubical wall she shared with Ruth. No more days when her only bright spot was useless flirting with Josh.

"I was a digital marketing executive in San Francisco. Can you believe that? It was a fast-paced life, full of big opportunities, and I hated every minute. There I was raking in all this money, but I was working such horrendous hours, I never had time to spend any of it. It hit me hard when I bought a boat and only got to take it out once the entire summer. One day, I cashed in all my stock, sold the house, the boat, and the Tesla, and walked away. Bought a one-way ticket to Colorado and joined the Faire. My parents think I'm nuts; but after the first season, I really stopped caring. I usually head down to the Caribbean in the winter months and chill out, waiting tables or something, then it's back up to the Faire come spring."

"And you don't miss the stability that your old life had? You're completely happy?"

"Stability is an illusion in corporate America," Claire said, hauntingly serious. "And yes, I'm more than happy! No more heart palpitations. No more anxiety. No more stress."

"How did you end up picking Ren Faires?"

"Doesn't every little girl want to be a princess?"

CHAPTER 23

Amanda didn't need an alarm clock to get her out of bed for work now; her excitement woke her up. She dressed quickly, grabbed a protein bar and banana, and was in her car at 7:15 a.m.

The sun beamed intently. She drove in circles in the Faire parking lot, trying to find a spot in the little shade the lot offered. The temperature felt like it was 90, and it was still early in the morning — not a good sign for the rest of the day. She was instructed at orientation to be at the Costumery by 7:30. When she stepped inside, she realized that 7:30 was the 'no later than' time, and most people had arrived quite a bit earlier.

"Excuse me," Amanda interrupted a petite woman who looked to be in charge. "This is my first day. Can you tell me where I need to go?"

"Over there." She pointed in one direction, while her body turned in the other. "I said *not* the pirate costume, asshole!" the woman screamed, startling Amanda. "How many times do we have to go over this, Brad? Your costume is on the back wall. Do you see it?" she continued talking several octaves too loud at the moppy-haired 20-something with vacant eyes and a mouth stuck in a soft open state.

"Sorry," she said, turning her attention back to Amanda. "It's a fucking madhouse around here. Go over there. Do you see Ann-Marie in the corner?"

"The redhead?"

"Yeah, she'll help you out." The woman was gone before Amanda could turn around to thank her.

"Where you workin', hon?" Ann-Marie called out to Amanda across the sea of women's bodies in various states of undress.

"Faerytale Fynery."

"Okay. You're on that rack. If you don't see a size that fits, call me." Ann-Marie's attitude matched the other woman's. It must be a survival tactic in this chaotic mess. She fought her way through the mass of women, then flipped through racks upon racks of heavily layered skirts and bodices with complicated ribbons dangling from them. *I can't imagine how any of these outfits could be comfortable in this 100-degree weather. I wonder how often they get washed? But I probably don't want to know.*

Right there, in the middle of the floor, she peeled off her sweaty shorts and T-shirt. She felt self-conscious standing in her bra and underwear amongst all the other women, especially when she realized that they were in plain sight of the men on the other side of the fitting room. She scanned the area, desperately trying to see Miles, but there were too many people. She fidgeted with the ribbons on the bodice, and was about to tear it apart in frustration when a set of fingers reached in and offered help.

"Hang on. Hang on. These things can be a bitch." Amanda looked up to see Claire's diamond nose piercing catching the light and sending glittering rays across her face.

"Thanks." The angel Claire had come to save her from the wardrobe demons.

"The newbies always look a little shell-shocked in wardrobe. Here, let me show you how these things work." Claire took the ribbons out of Amanda's hands, and began to expertly and quickly lace up her top. "There's a reason women used to have ladies-in-waiting. These dresses are impossible to get on by yourself."

"Totally," Amanda agreed and then started snickering at the sight of her small breasts being squeezed out of the bodice like they were about to explode. "I feel like a ketchup bottle!"

"After a few days, you get used to it." Claire smiled. "It will also take a while to get used to men talking to your chest instead of your face."

"Unfortunately, I already have experience there. My old boss in Chicago used to say hello to my boobs more than to me."

"Nice."

"What is wrong with men? It's not like we go around talking to their crotches."

"Seriously!"

"So this must be your royal court garb." Amanda admired Claire's ornate attire. A purple velvet dress with a gold v-shaped front bodice. Gold lacy puffs capped her shoulders. Pearls dripped from her neck and her hair was captured in a shimmery netting that connected with a glistening tiara. She truly looked like she had stepped out of another era.

Claire gathered up her bag and pointed at Amanda to do the same. "Now we go to makeup. Actually first, we'll find a locker for your stuff. Can you breathe?"

"I think so." Amanda tried to take in an extra big breath. It was tough.

On their way to the lockers, Claire introduced Amanda to Dwayne and Chris, the carny male fantasies, who pushed the big ribboned swing. Both of them had greasy long ponytails and buff bodies. They were generically good looking and Amanda could see how Claire found them attractive.

"Hey, babe. What's up?" Dwayne greeted Claire with a kiss on the cheek, and then pulled her into an embrace with a muscular arm.

"I want you to meet Keira."

Dwayne and Chris bowed in tandem, making Amanda feel like she was an important visitor. She realized that working there, she could at least pretend that chivalry wasn't dead.

"Charmed," Chris replied, kissing Amanda's hand. If she had to choose, Chris was definitely better looking than Dwayne. He had deep brown eyes that bore into her as he took her hand, and when he smiled, those eyes lit up, offering a dangerous vibe and a promise of adventure.

"We have to run along and finish our hair and makeup. Maybe we'll see you boys at Spur later today?"

"Definitely," Dwayne said to Claire before giving her another kiss.

"I hope to meet this fine lady again very soon." Amanda offered a polite smile, but she couldn't let puppy dog eyes distract her. Chris kissed Amanda's hand once more and walked away.

"Aren't they hot?" Claire asked when they were safely out of earshot.

"They're nice."

"Not your type?"

"Um, we'll see."

"Oh I get it! You like playing hard to get. Good for you! I've never been very good at that. Dwayne and I hook up from time to time. He's good in bed." Claire shrugged as they came upon the lockers. After snagging one of the last available ones, Amanda and Claire left for the makeup department where a bank of mirrors and desks were lined with endless amounts of makeup and brushes. Amanda cringed at the germs that must be spreading around from everyone using everyone else's brushes.

"Would you like me to braid your hair?"

Amanda thought back to how Celia used to braid her hair when she was a little girl, and how much she'd loved having her hair brushed and played with. It was one of the rare tender memories she had of Celia.

"Do you mind?" Amanda asked a little embarrassed to be so excited.

"Not at all. The makeup person is running late. The court has their hair and makeup done professionally. It's one of the bennies of moving up. I've got some extra time."

Amanda sat down and closed her eyes, luxuriating in the sensation of Claire brushing her hair. She hadn't cut it since her first session with Therese, and it was now just past her shoulder blades. She had toyed with the idea of chopping it off since arriving in Colorado. She'd forgotten how insufferable the heat was with longer hair.

Claire made two tiny braids around Amanda's temples and then pulled them together in the back and fastened them with a jewel-toned clip. Amanda looked in the mirror. There she saw Keira of the Forest of Forgiveness. The image caused her to go dizzy, but she fought it with all her might. As much as she wanted to regress, she couldn't give in to it, not there in the middle of the makeup department. The dizziness grew.

"No, no," she muttered to herself. Claire came around in front of her with a worried expression on her face.

"Are you okay?"

"Yes, just got a little light-headed for a second." Amanda tried not to let on that she had broken out in a full sweat.

"Do you have time for makeup? It's nearly nine."

Amanda looked at her watch and realized that she was running dangerously late. She was supposed to be at Faerytale Fynery at nine to review the merchandise before the Faire opened at ten.

"I have to run. I put some on this morning. It will have to do. Thanks for your help!"

"Wait for me in the Costumery before you leave today," Claire called as Amanda ran off, winding her way through the re-creation of old England.

****

Amanda quickly made her way to Faerytale Fynery, amazed that she still remembered where the store was from the orientation tour. The clapboard building glowed as the morning sun shone upon it. The entire front of the store was open, and Amanda wondered how they would lock up at night, or if they even had to. Pigeons nestled in the eaves and she pretended they were doves. Thank God she had left the land of gargoyles and steel far behind.

From the doorway, Amanda could see displays of flowered and ribboned tiaras shining in the sunbeams that streamed through a skylight. Mirrors for trying on the tiaras reflected the natural light and the space glowed warm and inviting. No more windowless offices and cubicle environments!

Amanda was greeted by a robust, jolly woman, whose smile was so vast that it caused her eyes to sink into her face. She instantly reminded Amanda of the Cheshire Cat. "You must be Keira!"

Amanda approached her, extending her hand for a shake, but the woman pushed it aside and pulled her into a bear hug.

"Yes. Are you Melinda?"

"Of course! Come in, come in," she sang the words, ushering Amanda into the shop. "Let's get you oriented around the store. We have a lot of merchandise to cover before the flocks descend." Melinda grabbed Amanda's arm and dragged her around the small space. "The flower crowns are our most popular items, particularly with little girls. Let's go in the back and I'll show you the wings."

On the far wall, hung angel wings in sheer luminescent white and rich and shimmery black. Amanda picked off a white pair that matched her body frame.

"May I wear these?"

"Now aren't you a little fairy angel," Melinda cried, seeing Amanda hold up the wings to her back. "You'll fit in beautifully here. Go ahead, put them on, and then let me show you around, familiarize you with the merchandise, so to speak, and show you how we dazzle the crowds. You know, this is nothing more than acting. We want to create an experience for the people who come here. Make them believe they really have stepped back in time. And if they buy something while they're here, then all the better! Right? Right?" Melinda's robust laugh filled the room. "Here, we invite the visitors to take the magic home with them."

Take the magic home. That really resonated with Amanda. She slipped into the angel wings and continued following Melinda around the store.

"I can't tell you how excited I am to be here. This is like a dream come true."

"Tell me, lass, what brought you to our wonderful Faire?"

The question felt so overwhelming. *Where should I start? So many things have brought me here. Should I actually admit that an Internet ad brought me? That my soul mate from 500 years ago is at the Faire, and I've come to find him? Or is that too big a heap of crazy to lay on Melinda, even though I suspect she might be a little crazy herself?* "I needed a big life change ... and who could turn down Colorado in the summer? It's so gorgeous here. And the Faire is so fun, and like you said, magical. It's a great place to recharge."

"Oh yes, honey," Melinda agreed without turning around to look at Amanda. She was frantically fixing a wand display that was precariously positioned. "The Faire is a place of complete reinvention. It's my sanctuary as well. So where are you from?" Melinda turned to Amanda with a feather duster and pointed her to a display in the opposite corner.

"Chicago."

Amanda took Melinda's cue and walked toward a display of magic wands.

"Never been. I'm from Humboldt County, California. Heard of it?"

"No."

"It's a slice of heaven. It's north of San Francisco. Otherwise known as pot country."

"Ah. My dad lives near Santa Barbara. Further south ... but I haven't spent much time there."

"Eek! Look at the time." Melinda moved back to explaining the pricing and appropriate sizing of the various tiaras: plastic versus silk, leaves versus flowers, cloth versus velvet, it seemed to be endless. They reviewed the angel wings and dragonfly wings, the magic wands, and the crystal orbs. Amanda thought, *it will be weeks before I can memorize it all. And oh, how things have changed in retail since my days at The Gap. There's no dial-up machine for processing credit cards; now, everything's swipe-based on iPads. The technology seems oddly misplaced in the Renaissance world. I feel like I should be accepting payment in gold and silver coins.*

"Look at that, the peasants have found their way!" Melinda cried, and with that came the first group of customers.

Amanda happily settled into her new role as faery angel sales clerk and descended upon a group of little girls as if she truly was an angel.

****

Following Claire's suggestion, Amanda planned to spend her lunch break watching Zora present on the Celestial Stage. When she read the schedule, though, she realized that Zora wasn't up again until 2:00 p.m. and she couldn't wait that long to eat. The other event that caught her eye was a jousting tournament. It was only a half-hour, which would leave her plenty of time to grab something to eat, watch the event, and return to work.

The jousting arena was on the opposite side of the Faire from Faerytale Fynery. She didn't know how long it would take to get there, so she stopped for a turkey leg and a Sprite from the Meadery to take with her before hustling her way across the entire Faire.

The arena was nestled at the bottom of a hill. Looking out from where she stood, she could see the mountains and valleys of Colorado laid out before her. The sun played with light and shadows off the evergreens in a way that captured her breath and left her stunned. She realized why people referred to Colorado as God's Country. Awestruck, she thought, *I've never seen nature look more beautiful.*

Amanda descended the hill toward the arena. The crowds were already taking over the grassy slope. A hyperactive musician banged on a series of massive bells, playing the theme to *The Exorcist.*

Not very authentic Renaissance music, Amanda thought, as the tingy music sent goosebumps down her spine. She'd been expecting bagpipes or mandolins as she marveled at the royalty stands that rose above the jousting field. Deciding she could get a better view away from the crowds, she walked to the opposite side of the field.

Settling onto the grass, she watched as heralds bugled on shiny brass horns announcing the arrival of the royalty. The heralds were clothed in red and white capes over rippled shirts and red velvet pants capped by white stockings. From her front-row spot, Amanda could see that, like her, they all had sweat glistening on their brows. The first to arrive were the ladies-in-waiting and princesses. Amanda recognized some of the people from the Costumery that morning. The transformation from shorts and T-shirts to royalty was incredible. She waved frantically at Claire as she walked by. Claire looked amazing after having had her hair and makeup done, a true princess. She smiled at Amanda, but she couldn't break character and wave back. Next, King Henry entered the procession, the only one besides Claire whom Amanda could identify for sure. He had a wife on his arm, and she wondered which one of King Henry's many wives this one was supposed to be playing. In fact, Amanda wondered if there was a replica Tower Green for beheadings, like she'd read about in her research of the time period.

"Good day, gentle folk," King Henry bellowed from atop his royal seat. "Today, we have come in the name of sport to witness the skills of four of our bravest knights in the land." The crowd clapped and screamed, as the knights in full armor galloped into the arena. The crowd cheered for certain names and Amanda quickly realized she'd missed something by arriving late. Her side was cheering for Sir Lancelot and Sir William. *Sir Lancelot? Roxie's sarcastic name for Miles. Probably just a silly coincidence.* She was so distracted that she completely missed hearing the name of the opposite side's knights, as they too were introduced.

"Sir Lancelot and Sir William are riding for Northumberland. Sir Thomas and Sir Christian are riding for Greenwich," The King continued. "Ladies, please now present your favors to the knights."

A few of the ladies-in-waiting approached the base of the scaffolding. The knights rode their horses to greet them. Amanda tried to discern which knight was Lancelot, but in full armor it was impossible to know. The women placed beautiful, brightly colored ribbons onto the knights' decorative lances: red and white was announced for Lancelot and William, purple and pink for Thomas and Christian. The knights returned to the center of the arena and turned to the king for direction. They looked so authentic, displaying their lances.

"May I remind my knights that this is to be a joust of joy and sport — there will be no bloodshed today," Henry bellowed from his place in the stands, and Amanda wondered if the knights ever actually got hurt performing in these mock tournaments. "Knights, please greet your people, and then return for the beginning of the joust."

The knights removed their helmets as their horses pranced around the inner edge of the arena. As Lancelot and William approached, Amanda stood up so she could get a better look, and hopefully, see if she could notice any defining features across the arena. As she was standing, Lancelot rode by her and his eyes locked on hers. Those blue eyes! From the Internet ad! From her regressed time as Keira in the Forest! They pierced a place inside of her like lightning, leaving her weak-kneed. Her breath constricted, every muscle in her body stiffened. *Could it be? His eyes are the same lucid blue, his thick black hair the same I ran my fingers through.*

"I see we have been graced by a number of lovely ladies this fine day," Lancelot said, not releasing Amanda from his gaze. Her legs trembled, and she started to feel light-headed the way she did right before a regression. He continued prancing, back and forth, and a woman standing next to Amanda nudged her in the arm.

"I think Sir Lancelot was looking at you," the woman said with a wink.

"Yes, I think he was."

CHAPTER 24

The Faire closed at six P.M., but by the time she and Melinda straightened up the store, Amanda didn't make it back to the Costumery until almost seven. She looked for Claire, but couldn't find her anywhere and cursed herself for not exchanging phone numbers. There was no way to reach her until they ran into each other again.

I have to know if Claire knows Lancelot. Lancelot! The way he looked at me, like he knew me on a soul level. He does know me on a soul level. Is it really this easy? Have I already found him?

Amanda had finally gotten back into her normal clothes and unbraided her hair when she noticed that nearly everyone had already left for the day. She wondered how the others changed so fast. On her way out the door, she found a photocopy of a staff directory lying on a table. She picked it up and flipped through the booklet on the way to her car. The brochure listed all the real names of the actors in the Faire. Amanda immediately turned the page to the knights and looked up Lancelot. Steve Thrasher. Gross.

Sir Lancelot is Steve Thrasher? What a terrible name, so harsh. She particularly hated the name Steve. She had a stalker in junior high named Steve.

Amanda put her Bluetooth in and looked up Therese's number on speed-dial. She had to tell Therese that she'd found Miles, but instead of Therese's familiar voice, Amanda heard a recorded operator say, "You have reached a number that is no longer in service. Please check the number and dial again." Amanda tried manually dialing the number three times in a row, thinking that she might have programmed the number wrong, but each time she got the same recording. In desperation, she sent a text. It didn't go through. She tried an email. Undeliverable. Amanda started the car and sped out of the empty parking lot.

Back at her apartment, Amanda tried a new round of emails, texts, and phone calls. *Nothing works. This is crazy. How can someone simply vanish? Did something happen to Therese? Has she died? It's not like Therese's family checked on her. Heck, I've never even seen another client leaving Therese's office or waiting after my appointment.*

Maybe I'm truly going insane. Is this how it happens? First, I lost the bracelet. Now, I can't find Therese. Did I dream the entire last six months of my life?

She was too upset and nervous to concentrate on making dinner, so she headed down to the pool. A cool-down sounded good anyway, since her apartment didn't have air conditioning. She couldn't imagine having a place without air conditioning back in Illinois. Even with no humidity, Colorado was hot. The dry heat simply felt like being an oven.

****

Amanda tried to lose herself in an article in *Esquire* on how to prepare for the fall fashions, but it wasn't working. Besides, seasonal fashion likely no longer applied to her anyway. *Where the hell has Therese gone? Did she ever even exist? Maybe I should fly back to Chicago. Go and check out her office in person, confirm that it's empty and that I'm truly alone on this journey. Or maybe, just maybe, I can beg Roxie to check up on her. That would be a tough sell.*

She took a deep breath and opened the keypad on a new text: "Can you call me? I need your help."

Twenty minutes later, her phone started playing an old 80s Madonna tune — Roxie's custom tone. A 40-something lady at the opposite side of the pool turned to smile at the sound of it. Amanda loved to see who reacted when it rang; it was almost always a Gen Xer.

"Thanks for calling."

"What do you want, Amanda?"

She knew it was going to be a tough call, but ouch! Roxie's hostility was at an epic level. *Amanda*, her name, hung in the air — a weird hangover from another life. She hadn't been called that in over a week; it was already beginning to feel like an outdated childhood nickname, the way a Suzie one day grows into a Suzanne.

"Hi to you, too."

"Don't play with me. You've been gone over a week and I just now hear from you? No 'I made it okay' phone call. No 'I'm having a great time, wish you were here' text. Since you've been gone, I've gotten one emoji thumbs-up from you. That's it. You know Celia and I are worried. We're thinking about coming out to check up on you."

"You've been talking to my mom?"

"Of course I have; you've freakin' gone off the deep end!"

"I'm going to ignore that. Listen, I really need your help. I've been trying to call and email Therese, my past-life therapist, and I can't get through. Could you swing by her office and let me know if her name is still on the door. I think maybe she closed her office."

"Hell no! I'm not helping you if it involves that woman. She's the reason you're in this mess. She's turned you into looney tunes."

Amanda pulled the phone away from her head for a moment while she rubbed the bridge of her nose with her thumb and index finger.

"And your mom and I are worried that you're not eating," Roxie continued.

"You guys are being completely ridiculous! I'm fine. Come on, Roxie, if I can't turn to you, I have no one. Don't do this to me."

Silence.

"Roxie, I'm sorry I haven't called. I really need you now. Will you help me? I know this is all really weird to you, but it would mean the world to me if you could help. Can you do this for me?"

"Fine," Roxie sighed. "But you have to tell me what's so important."

"I found Miles."

"What?"

"He's here. He's at the Faire."

The phone went silent.

"I should tell Celia about the whole past-life regression bullshit."

"No! You can't. Please don't tell her anything. You're the only one who knows. The only one I've trusted. Please! She'll have me checked into a mental institution. She won't understand."

"Exactly."

"Look, I know you don't understand either and I know it sounds insane, but you're the only one I can trust. I need you, Roxie. Please help me out, and see if Therese is still there. We're always there for each other. Always."

"Okay, I'll do it. I'll call you and let you know what I find out," Roxie acquiesced before changing her tone. "So what's he like?"

"Miles?"

"Yeah, your knight-in-shining armor, Lancelot?"

"Funny, that's actually his name at the Faire."

"Seriously?"

"Yes, he goes by Lancelot. Well, at the Faire anyway."

"That's really weird," Roxie said. "So what's he like?"

"I'm not sure."

"What do you mean?"

"Well, I haven't actually talked to him yet."

"You're ridiculous, Amanda. You know that? I'll head over to Therese's office after work tomorrow. I'll call you and let you know what I find out."

"Thank you. Thank you. I owe you."

"Oh, yes you do." Roxie hung up before Amanda could say goodbye.

****

She'd passed much of the day at the pool and running errands, and by 4:30, Amanda finally felt hungry. After finding some lettuce, crackers, and a can of tuna to serve as dinner, she headed out to the liquor store down the street to pick up some wine to pair with her meal. *What complements canned tuna? Maybe a chilled rosé?*

She opened the door to the liquor store and saw a weathered man with a long scraggly ponytail, sunken bloodshot eyes, and arms that looked like heroin receptacles peppered with tiny scars and laced by a few bruises. He sat on a stool behind the check-out counter reading a tattered paperback with its cover missing. He reeked of cigarette smoke.

"Well, hello there, sweet thing." *His voice should be creepy, but for some reason it's oddly ... sexy? No, but ... well?* Amanda contemplated turning around and leaving but a vague curiosity made her stay. *There's something familiar about him. I can't put my finger on what it is. It's not his voice, although there's a comfort in the smooth way the words roll off his tongue. It isn't the way he looks; there's nothing familiar there. It's his presence, his vibe.*

"Looking for something ... special?" His eyes lit up as they fixed on her.

"Not really," she said ducking into the next aisle. She found her way to the back wall, to the refrigerated section. She knew nothing of wine, so she grabbed a $10 bottle of rosé, the one with the prettiest label. As she approached the front of the store, wine in hand, the creepy guy propped his shaky arms on the counter and drilled his stare into her.

"I'm your neighbor, Jerry."

"Really." Amanda used her non-committal, urban defensive tone, even though chills ran down her spine. She and Roxie had once taken a self-defense class, and she was trying to remember what to do. *Did we cover creepy-guy-in-a-store conversations?*

"I've been watching you. You're real pretty." That was when she recognized him. She wanted to run away, but she didn't. "What's your name?"

Amanda should have made up a fake name but if he was her neighbor and had been watching her, he would figure out her name soon enough. "Keira," she relented.

"Of course. Keira."

"How much?" she asked while slamming a twenty dollar bill on the counter.

"She comes skimmin' through rays of violet. She can wade in a drop of dew. Um, um."

"What was that?"

"It'll be $12.20 with tax."

Amanda got her change and quickly walked away.

"Good bye, sugar," Jerry called. "It's nice to have you back."

Amanda didn't say goodbye, but walked as quickly as she could to her apartment, locking both the deadbolt and the chain. *What a freak*, she thought, launching Netflix and curling up on her futon.

CHAPTER 25

"So, do you have a special someone in your life?" Melinda asked, dusting off the display shelves, looking like a fairy godmother, with her flowing dress that hung like a muumuu over her large frame. A flowered tiara held her oversized dark-brown curls in place, and she wore an intense green eye shadow that glistened off the reflection of the lights in the store. Overall, she had a wild look that announced *I am my own person, and I don't give a hoot what anyone else might think.*

"No, not really." Amanda tried to play the conversation cool and not tip her hat that she was in a 600-year-old relationship with someone she'd never actually met. She busied herself rearranging the fairy wings. For some reason, the workers who had helped stock the store at the beginning of the season put the children's wings at the very top of the wall and the adult wings at the bottom. After only one day of having to constantly pull wings down for little kids, Melinda and Amanda knew it wouldn't do.

"What does 'No, not really' mean? I take that for a 'Yes' with an interesting story."

"There's someone I like, but he doesn't know me. Not yet anyway."

"Someone here at the Faire?"

Amanda thought long and hard before answering. *Maybe Melinda knows Miles. Perhaps she can even help broker an introduction.*

"Yes. He's one of the knights in the jousting tournaments."

"Which one?"

Amanda diverted her eyes.

"Come on now, you can't tease a poor old woman. Out with you!"

"You're not an old woman."

"You're sweet, but I'm not letting you off the hook on this one."

"Okay, it's Sir Lancelot."

"I knew it!"

"What do you mean, you knew it?"

"All the ladies fall for Sir Lance. How do you think he ended up with that name?" Melinda giggled. "Be careful, my girl. You're blonde, skinny, and naïve — totally his type. He's infamous for his summer flings, but all the women walk away with a broken heart. He's a total player. Mmm, he is a hottie, though! I wouldn't mind a romp in the hay with him."

Amanda wanted to explain to Melinda that she was Keira. She wasn't just a new blonde here for the summer. She was the one Lancelot had been waiting for. There would be no more flings. But it was too soon for that. Melinda and everyone else, including Lancelot, would see it over time.

"Remember he's a pretty butterfly who can't be captured," Melinda warned. "Have fun, child."

Amanda looked up and the first customers entered the store.

****

Amanda timed her lunch break so she could return to the jousting event. She knew it would be a while before she made time for Zora the Fortune Teller or any of the other novelty acts for that matter. There were so many things she wanted to do at the Faire. She had noticed many of the other women in the Costumery sporting henna tattoos. The idea of a tattoo of any kind, real or temporary, had never appealed to her, but now she decided she wanted one. Now was the time to start doing a lot of things she never would have done before.

Amanda arrived at the jousting early enough to get a good spot, front and center. The royal pageantry began their march and she quickly spotted Claire in the parade. She still couldn't figure out how she had missed her at the Costumery that morning. Claire looked amazingly radiant and Amanda wondered how her mousy looks could transform so dramatically. It made her realize how much makeup, hair design, and costuming could do to transform people, just like in the movies. And there was always plenty of jewelry.

After the royal court made their entrance, the knights entered the arena on horseback. The horses were clothed in royal sheaths that matched the colors the knights wore. Amanda didn't know her breeds, but the ones used in the jousting were absolutely stunning. The 'good' knight was dressed in white, and his horse's coloring matched perfectly. Amanda immediately spotted Lance, who was on the 'bad' side, riding a dark-brown steed. He looked incredibly regal, back held strong, and head high and proud.

As the knights galloped by, Lancelot once again made eye contact with Amanda. It was almost as if he was looking for her in the crowd. He stopped his horse in its tracks and smiled broadly. Amanda held his gaze. She knew his eyes were saying, "I will find you." She could barely contain herself as she watched him canter away.

****

By the end of the day, Amanda was beat. The screaming kids and relentless crowds really took their toll on her. She forgot how exhausting retail could be. It seemed there was no particular busy time, it was just a constant stream of people offering very little time to rest.

She entered the Costumery and loosened her tight bodice, allowing herself to finally take a full deep breath. She was lost in thought and wasn't paying attention to where she was going when she walked smack into someone. "Sorry," Amanda muttered.

"It's okay, I wanted to meet you."

As Amanda made eye contact with Lancelot, she nearly tripped. *Holy crap. He's here. Standing in front of me.* She felt woozy. Her search had led her to this moment. *He's here. And he said he wanted to meet me.* "Hi," she managed, stabilizing her shaky legs.

"I'm Lance." He extended a hand. His smile had a devilish, playful feel as his eyes wrinkled into beautiful rays.

He's here, right here in front of me. My plan worked. It worked! "Keira," she said, offering her hand in return, slightly afraid to touch his. *What if I regress? Or worse, what if he disappears like Therese and all of this is merely a dream?* Amanda felt a pulsing heat pass through them, and it instantly brought Keira's life into full bloom. She could feel what it was like to be lifted onto his horse at the Abbey and taken to the Forest of Forgiveness. She could sense what it felt like to lie in his arms and make love to him. Amanda knew that she had found the man she had been searching for. *Has he been searching for me too?* she wondered as she asked, "So you go by your faire name?"

He grinned. "What man wouldn't relish pretending to be Lancelot?"

"Umm," Amanda stammered.

Lance smiled again, and Amanda wanted to rip his clothes off, right there in the middle of the Costumery. She had never wanted a man so badly in her life.

"Do I know you from somewhere?"

"I'm new." Amanda fidgeted with the ribbons on her bodice.

"It's just ... you look so familiar. I saw you in the stands at the jousting a couple of times this week."

Amanda blushed.

"So where do you work? Who are you? Do you want to grab a drink?"

Amanda laughed nervously. "I work at Faerytale Fynery. I'd love to have a drink."

"Great. There's a bar in Larkspur where all the Faire employees chill after work, Spur of the Moment. Have you been there?"

"No, but I've seen it. I love the name." *Particularly appropriate at this moment,* Amanda thought, but didn't want to seem like a complete idiot by saying so. "Let me get changed."

****

Lance suggested that she follow him. Pulling out of the parking lot her phone played *Like a Virgin*. She answered and pressed the speaker button "Hey, Rox."

"So I went to Therese's office today, but she's not there."

"Seriously?"

"She's gone. No nameplate, no nothing. She wasn't there."

"Are you sure you went to the right place? 1818 N. Wells, Suite 404?"

"Yes, I went to the right place," Roxie snapped.

"Jesus."

"I have to run. I have a date tonight, and he'll be here any minute. Of course you wouldn't know that, though, because I haven't even told you about Izak. You don't really know anything about my life anymore."

Amanda sat there dumbly staring ahead, her eyes tracking Lance's taillights.

"Are you even there?"

"Yeah."

"Goodbye, Mandy."

Therese and Roxie swirled in her mind for the rest of the short drive to Spur. Once parked, she texted Roxie a string of emojis that she hoped to lessen the sting of the call. *I wasn't there for Roxie. Tomorrow. I'll call tomorrow and ask about Ian or was it Isaac? Some guy named I.*

And then there was Therese. The lack of Therese. *How could she have vanished? Where has she gone? Has she been kidnapped? The whole last six months of my life is beginning to feel more and more like a dream. This must be what it feels like to go mad,* she decided. She breathed in slowly and deeply, exhaling fully. She wiped her face with her hands and took another deep breath before following her Lancelot.

Lance and Amanda grabbed one of the few remaining tables in a corner of the musty, hot bar. Amanda spotted Claire from across the room and waved to her. Claire waved Amanda to join her, Dwayne, and Chris but Amanda pointed to Lance. Claire violently shook her head no and raised her eyebrows in full alarm, but Amanda waved her away.

Amanda studied Lancelot's face, impressing details into memory, as if she would need them to carry her through for the next 600 years. He ran a hand through his thick hair, pushing it off his forehead with an air of confidence that grounded her. The hair immediately fell into waves framing his strong jaw line. And those eyes! Miles's clear blue penetrating eyes. She'd found him! And here they were, sitting in a bar in the middle of Colorado, a million miles away from Renaissance England.

"Where are you from?" he asked. A waiter came by with two waters in plastic 70s era Coke cups. Amanda smiled when she noticed they had bendy straws.

"Chicago."

"I thought so. I spent a summer there."

"Can you hear an accent?"

Lance nodded and smiled. *That smile!* "So what brought you out here?"

Amanda choked on her water and nearly spit the mouthful back into her cup.

"You okay?"

"Yes, sorry. Swallowed wrong."

How can I maintain the cool necessary to pull off this conversation? He's sitting right in front of me. Right. In. Front. Of. Me. It's all too much. I'm not a good enough actress to pull off this performance.

"I quit my job and moved last week. I came to work at the Faire," *and to find you*, she thought, but didn't add it.

"Nice. A Faire groupie."

"Virgin Faire groupie. It's my first time," she said, thinking back to Claire's comment. Nibbling seductively on the tip of her straw, Amanda tried to remember some of Roxie's favorite flirting moves: nibble straw, pull and curl hair around finger, rub foot along man's calf, although that last one felt a bit premature — a big gun to be held in reserve, the finale of flirting.

"I like virgins." He had that knowing grin, running his hand through his hair again.

Amanda blushed and took another drink of water, thinking back to their encounter in England, that day by the pond. "How about you? Are you from around here?"

"Sort of, I grew up in the Springs. I come back here in the summer. In the school year, I live in New York. I teach drama in the Bronx. My kids are at-risk and super-low-income. I survived the last two years on an NEA grant. I've reapplied for it again, but they haven't given me any word. If it doesn't come through, I'm not sure I can afford to go back. The stipend they pay teachers is a joke, and the city is crazy expensive. It's only by the mercy of the heavens that I've survived this long."

The waiter returned and they ordered two beers, a stout for Lance and a raspberry wheat for Amanda. Being in the middle of nowhere, Amanda was amazed at the microbrew variety the bar had. She hadn't seen an equal selection at even the trendiest bars in Chicago. "Sounds like a really cool job. How did you ever decide to teach theater? And in the Bronx, did you say?"

"It's what a theater major does after college. I knew I was never going to cut it in the real acting world. I was infected with the acting gene, and it needed an outlet. Working here helps too."

Amanda smiled, realizing that Lance hit two of her guesses as to why people worked at the festival: school teacher and frustrated actor. Claire fit her other guess — gypsy.

"So where are the Springs?" Amanda asked, but what she really wondered was, *how could fate have sent us both to the same place out of all the Renaissance Faires in the country, let alone the world. How does the universe know how to connect souls? Did we make a plan when we were in spirit form to meet up? 'Okay, see you in the summer of 2019 in Colorado. We'll pretend we're re-living our old life by playing in the Renaissance Faire.*

'Oh yeah, sweet. That sounds like tons of fun. See you there.'

Amanda chuckled.

"It's actually Colorado Springs, just a little south of here," Lance continued; she hoped she hadn't missed key details while ruminating on their celestial hangout. "My folks moved us out here from Boston when I was in junior high. As much as I feel at home on the East Coast, I still need my mountain fix, and it's a nice excuse to come home and see the family. New York is brutal in the summer anyway. I can't take the heat and humidity or the terrible city smells, like rotting garbage and diesel fuel."

"Yeah, I went to New York in July once," Amanda wrinkled her nose in camaraderie.

"Besides the Faire is like a second home. I've been working this place since high school. I'm kind of a legend," he laughed, but Amanda's guard went up. Melinda's warning rang in her ear. "I love riding the horses. Finding beautiful women, like you, isn't so bad either." He grinned. "I don't know a better way to spend the summer." He tossed his head back to polish off his beer, then signaled the waitress. "So, did you leave a lonely boy at home?"

"No. No one's waiting for me." Amanda thought about Josh, who was probably flirting with her replacement. The image didn't bother her. She was finally aware that Josh was simply a temporary distraction until she found Miles. "But I bet you have a ravishing Latina waiting for you in New York? Maybe a European model?"

Lance shook his head and laughed a little, "Nope. I'm here free and clear." Their eyes locked and Amanda nearly blurted everything out to him right then and there.

"I need to see you again," Lance started. "I have someplace I have to be tonight. Are you free tomorrow? I'd like to take you out. You know, on a proper date."

"I am." *I'm free forever.*

CHAPTER 26

The doorbell rang at ten minutes after seven. Amanda had nearly completed her makeup, which was a minor miracle, considering she'd barely made it home in time to get ready for their date. *Our date!* Her stomach quaked. *Miles is at my door. It worked. I've actually moved to Colorado and literally found him! But now that he's here, what next?*

A spritz of her new jasmine perfume from the Faire and a final brush of blush, and yes, she was ready to open the door. She hesitated and took in one last full breath before turning the knob. Thoughts raced through her mind: *Why can't I locate Therese? She never prepared me to meet Miles in this lifetime. I still need her guidance. There's no way I know how to do this on my own but now what choice do I have? I'm about to go on a date with my soul mate.*

Lance stood outside her door, carrying a bundle of red roses. He was dressed in a midnight-blue, long-sleeved silk shirt that accentuated his eyes. *And those pants. Wow, very form-fitting black jeans. I can't wait to catch a view of those from the back,* she thought as she sank into his blue eyes and instantly felt transported back to Keira's world, in the same way she had yesterday in the Costumery.

Lance leaned in to peck Amanda on the cheek, causing her to become enveloped in the smell of his peppery, rich cologne. She inhaled deeply and decided at that moment that she would put aside her good-girl rule and sleep with him before the night was through. It would be a test of will to make it through dinner.

"Thank you. Did you find my place okay?"

Lance nodded. "You look great."

Amanda was wearing her favorite summer pants, white silk that had steamed out nicely in the humidity of the bathroom, a last-minute salvation since she learned, a little too late, that her furnished apartment was furnished with an ironing board, but no iron. The fitted black bodice, with lace overlay, hid wrinkles well, so she was safe there, and her pink cashmere wrap was good for dressing up any outfit and dealing with over-air conditioned restaurants.

There was a moment of awkward silence. Amanda felt overwhelmed by all that was happening. "Please, come in." She ushered him in to her tiny apartment.

"Nice place."

"Cozy, huh? I never thought I'd be back in an apartment the size of my college dorm." Amanda fumbled in the kitchen for something that would serve as a vase, finally settling on a clear plastic pitcher covered in tiny yellow daisies.

"We've all been there at one time or another. I'm staying at The Highlands. It's just a few miles from here. I've got one of their killer one-bedroom units, with a view of the mountains. I've learned after enough years of working the Faire that you have to come early to snag the premium places." Lance held his arms behind his back like an eager schoolboy.

Lancelot, Miles, the man of my dreams. The man of many lives worth of dreams. Here he is, standing in my apartment. Her eyes teared up, and she was thankful she'd thought ahead and put on waterproof mascara.

"Actually my apartment in New York isn't much bigger than this."

"Oh right, you'd said you teach in New York."

Lance nodded. "So, are you ready to be kidnapped, Princess Keira, and taken aboard my pirate ship?"

"I am, but I thought you were a knight?"

"I am a man of many faces." He stared at Amanda with a knowing smile.

Amanda locked up her apartment and followed Lance to his car. Everything felt so naturally comfortable and familiar that she half expected Maraza, Miles' horse, to be tied up by the bike racks. *Wouldn't it be grand to ride off with him into the sunset, my arms wrapped tightly around his body? Well, maybe not in white silk pants.*

Lance drove a very sleek black Audi. Amanda wondered how he could afford such a car on an inner-city teacher's pay, but decided she didn't care. She felt like Cinderella approaching the magic pumpkin. Lance opened the door for her and she slipped inside.

"So where are you kidnapping me to, Pirate Lance?"

"Well, my princess, you have your pick. There's a swanky Italian joint in the Springs that is my hidden island safe haven. Then, there's a dirty pirate pub in Larkspur that's full of truckers and chain smokers and other ill-begotten sots. Finally, there's Applebees in Castle Rock, chock full of screaming, whiny brats I kindly refer to as crocodile bait, all supposedly supervised by under-sexed parents. What strikes your fancy?"

"Let me see, I think I'll go with the hidden island haven. It sounds too special to pass up."

"Oh, and it is, my virgin maiden. That is what you told me yesterday, right?" Lance raised one eyebrow and placed a hand on Amanda's thigh, causing a rash of goosebumps across her body.

"Yes." Amanda burst into nervous laughter. "So, is this perfect Italian spot where you take all of your Faire maidens?"

"No, no, no, it's reserved for special ones, like you." He gave Amanda's shoulder a quick rub. Lance was very tactile, Amanda noticed, and she rather liked it. "Actually, it's a favorite of my family's. You know, birthday dinners, graduations, retirement parties, that sort of thing."

"Oh now, that doesn't sound like a pirate's life."

"Really? You aren't familiar with the strong family traditions of pirates?" Lance laughed as well, having a hard time keeping up his own charade. "So tell me more about you. I want to know everything," he insisted in a way that made Amanda uncomfortable.

"Like what?" Amanda was getting frustrated with her nervous laugh, but couldn't help herself. She thought back, and sadly, had a hard time even remembering when she'd had a date that she was this excited about. *There were a few lame attempts off a dating site Roxie insisted I try, but they all ended rather non-eventfully. Even my first date with Ryan didn't invoke this much anticipation. The only one that really jumps to mind is Jared Kline – the snare drummer in high school. Oh, was I excited when he asked me out. That was it. That was my last really high anticipation date, but that was high school. Shouldn't I have outgrown the awkwardness by now?*

Talking about my life before Colorado is the last conversation topic that interests me. I want to ask Lance what he's been up to since the 1500s, but I can't think of a way to do that without sounding crazy. I wonder if we knew each other in lifetimes in between. The era of pirates is right smack in the middle of my two known lives. Perhaps I really was with him in pirate times. If I could only find Therese! There are still so many unanswered questions.

"Tell me anything. I don't know. Do you have any brothers or sisters?" Lance asked, keeping his eyes focused on the road, but glancing at Amanda every now and again with a sly smile.

"No. Well, technically, my dad has kids with his new wife, but I don't count them as siblings. What about you?"

"I have a sister who lives in Vail. She used to work up there as a ski instructor. Now she's married to a real estate developer. You know, typical ski bum-turns-soccer mom story."

"Suburbia in the mountains, huh? How many kids do they have?"

"Three, and they're all under twelve. Two boys and a girl. A lot of family."

"Not much into kids?" Amanda asked, unsure of whether or not that bothered her. *Did Miles and I have children during Keira's time? I always assumed kids with Ryan – that would have been a package deal – but now, with this new lease on relationships, maybe kids could be a possibility instead of a given.*

"Kids, umm, not really my thing. I'm still too much of a kid myself. I'm a killer uncle, though."

"I bet you are! Are your folks still married?"

"Yep. Going on forty years. Hard to believe that kind of commitment even exists anymore."

Amanda thought back to meeting Miles in the Forest of Forgiveness. *That was several hundred years ago and it wasn't our first meeting. Commitment seems to mean a whole lot more than just one lifetime.*

****

It wasn't long before they arrived at the restaurant. The entrance was tucked away in a secluded alley. At first, Amanda was apprehensive. *Maybe this is a secret mafia hangout. He's probably on a 'special assignment' and I'm his decoy for the night. That might explain how an inner-city drama teacher got his hands on a brand new Audi. No,* she quickly corrected, *this is Miles. He wouldn't do anything to put me in harm's way. It isn't in his DNA. But I still can't figure out how he got the car.*

When she stepped inside the restaurant, her worries melted away. The interior was styled as an Italian villa square, replete with a fountain in the center, appropriately speckled with pennies. The floor was cobblestones and difficult to tread in heels. Decoration ivy strung from the ceiling and framed the archways that led into each room. Sconces holding gas lamps hung on the walls, casting cascades of light and dark. Every nook hid a private table. Amanda couldn't have thought of a better place for their first date.

"Pretty cool, isn't it?" Lance whispered in her ear.

"It's incredible."

They were seated in one of the private alcoves in a red velvet booth. As they snuggled in together and opened their menus, a robust Italian man with a balding head and escaping chest hair came right up to their booth and bellowed *That's Amore*. Amanda flashed back to *The Lady and the Tramp* and enjoyed the idea of her and Lance being cartoon dogs in love in a back alley. *In our private cove, we could probably get away with each taking an end of a piece of pasta and chewing until our lips meet in the middle.* She scanned the menu for linguini.

"I recommend the lobster ravioli tonight or perhaps the filet mignon," the waiter said with an Italian accent. "Both excellent choices and specially prepared by our chef." Amanda suppressed a giggle. This was turning out to be the Disney World of Italian restaurants.

"Thank you." Lance dismissed the waiter.

"Do you have a favorite dish?"

"Everything here is good. It just depends on where your tastes go. I'll probably have the filet, but get whatever you want. Should I order a bottle of wine?"

"Anything red."

"A woman after my own tastes." Lance glowed as he read the wine menu. "So, I'm still stuck on why I feel like I know you."

Amanda felt a lump form in her throat.

"Are you sure you haven't worked for the Faire before?"

"Nope, I'm sure. I guess I must have one of those faces."

"Maybe," Lance said distractedly. "So what brought you to Colorado and the Faire?"

Feeling better rehearsed this time, she didn't choke on her words or feel like she was going to say, *"You! I saw you in a pop-up ad and knew I had to come find you!"*

"Basically, I needed out of Chicago and I always wanted to come to Colorado." Amanda avoided making eye contact. She felt slightly guilty about her exaggeration of the truth. Colorado had honestly never crossed her mind before seeing the ad that day. "The Renaissance Faire looked like a fun way to spend the summer. You get to be outside. You know, it's like camp. And it let me put off the whole decision about what to do with my life for at least a few more months."

"I hear you. That's how I got started with all of this. After high school, I continued working the Faire during college, as well as the summer after college. Next thing I knew, it was something I did."

The waiter returned with a basket of breadsticks, and Lance ordered a bottle of Merlot. Amanda thought about Celia's wine snobbishness, and how mortified she would be if she saw her daughter now. *Celia always said, "Merlot is for people with no taste and no budget." But I don't have as developed a wine palate, and as long as it isn't in a jug, it's good enough for me.*

When the waiter returned with the wine, Lance raised his glass to Amanda.

"Cheers," he said as they clinked glasses. "To a great summer."

"Cheers," Amanda said. *And to finding your soul mate.*

****

As Lance poured the remains of the bottle of wine into Amanda's half-full glass, she started to feel tipsy.

"You'll have to finish it," Lance said, setting the empty bottle on the table. "I have to get us home."

"I thought you were supposed to watch how much you drink when you're getting used to the altitude?"

"That's an old wives' tale," Lance winked, "and you've already been here for a while. Drink up, babe." He leaned over to kiss Amanda on the forehead. The press of his lips against her skin brought on a new level of desire. *No one's ever compared to this. Not Ryan, not Josh, not even high school Jared. This is a whole new level.*

****

Amanda had sobered only slightly by the time they pulled up to her apartment building. Lance parked the car in a visitor spot and left the engine running. *It's time to make my move.*

"I had a nice time tonight," Lance said, placing a hand on Amanda's leg, just above her knee. His touch triggered a tingly sensation between her legs.

God, how I want him, she thought. "Me, too," she whispered. *Game on.* "Would you like to come up for a drink?"

Lance turned off the engine. "I'd love to."

"You know, I invite you up for a drink, but I don't even know what I have. My cupboard's rather bare," Amanda giggled as they walked up the stairs to her apartment.

"We can run out if we have to. I'm pretty sure there's a liquor store not far down the street."

"Yes, there is." Amanda thought of the strange encounter with the liquor store clerk, and hoped they wouldn't have to go there.

Once inside, Amanda fumbled around the cabinets. "Oh yeah, I forgot I have a bottle of vodka. Not sure I have anything to mix it with, though."

"We can do shots, pretend we're in Russia," Lance smiled as Amanda drunkenly giggled. "You laugh, but I went there once with a college group, and that's my only memory – shots before bed. Every. Day. The nightly drinking wiped out all other memories."

"Do they really drink that much vodka?"

"They do. It's incredible."

"It's so funny how those stereotypes are true. I went to Ireland with my ex a few years ago and everyone drinks Guinness, like *all* the time."

"Yup. I've been there too. Saw the same thing. Worked out well for me, as I tend to love Guinness."

"And I loved the Irish coffees and Baileys. Speaking of drinking, I have to go to the bathroom. Here's the vodka if you want some, I don't have anything but grapefruit juice to mix it with."

"Grapefruit juice is a perfect mixer."

"Okay then, knock yourself out. I'll be right back."

Amanda sat on the toilet for several minutes. She re-spritzed her perfume, even opening her top and spraying her chest. She touched up her eye shadow and tried to calm her nervous system. Amanda smiled at herself in the mirror. *Tonight's the night you've been waiting for*, she reminded herself. *Be present, be calm, be ready. He's here. Your soul mate is in the next room waiting for you.*

Amanda opened the door to see Lance had reclined the futon and music was playing through her Bluetooth speaker. The overhead light had been turned off, and the only glow came from the light over the kitchen sink. She missed the LED strip she'd installed in her Chicago apartment. It would have been perfect mood lighting.

Lance was sipping his drink; an extra cocktail sat on the coffee table waiting for her. The first two buttons on his shirt were undone and his sleeves were rolled up. She saw a few chest hairs peek out from the top of his shirt. *Deep breath*, she told herself, *pacing, pacing, don't dive on top of him.* She propped her wobbly body against the door frame. Her thighs started to shake. Everything was happening so quickly. And she was still so very, very, tipsy.

"You're so gorgeous," Lance whispered as Amanda sat down next to him. He leaned in close to her face and kissed her gently on the lips. Adrenaline coursed through her whole body. She pulled him closer. She wanted to hold onto this moment for as long as she could: the feel of his lips, the slip of his tongue into her mouth, this would be the best kiss of her life. She needed to etch all of this deep into her memory.

"Wow," he exhaled as they pulled away.

"You're real!" She pulled him toward her, madly kissing his cheeks and neck, nibbling on his ear.

"What did you say?"

"You're such a great guy. I'm glad I found you," she quickly corrected. Amanda pulled Lance on top of her and together they fell backward onto the bed.

Lance pressed his lips to Amanda's neck and she writhed in pleasure. He let a hand fall down and grabbed her between the legs, gently massaging her upper thigh. She thought she would explode with desire. Her fingers frantically unbuttoned his shirt and unbuckled his belt. *Fade into You* by Mazzy Star ended, and Amanda listened for the next song. He had good taste in music. Coldplay. She couldn't remember the title, but she loved the track. She teared up as the opening music struck a chord across her heart. *This moment. This is happening.* As the music crested into lyrics, Lance's fingers found her nipples. A pulsing sensation throbbed inside her. She pressed herself harder against him. Urgently removing their clothing, they let their hands explore every angle of each other's bodies.

Lance pressed his lips to Amanda's ear and whispered, "I want to be inside you."

Amanda spread her legs and arched her spine. The next song began and Amanda's muscles followed the tune, contracting around him and holding him tight. As they climaxed together, Amanda regressed.

****

Keira is in a four-poster bed in a cold, stone building. Miles is hovering above her naked body, moving up and down as he enters and reenters her. Everything about his body is so familiar to her now: the hair formation on his chest, the movement of his Adam's apple. Closing her eyes, she can identify him by his smell and then the smell they make together. She is warmed by his body and feels at peace in this place.

****

Amanda opened her eyes and looked around wildly to see if Lance had noticed anything. He was sound asleep beside her. *How long was I under? Did he see me go?* Her heart raced, her mind panicked. He was clearly asleep; there was nothing that needed to happen. Fresh tears moistened her face. She curled up next to him, and fell asleep on his familiar shoulder.

CHAPTER 27

Amanda awoke to a note, and her heart sank. *A note just like every other one-night stand? Did last night matter to him at all? I regressed! That has to prove this was some kind of freaking out-of-control cosmic soul connection, right? But no, I'm left with an empty bed and a 'wham-bam, thank-you, ma'am' letter.* She read the note for the fifth time that morning:

Princess Keira,

Thank you for a wonderful night.

I hope to be able to kidnap you again sometime in the near future.

Your knight in shining armor,

Lance

The last part made Amanda want to vomit. *I bet he uses that as his pick-up line with all the women he sleeps with. How am I going to make him understand I'm not just another fling? He probably saw me regress. It probably freaked him out so much that he got spooked and took off before I woke up. I can only imagine myself, eyes rolled back into my head and mumbling. What guy wouldn't head for the hills?*

****

Amanda was late getting to the Costumery and frustrated that she hadn't had time to stop for coffee. Her only option would be to grab some of the crap coffee they brewed in the back of the Costumery. *That pot got made around 5:00 a.m. and sits so long it's almost always slightly burnt. After last night, there's no way I'll make it through the day without a lot of caffeinated assistance.* Needing the energy more than the taste, Amanda filled a Styrofoam cup and added extra sugar and powdered creamer in hopes that would tame the bitterness.

"Claire!" Amanda called, spotting her not far from the coffee.

"Hey, sweetie!"

"Where have you been? I've been looking for you for the last few days."

"Food poisoning."

"No!" Amanda clasped her hand to her mouth. She couldn't even hear those words without thinking of the fish she'd eaten the night of her junior prom.

"Today's my first day back at work." Claire took a big gulp of coffee.

"You poor thing. I don't think I'd have been able to handle that coffee after a bout of food poisoning," Amanda responded.

"Feel pity for me, please. It was truly nightmarish." Claire shook her head like she was shaking out the remaining toxins. "So what's up with you? Running late, I presume?"

"Yeah, I had a date last night."

"Oh! Carny-fantasy, Chris? He did have eyes for you."

"Actually, no. Lancelo ... I mean Steve Thrasher," Amanda corrected, figuring Steve was more appropriate, as much as she hated his name. To her, he would always be Miles, or at least Lance.

"You didn't go out with him, did you? Oh jeez." Claire didn't look so good. She covered her mouth and Amanda worried she was going to be sick again.

"No, I did. We had a really lovely night last night."

"You slept with him too, didn't you?"

"Well ... "

"Ugh, Keira. Everyone has at least one really lovely night with Mr. Thrasher. I wish I could have had a chance to warn you. I saw you at Spur with him, but then I got sick. He's ... he's ... " Claire looked around as if to confirm that no one was listening, " ... just don't go out again, okay. He's not good for someone like you."

"Someone like me?" Amanda snapped. *Exactly what vibe have I been giving off, lost farm girl in the big city? I can handle myself quite well, thank you very much.*

"I'm sorry, I didn't mean that. It's ... Steve's a total player, like he wrote the book on it. Don't fall for him." Claire lowered her voice when others entered the coffee area. "He'll break your precious little heart. Please promise to stay away from him."

"It's okay," Amanda whispered. "I can handle it. Besides, Melinda already gave me the same lecture." Amanda tried to remain cool. *Is there anyone here who won't warn me about Lance?* "I'm a big girl." Amanda tried to hide the creeping anxiety she felt. *What if Claire was one of Lance's previous flings? And who else at the Faire? Now I won't be able to walk around without wondering if some cute, young thing has shared Lance's bed.*

"I don't want to see you hurt," Claire responded with an edge to her voice that suggested she was hiding something. "You're very sweet."

"You sound like you speak from experience." Amanda eyed Claire warily.

"Bye, hon!" Claire sang, kissing Amanda on the cheek. "I gotta run to makeup, and you better get dressed quick if you're going to make it to work on time."

****

When Amanda spotted Melinda standing outside Faerytale Fynery, she checked her watch. "I'm not late, am I?"

"Heavens, no! I was hoping you'd be in early enough so I could hear all about our first romance of the season! It's really what keeps me coming back each year. I love to see the soap opera unfold." Melinda had already shared with Amanda quite a bit of historical faire gossip, such as who had slept with whom, and even more interesting, who had cheated on whom. Since Melinda knew Amanda was after Lance, she never offered to disclose Lance's past.

"How do you know I have anything to share?" Amanda felt herself blush.

"Oh please! You have sex written all over your face." Amanda immediately thought of Roxie. She wanted to correct Melinda and explain that it was 'love' written all over her face. *I've found my soul mate. How many people can claim that — and with such certainty?* Before Melinda could ask any more questions, Amanda was saved by the day's first group of customers.

****

At lunchtime, Amanda made her way to the jousting arena and stood in the perfect position to get a clear view of Lance. The tournament began with the usual pageantry, and Amanda's anticipation built as it came time for the knights to gallop into the arena. She and Lance would soon share that amazing eye contact connection, validating that it was so much more than a one-night stand. It had been the first night of forever.

Lance removed his headpiece and cantered past his waiting fans. *He must relish all this attention.* He made eye contact with her like he had the first two times she'd seen him, but this time there was no smile, no wink, no acknowledgement. Her stomach clenched. She stood stoic, an utter fool. He might as well have thrust his lance into her heart. He rode away, smiling at the other women in the crowd. A rogue tear escaped. She felt cheap.

Stupid! Stupid! She scolded herself. *Why did I give it all to him on the first night? I know better, damnit! It's the cardinal rule of dating.* He rode past Amanda again, and didn't even look in her direction. *That's it. It's all so very typical. I meant nothing to him. He didn't get it at all.*

The massive bells chimed a tune that was probably a part of a symphony, but Amanda only knew it from a TV ad that ran at

Christmas. The whole experience felt surreal under the hot Colorado midday sun. She felt like curling into a shell and hiding. *Was I an idiot to think he'd fall for me so easily, and worse, stupid to believe in destiny?* She gathered up her dress so she wouldn't trip, and raced back to Faerytale Fynery as fast as she could.

****

As the day closed, she left a few minutes early, pretending to have 'female problems.' Melinda tried to get her to take some pot. "It really helps with cramps," she'd insisted.

Amanda turned it down. She hadn't been at the Faire more than a few days before she'd realized the entire establishment was basically an elaborate drug den. Everyone was buying and selling from one another whatever wasn't already legal in Colorado. Drugs had never been of any interest to her. After trying Ecstasy at a party one night in college, and waking up naked next to a guy she hated, she decided being high was not a good thing. She vowed never to move beyond alcohol again.

Amanda said goodbye to Melinda and made a mad dash for the Costumery. She felt a need to get out of there before she saw Claire, who would say "I told you so," or Lance, who would say nothing at all. She wanted to grab her latest copy of *Vogue,* lay by the pool, and try to forget why she'd ever come to Colorado in the first place. She tried to recall what the penalty was for breaking the lease on her apartment, thinking, *perhaps it's time to put an end to this charade and head back to Chicago where I belong. Therese disappearing the way she did only reinforces the idea that this is all a big sham. None of it is real. It's merely my mind playing games with me.*

****

Amanda lay on a chaise lounge by the pool with her eyes closed, picturing herself in that ad for the condos in Florida.

Even at seven in the evening, the sun was still strong, and she luxuriated in the warm, penetrating rays. She relived every part of last night's date in her mind. The time in the car where she'd felt so warm and safe sitting next to Lance. She thought back to the restaurant and how he'd fed her a piece of chocolate cake and wiped a crumb off her cheek. She could still feel the intensity of his eyes, and oh, the weight of him on top of her! The smell of his cologne gave her shivers. *Did it really happen? If I left Colorado now, no one could take away the memories of our night together. But if I left, I'd also never know if I could have turned the situation around. I wouldn't know if I could find a way to make him realize that I'm his Keira, that we have a deep history together, and that I'm not just another fling. No, I can't leave. I've come too far to give up so easily. Besides, aren't I doing this as much for him as for myself? If I don't make him wake up to the reality of who I was in his life, then he too could risk his only chance at true happiness this time around.*

The warm sun, on top of the long day, lulled Amanda to sleep, but after a few moments, she was awakened by someone breathing above her. Her eyes flew open to see the creepy guy from the liquor store hovering beside her lounge chair.

"Yes?" she asked, in a tone that sounded eerily like Celia's 'city voice.' She looked around to see who else was at the pool. There was only a Hispanic grandma with grey hair watching a toddler splash in the shallow end. She probably wasn't going to be able to come to Amanda's rescue. Amanda felt violated. She pulled the magazine up from her stomach to cover her bikini top. "Can I help you?"

"Tell me your name again." He sat down on the lounge chair next to hers.

Amanda knew she should gather her things and leave, but for some reason, she couldn't bring herself to go. He smelled like cigarettes and patchouli, a combination that grossed her out. His eyes had a crazed look that Amanda presumed came from drug use. *Is everyone in this state high?*

Yet, at the same time, there was something compelling about him. He was gentle in the way he spoke. It was his mouth. He had tender lips that moved like Miles'. He sounded like him. That's it. She was definitely going crazy.

"Keira," she heard herself say the word, but it was like she was under a spell.

"That's right, Keira." He massaged her name in his mouth. "Keira. Keira of the Forest. Beautiful, enchanting, mystical Keira."

Keira of the Forest? What the hell? Amanda's nerves spiked. She noticed that the grandma and toddler on the other side of the pool had left. *Now it's just me and creepy stalker dude. What was his name? Jerry, that's right.* She sat up and in so doing, removed the magazine that was covering half her body and placed it in her bag.

"Yeah, you're really beautiful." His eyes walked up and down her. She could feel him scouring every tuck and shadow on her body. She reached for her cover-up and quickly pulled it on over her bikini. She should leave, but she didn't. There was something weirdly appealing about him checking her out.

"I was about to head upstairs." She gathered her sunscreen and water bottle and tossed them into her bag.

"But you just got here."

He was watching her again.

"Jerry, is that your name?" She was fully lucid now, and her sanity quickly returned.

"Yes," he smiled dreamily, completely oblivious to Amanda's shift in mood.

"Jerry, stop watching me. If you don't leave me alone, I'm going to call the police. Do you understand?" She nearly laughed at herself when she looked down and realized she was holding her phone as if it were a gun.

"Oh, Keira, don't be like that. Queen Isolde would be so upset."

Amanda froze. Cautiously she turned around again, her phone still poised like a weapon.

"What did you say?"

"Remember, if you plant ice, you're going to harvest wind." Jerry hummed as he stood up and started walking toward the parking lot.

"How do you know Queen Isolde?" Amanda called after him. "Wait, you can't leave. You have to tell me how you know Queen Isolde!"

Jerry walked faster and Amanda followed him, trying to put her flip-flops on while she ran. He slipped out through a side entrance Amanda had never noticed before. She tried to follow, but the gate was locked. By the time she made it through the entry to the pool, she was a good ways behind him. She saw him heading down the alley that separated the apartment buildings. She knew that following him could mean walking into a dangerous trap, but she couldn't let him get away. She ran after him, so focused on not losing him that she didn't notice the gravel in front of the pool house and tripped on her flip-flops, landing face down on the stones.

"Dammit!" she hissed, pushing up from the gravel. She looked down the alley, but he was gone.

Perhaps this is all a regression, Amanda thought, limping her way back to her apartment, patting a bloody spot on her knee with the edge of her towel. *Why did Therese have to disappear? How am I supposed to understand any of the completely crazy shit that's happening in my life if I don't have her guidance?*

She could hear Therese's voice in her head, "You know the truth. Close your eyes and open your mind; it will come to you." But Amanda was very aware that she didn't know the first thing about what was happening to her. Dejectedly, she unlocked her door. There was only one thing that sounded vaguely appealing. She stepped inside, took off her cover-up, and in her damp bikini, she opened the bottle of vodka, pouring what was left of it directly down her throat.

CHAPTER 28

Amanda's head pounded. The empty bottle of vodka stood guiltily on the counter. *How much was left before I decided to polish it off?* Panic set in. She frantically jumped in the shower to get ready for work, but halfway through shampooing her hair, she realized it was Monday, a day off. She finished her shower, dried off, and crawled back into bed.

As she lay there, trying to regain control of her day — if not her life — she decided to throw on some clothes and drive over to Jumpin' Java for a pick-me-up latte. *Once I have a good coffee in hand, I'll chill by the pool and keep an eye out for Jerry. I've got nothing better to do while I wait for this hangover to wane.*

****

Amanda lifted the gate latch and entered the pool area, carefully balancing her coffee, magazine, and towel while maneuvering the creaky latch back into place. As if he knew she was looking for him, Jerry was there waiting, stretched out on a chaise lounge, eyes closed, soaking in the Colorado rays. Amanda spotted an open chair next to him. She walked in his direction and her phone rang. It wasn't a pre-programmed song, so it was someone who normally didn't call. She let it go to voicemail and walked over to confront Jerry.

"Hi." Amanda dropped her magazine and towel on the empty lounger.

"Hi." Jerry's eyes darted from her to the pool.

"Why did you run away from me yesterday?"

"I was late for work, Keira." He held onto her name, as if savoring it in his mouth. A wave of desire flooded Amanda. *What the hell? He's a drunk, a druggie; this is no one to pay any attention to. But then why am I eyeing his tanned, skinny legs, their soft blonde hair glistening in the sun? I'm not actually attracted to him. I just can't be.* Her phone beeped with a message. She ignored it. Jerry's answer was stupid, but she didn't really care. It wasn't the question she wanted answered anyway.

"Tell me how you know Queen Isolde."

"Who's Queen Isolde?"

"Yesterday, you told me Queen Isolde would be mad if I didn't treat you well. Don't fuck with me," Amanda said in that bitchy city voice that did not come naturally. Roxie had always told her that if she used it, she'd attract more men. *I wonder if I'm trying to scare Jerry away or draw him closer. I can't separate the feelings.* "Tell me what you know. How do you know her name?"

"I don't know what you're talking about," Jerry insisted, lying back, not a care in the world.

Amanda's phone beeped again.

"Yes, you do. Please. Tell me how you know Queen Isolde. This is really important."

"Look lady," his tone changed as he sat up and looked directly at her. "I don't know what you're talking about." He raised his voice enough that a few other pool goers looked their way.

"But yesterday ... " Amanda began in a hushed voice. She stopped herself, realizing that Jerry wasn't high. His eyes weren't bloodshot, and he didn't have that far-away, crazed look, like he had the two other times she had talked to him. He was just a normal man, in desperate need of a haircut and cologne. She looked at his chiseled face, long and narrow and on the gaunt side. He'd probably been attractive when he was ten years younger and twenty pounds heavier. Amanda was drawn to a scar across his left cheek and wondered if it might be from a knife fight. "Would you want to go out tonight?" she asked.

Jerry looked shocked, and then responded with a sly grin that completely unnerved her. "You want to go out?" His eyes glistened as he questioned her offer.

Amanda thought of Keira and her quest to make sense of everything. *I have to know. I have to get him high or drunk or both. That's the only chance I have to learn anything.*

She immediately regretted the invite. *But he knows Queen Isolde*, she reminded herself.

"Meet me at the liquor store tonight at nine. I get off work then. I'll take you to a bar nearby that I like." He stood up and left. He hadn't even brought a towel with him.

A bar he liked nearby. Ah, the trucker bar, Amanda recalled Lance's description of the area hot spots. *Lance.* She hadn't thought about him in hours. *Wait! My phone! What if that was him calling?* "See you later," Amanda called, settling on an empty lounger.

"Keira, it's Lance. Sorry I missed you, babe. Are you free tonight? Call me." *Lance wants to see me again. Maybe it wasn't a one-night-stand after all. I must have been overreacting.* Her heart fluttered in wild anticipation. *What should I wear? What will we do? Will I regress again if we have sex? Wait. What about Jerry?* She looked around, but he'd already disappeared. *Why the hell did I agree to meet him? I don't have his number, and I'm not exactly sure which apartment is his. I'll have to stop by the store and tell him something's come up. I can't say no to Lance.*

****

Amanda had left Lance two voicemails, but hadn't heard back. To make use of the empty time, she rushed through getting herself cleaned up and showered, and was sitting in her apartment, waiting for him. She decided to wear her favorite jeans, a black tank top, and a pair of high-heeled black sandals with rhinestones that Roxie had made her buy.

She had chickened out on confronting Jerry, and instead left a note at the liquor store late in the afternoon when she was fairly certain he wasn't in yet. She felt horribly guilty. *Maybe if Lance doesn't show, I'll go back to the liquor store and explain that I'm available after all.*

She went to the bathroom and thought she heard her phone ring. She came flying out with her pants unzipped, and checked her phone, but there were no missed calls. At 6:40, her phone finally rang.

"Hey babe, it's Lance. Sorry I didn't call sooner. I was hiking and just got back into cell range. Did you want to get together tonight?"

"Sure." Amanda tried to play cool, all the while her heart raced at the sound of his voice.

"Great. Let me stop home and shower first. See you soon."

CHAPTER 29

Lance arrived at 7:30 carrying a bottle of wine and a pizza. "Hope you like pepperoni," he said, setting the box on the counter.

"You're very into Italian, aren't you?" Amanda opened the lid and inhaled the aroma. She didn't have the heart to tell him that processed meats were not high on her list of favorite foods.

"Very odd for a nice Irish boy, eh?"

"It's America. We're all a big melting pot." Amanda placed two plates on the counter and dished out a slice on each. "I'm starving. Ready to dive in?" Without dining room furniture, let alone a dining area, the futon and coffee table had to serve all entertaining purposes. "So where did you go hiking?" Amanda impressed herself, sounding like such a local, recognizing that she'd have no clue what he was talking about when he answered.

"Spruce Mountain."

Amanda reached for the wine glasses, and gave a polite nod. It kind of sounded familiar. She was working hard to play it cool, still frustrated with the way he'd handled things after their first date.

"I thought you might call yesterday," Amanda worried she sounded too needy. She knew so much more about their relationship than he did, it was hard to let the conversation flow naturally. "Isn't that what nice Irish boys do?" she added as a joke, hoping that conveyed the right tone.

"I tried." Lance shrugged his shoulders and took another big bite.

"Didn't you see me at the jousting?"

"Oh, I guess I didn't."

The bastard is flat-out lying. Or is he? Maybe he really didn't see me. What does, 'I tried' mean anyway? If he'd tried to call or text, his number would have shown on my phone.

Lance's phone rang. He leaned into her to retrieve it out of his back pocket and placed a kiss on her neck in the process. Amanda drank in his cologne. He looked at the number before turning it off and setting it on the coffee table

"Another one of your female fans?" Amanda's attitude came out before she could think. *The fastest way to scare off a man is to act clingy after the first date. I know better! He's here in my apartment, spending the evening with me. What else matters?*

Lance set both of their plates on the coffee table and drew Amanda into his arms. "I'm sorry I didn't call yesterday. Got wrapped up in life. How can I make it up to you?" He ran kisses down her neck, letting his tongue swirl on her skin and releasing an internal flood within her that felt like a dam had burst wide open.

"I'm sure I can figure something out." She took a big sip of wine and swallowed it along with her frustration. She wanted him. She would hate herself if she pushed him away.

"So, have you been skinny dipping yet?" Lance's view shifted to the pool.

"No." Amanda giggled. She'd never been skinny dipping in her life, but she refrained from sharing that detail. She tried to figure out if the overall concept didn't appeal to her, or if she'd never been asked by the right person.

"Well, let's get some wine in us and go for a midnight swim."

"We can discuss it more after the wine," Amanda replied, noncommittally, topping off her glass.

Amanda and Lance watched a new show on Netflix while they finished their pizza. About halfway through, Lance was taking off Amanda's shirt and spending more time kissing her than watching the screen. The kisses multiplied and they never did finish the show.

"Ready for a clean-up in the pool?" Lance suggested as he pulled his jeans back on and turned off the TV.

"That is so gross."

"Come on. Please?" Lance's long black lashes batted wildly.

"You're really serious?"

"Yeah. It'll be great. Besides, it's a full moon. We have to go. I think there's a rule about that somewhere."

"I don't think so. It's cold out there. The nights don't stay warm here like they do in Chicago."

"The pool's heated."

"How do you know?" Amanda's mind raced to Claire and Melinda's warnings. *Crap, he probably did this same thing with previous year's flings, probably in this same pool. Does that matter? What if he did? Ugh, I wish he was the 'virgin.'*

"Come on, don't be a wimp. It'll be fantastic." Lance tugged on Amanda's stiff arm.

"I don't know ... "

"Please?" Lance got on one knee, in full-on proposal stance, hands placed together in a praying motion at his heart. Amanda couldn't take it.

"Hang on, hang on. Let me throw on a T-shirt and shorts."

****

Amanda and Lance entered through the locked side gate Jerry had used to escape. Lance pulled out a pocket knife and picked the lock efficiently. The gate opened without making a sound.

"You've done this before, haven't you? Could you get arrested for skinny dipping? Would they give you clothes for your mug shot or just an old police station towel? Or maybe an orange jump suit?"

"Shhhh."

They made their way to the deep end, after leaving their clothes in a pile by the back fence. The water looked radiant under the light of the full moon, and Amanda was glad Lance had talked her into doing this.

"Isn't this awesome?" Lance treaded water in front of her, his voice low and sultry. *Everything about this night is awesome.* "I was captain of my swim team in high school. The water's like my second home."

"I'm not much of a swimmer." Amanda realized that for all the times she had come and sat by the pool, she'd only gone in the water once. "I'm more of the girl-who-lies-by-the-pool-with-a-magazine type."

"I'm sure you do a fine job at that." Lance pressed his body against hers, pinning her to the side of the pool. She could feel him get hard, and she let her body fall into his.

"You're the type of girl I could fall in love with, Keira."

Lance's words sung in Amanda's ear. Her heart raced at the word Love. Her heart raced at the way he said her name. Her heart didn't stop racing around him, it just tried to keep up and stay present. "You're just saying that to get into my pants," Amanda teased, continuing to lean into him.

"You don't have any pants."

Amanda found herself ready to tell him everything. Right there, under the moon and the stars, she wanted to confess it all. "I have something to tell you." She took a deep breath. Then a car pulled into a spot by the pool, its lights shining on Amanda and Lance through the metal fence. The driver left the car lights on as he stepped out.

"Shit, it's the apartment manager. What do we do?"

Lance covered Amanda's mouth with his hand.

"Who's in there? The pool is closed after dark. No one's allowed in there."

They watched as the manager left the fence and made his way around the building. She and Lance rushed out of the pool and made a move for their clothes as silently as they could, Amanda cursing under her breath. They could see the manager enter the pool house. He was probably going to turn on the flood lights and they'd be totally on display, in their full nakedness.

"We'll have to jump."

They eyed the six-foot chain-link fence.

"I can't climb that!" Amanda shivered, trying to pull her shirt over her wet body. The air was freezing.

"Well, it's that or we're getting caught." Lance put Amanda on his shoulders and she grabbed hold of the top of the fence. She vaulted to the other side like a gymnast and crashed into the bushes. The shorts she was holding flew out of reach.

"Ow!" she hissed, quiet as she could. "This bush is prickly!" She started hysterically laughing and crying.

"Get out of the way, here I come." Lance was laughing so hard that he could barely make it over the fence. He tossed his clothes into the bushes and climbed. Next he came flying over the fence, penis dangling in the air. Amanda's side ached from laughing so hard. The flood lights came on as he crested the fence.

They lay silently laughing together, huddled below the bushes. They could hear the manager mutter under his breath.

They hid for a good five minutes before the manager eventually turned the lights off and left. Then Lance rolled Amanda onto the grass and they made love beneath the bushes, under the full moon.

CHAPTER 30

When Amanda awoke, Lance was there, sleeping quietly on her futon. From where she lay, she spied a piece of paper, slid under her front door. Trying not to disturb him, she eased out of bed to retrieve the note.

> Beautiful Keira,
> I'm sorry you weren't feeling well enough to join me last night ...

Amanda cringed; in the fun of last night's escapades, she'd forgotten about Jerry. I should have gone with Jerry and told Lance I wasn't free. Don't guys like women who play hard to get? That's what Roxie always said. But Lance is the one I've been looking for; I only came to Colorado to find him. And last night was amazing. Again. He's more than I ever dreamed.
Amanda read on:

> She's got everything delightful, she's got everything I need,
> a breeze in the pines
> and the sun and bright moonlight,
> lazing in the sunshine -
> yes, indeed.
>
> Jerry

These strange sayings of Jerry's have to have meaning. And how does he know Queen Isolde? I need to find the answers to these questions. Amanda folded the note and hid it in her purse. She would show it to Claire when she went back to work tomorrow. Maybe she could make sense of the weird phrases.

Amanda watched Lance, sound asleep and naked in her bed. She still couldn't believe it was all happening. Sitting on the edge of the futon, she rubbed her hand across his tanned, muscular back, tracing her finger along the muscles he used to pull the horse's reigns in the jousts.

"Morning," he whispered, slowly opening his eyes.

"Morning. Did you sleep okay?"

"Mmm," he sighed, rolling over and looking disoriented. "What time is it?"

"Nine-thirty, but who cares? It's Tuesday, and we have the day off." Amanda had thought of a thousand things they could do with the day, but if the only plan included lying in bed and making love until dinner, she was fine with that, too. She was making up for her months of abstinence.

"I have to get going." Lance pulled off the covers and wiped his eyes with his knuckles. The thrill of seeing his smooth, toned body caused more excitement in Amanda. Lance had a smattering of hair on his upper chest and forearms, and a little on his legs, but that was it.

"Oh no, you don't," she toyed, grabbing his waist and pulling him back on to the bed.

"No, really I have to go." He gently but firmly pushed Amanda away from him and gathered his clothes. His shirt was on a bar stool, his pants on the other side of the bed. It looked like a tornado had come through the apartment and scattered clothing everywhere.

"Don't you want to stay for breakfast? We could have lazy sex all day."

"I'm sorry, babe, but I can't. I've got a standing tennis appointment with a friend."

"Tennis?"

"Yes, don't mock me. I like it."

"Well, cancel it." Amanda exposed her thigh, giving a flirty, baby-face pout. Her finger trailed the length of her leg, seductively, hopefully.

"Have you seen my other sock?" Lance ignored her, holding up a white sport sock.

"Is there nothing I can tempt you with? Coffee, pancakes – maybe a steamy shower for two?"

"Look, this is a good friend, and I can't cancel at the last minute. Besides, I'm already late. He's probably there waiting. I'll call you later today. Maybe we can get together for dinner or something. Oh! There it is." Lance reached under the futon and came up with his other sock.

Amanda was beginning to doubt everything all over again. She sat up fully and drew her knees to her chest, then pulled the sheets in tight so they completely covered her body, forming a cocoon.

"I'll call you later." He leaned over and kissed her on the forehead.

Amanda stared at the door for minutes after he left, and hoped Jerry didn't see Lance leaving her apartment. The endless questions started looping in her mind again. *Is Lance really into me or simply playing me? What's the deal with Jerry, anyway? Is he for real or a figment of my imagination?* Her head spun from the questions and then she remembered the Rilke quote she loved, the one about living the questions, and wondered if she ever would live into the answers. She was beginning to think that the answers were simply disguised as more questions.

****

An hour later, Amanda was at Jumpin' Java, getting her usual and seeking out a quiet table up front. The morning sun poured in through the window, as she played on her phone excited to not think for a while and drown herself in something mindless, like

Pinterest. Not more than five minutes later, she felt a tap on her shoulder.

"Good morning." Amanda looked up to see Claire's bright face.

"Oh, hi!"

"So you're a fan of this place, too?" Claire set her purse over the back of the empty chair at Amanda's table and sat down.

"I tried The Grounds when I first got here."

Claire shook her head, violently, in response.

"Yeah, that's what I thought too."

"Let me go grab a drink. I'll be right back."

Claire returned with a mocha topped with a mountain of whipped cream. Amanda looked down at her soy latte and wondered if she should have splurged.

"So whatcha up to today?" Claire asked, taking a sip of her drink and ending up with whipped cream on the tip of her nose.

"I don't really know. I hadn't made any plans. I suppose I should check out the mountains, maybe go for a drive or something."

"No plans with loverboy?"

"Maybe."

"He hasn't broken your heart yet, has he?"

"No," Amanda said, and then with a renewed energy that surprised her, she added, "I'm not going to let him."

"Good luck with that," Claire laughed. "So this week is royalty review."

"Royalty review? You have to explain that one."

"It's this team-building sort of thing we have to do. I asked if we can behead the king as part of it, but no one thought that was very funny. King Henry's such an ass! So I have to go in at noon. Can you believe that? We have to work on our day off. If I didn't have this stupid thing, we could hang out."

"Maybe another time?"

"For sure."

"Claire, can I ask you an odd question?"

"Okay."

Amanda retrieved Jerry's note from her purse and handed it to Claire. "So there's this guy at my apartment complex who likes me. He's a little on the crazy side. I was supposed to go out with him last night, but I ditched him when Lance called. He slid this note under my door. Every time I talk to him, he says eerie things like the line in the note. Do you have any idea what this means?"

Claire held the note and read it a few times before looking at Amanda. "Yeah, it's lyrics from a Grateful Dead song."

"Really?"

"Uh-huh. I used to be a Deadhead, once upon a time."

"So he's just a Deadhead?"

"Looks like it. That's pretty creative. What's his name?"

"Jerry."

"As in Jerry Garcia?"

"No!"

"Could be. Have you asked if that's his real name?"

"Like maybe he thinks he's Jerry Garcia?"

"You said he was crazy. Why were you going to go out with him? I thought you liked Lance."

"Long story."

"I have time," Claire said, then looked at her watch, "Oops, actually, I don't." She downed her drink and put her purse on her shoulder. "Well, enjoy the day off for me. If you're looking for something to do, you might want to check out Garden of the Gods in Colorado Springs. It's a great place to go hiking."

"Thanks." Amanda nodded to Claire, knowing full well she wouldn't be taking her up on her suggestion. She wasn't sure she'd ever been hiking.

"See you tomorrow."

****

Amanda was half asleep by the pool, her *Vogue* blanketing her belly, when she felt a tap on her shoulder. Her eyes flew open to see Jerry hovering above her.

"Are you feeling better today, Keira?" He was bent over, lightly touching Amanda's forehead, like Celia might have done when she was very young. He still held onto her name when he spoke to her. He held it for far too long.

"I am. Thanks." Amanda pushed away his hand. "I had a nasty headache," she lied.

"Can you go tonight? I get off at the same time." His eyes looked eager and ready to devour her. *I have to make time to do this, to find out what he knows. But what if Lance calls? I can't cancel on Jerry twice in a row. If I say yes, that's it; I'll have to go through with the date.* "Yes, that would be great. Should we meet at the same time at the store?"

Jerry nodded, then took her hand in his, lifted it to his mouth, and kissed it tenderly. His soft lips pressed against her skin and she swore she felt a hint of tongue. A jolt shot through her arm, connecting straight to her core. It was horrifyingly arousing. *What the hell is happening? Did Lance unlock my sex drive, so now everyone is turning me on?*

****

An afternoon hasn't dragged on so badly in months, Amanda thought, eyeing her phone. *I just want to get to the other side of this date. No call from Lance, so I didn't have to turn him down. At least that's something, although the lack of communication is troubling.*

Amanda approached the store. Through the window, she could see that Jerry had stepped up his game. He was wearing nice jeans and a black button-down shirt. With a rose in his hand, a single yellow rose, she could almost mistake him for someone worth dating.

Amanda considered turning off her phone so she wouldn't be tempted to answer if Lance called. Then, she surmised, she could make plans to meet him later – that is if he even called.

"Ah! Beautiful, enchanting, Keira. You look as angelic as ever." Jerry's eyes walked over Amanda, from her gold hoop earrings down to her platform sandals. She twitched under his stare. He was high, and although she reminded herself that was what she wanted, a major ripple of regret ran through her. *Am I truly prepared to spend a night out alone with him?*

"How about I drive?" Amanda offered after noticing his bloodshot eyes.

"Lead the way." He bowed to her with the rose in his teeth, matador style. She was surprised he didn't work at the Faire. He seemed to be dripping in chivalry.

"Where are we going?" Amanda asked, pulling her rental car out of the parking lot.

"I was thinking we could go to Spur of the Moment!" Jerry slurred, "It's a happenin' joint in Larkspur."

"Umm ... could we go somewhere else, maybe?" Amanda cringed at the idea of going there with Jerry. Who knew who she might run into? If she wasn't careful, Baldwin the Fool would soon be talking about Keira's new sexpot, the greasy hippie.

"Well, I, well, don't ... " Jerry appeared to be on the verge of an epileptic fit. Amanda panicked.

"That's fine. Never mind. I know where it is. We can go there." She thought through the interior of the bar and where they might be able to sit and, more importantly, sit but be hidden. She remembered the table where she and Lance sat at their first pseudo-date. It was in a corner by the back door. It would do.

Amanda entered the Spur with Jerry. Fortunately, it was still early enough that it was fairly empty. Amanda spotted the table she had been thinking of and quickly directed Jerry there.

A waitress came around to take their drink orders. Amanda ordered a pale ale. Jerry ordered a Long Island iced tea with a whiskey shooter. Amanda was fairly certain she hadn't had a Long Island since college, when consuming as much alcohol in the shortest time was the goal.

"Is that all you're having?" Jerry asked after the waitress walked away.

"I'm the designated driver, remember?" *And I'm here to get you drunk, so you'll talk, not me.* "So tell me about Queen Isolde." She didn't want to waste a minute of their time together.

"Ah, my dear, Queen Isolde 'comes skimming through rays of sunshine ...'"

"Jerry, how about we have a conversation without any Dead lyrics. Just tell me about Queen Isolde," Amanda's voice lowered, sensitive not to call undo attention to their corner.

Jerry sat there, humming a tune and nodding his head with his eyes closed. A few moments later, the waitress brought their drinks. *Maybe I need to flirt with him, loosen him up a bit first.* She let her hand brush his and he lit up – presto! She felt as easy as Roxie.

"It's so nice to be with you," he murmured.

Jerry's dream tone made Amanda more and more angry. She didn't have time for his drugged-out ramblings and pushed on; "So, were you in the Forest of Forgiveness?"

"Aren't the trees beautiful?"

"In the forest? Yes, they were very beautiful. Were you there at Queen Isolde's cottage? Were you one of the fairy folk?"

"Fairies. I wish I had wings. Don't you?"

Amanda wished she had a club to clobber him. She ran her hand through her hair in frustration, tipped her head to the side, took in a deep breath, and continued. "I don't know if the fairy folk actually had wings. Do you remember Maraza, the unicorn?"

Jerry got teary-eyed, and Amanda hoped she had found an entry point.

"Are you sad about Maraza?"

Jerry wouldn't answer. His head was bent down, staring into his drink.

I'm either losing him or cracking him open. Perhaps Jerry was Maraza? Can people actually trade places with animals? That would explain why he hasn't really made much of himself in his present life. Perhaps he's learning to be human. God, do I need to be able to talk to Therese! Where has that woman gone?

"Do you like horses?" Amanda continued, trying a new angle, but nothing was working and a half-hour of useless talk went by. The waitress brought another round. She didn't know how he was still sitting up straight. She also didn't know how the alcohol was mixing with whatever drugs he was on. She prayed he would remain conscious until she was able to dump him back at their apartment complex.

"I have to go to the bathroom. I think I have something in my eye," Jerry said as he stumbled out of the booth and lumbered his way to the restroom.

He was gone for an uncomfortable amount of time; Amanda was contemplating sending someone in to check on him when he finally returned as though nothing was wrong. She tried to pick up the conversation where they left off. For the tenth time in so many minutes, she stopped his foot from feeling up her thigh.

When Amanda polished off her second beer, she looked down at her watch. It was past 11. She didn't want to lead him on any more than was necessary. His hair shone in the light of the neon Budweiser sign that hung in the window above where he sat. Amanda could almost feel how greasy it would be to the touch. She also missed Lance terribly and wished he would call. She'd started to call him a dozen times throughout the day, but never pushed the button. They'd only really had two nights together, even though it felt like so much more, but now, he needed to seek her out if their relationship was going to work.

The next time Amanda looked toward the door, she saw Lance enter the bar. She fought an urge to call out to him because she didn't want him to see her with Jerry, but it was so hard not to run to him. He was with two other men she recognized from the Faire; one of them was another knight.

Jerry had moved his hand under the table and started to massage her knee. She slapped it away. Then she saw Lance walk up to a Mediterranean-looking brunette with long, straight hair that fell halfway down her back. He brushed her hair to the side before kissing her on the neck. She tossed back her head and turned to face him in a classically executed flirt. She was stunning – cat eyes and high cheek bones. *No woman has a right to be that beautiful. How could I ever compete with that?* Amanda's beer, mixed with acid from her stomach, crept back up burning her throat. She used all her willpower to keep it down. *What am I thinking? I mean nothing to him. He is a player, like everyone warned me, and here I am on the heartbreak fast-track and stuck with a junkie who thinks he's Jerry Garcia.*

"Excuse me. I have to use the restroom." Amanda barely got out of the booth before bolting for the back of the bar.

Sitting on the toilet, she bawled her eyes out, contemplating her next move. *I'll tell Jerry my headache returned, and I need to leave. It's incredibly ironic that my 'headache' has become a metaphor for Lance. 'Pain in the ass' would be more appropriate.*

I'll take Jerry home and then go straight online to see about booking my miles to go back home. I have to get out. Not just of the bar, I have to get out of Colorado. Why did I ever believe that after a night or two with me, Lance would have an epiphany, set aside his ways, and love only me? I was so naïve to believe in this stupid fairytale story I've bought into.

Amanda returned to the booth and quickly explained her headache to Jerry. He begrudgingly left his drink half-full and followed her toward the front door.

As she approached the front of the bar, she made eye contact with Lance.

"Wait a sec," she heard him say; then she saw him leave the woman's side, and walk towards her. Amanda pulled the door handle open to leave, but Lance stopped her.

"Where you going, babe?" Lance asked, acting all nonchalant, trying to plant the same kiss on Amanda's neck that he'd left on the brunette's. *Who kisses hello on the neck?* She pulled away, leaving him hanging in mid-air.

"Leave me alone!" Amanda released herself from his grip and took a step out the front door.

"What the hell's wrong with you?" Lance grabbed her arm and pulled Amanda back into the bar, holding on in a possessive way that confused her. Then, spotting Jerry, Lance dropped Amanda's arm. "Sorry. Didn't see you were with someone."

"Fuck you," she hissed and staggered slightly. She had a hard time keeping steady — her nerves were a wreck.

"Excuse me?" Lance's eyes had formed into little slits that stared at Amanda with a hatred so intense, she wanted to cry and take it all back. His presence towered in the doorway above her.

She had hurt him. He cared. "Last night, I was someone you could fall in love with and today, I'm another one of your scores? Is that it? There's always someone prettier waiting for you?" Amanda pushed Lance's chest, forcing him to land on his rear.

"I thought you were sick last night?" Jerry finally spoke up, looking disoriented and confused.

Amanda was caught off guard. She'd nearly forgotten that Jerry was there. She ignored him. He'd drunk so much he wasn't likely to remember anything from the night anyway.

"Who is this creep? Is this your boyfriend?" Lance teased, as he regained his balance and stepped back into the archway of the door.

"Go to hell."

Lance shook his head and walked back into the bar.

"He's a friend," Amanda called after him.

"A friend who brings you a rose?" Lance looked down at the flower in Amanda's hand.

With the front door open, Amanda felt every eye at the bar on them. Jerry made a lunge at Lance, but Amanda blocked him. Jerry slipped and fell in a heap by her feet. *Poor Jerry doesn't need to get caught in the middle of this. I have to get him out of here. But I have something I have to do first.*

Amanda grabbed hold of Lance and swung him around to face her. "You don't have a right to question me," she said harshly, shocked at the power of her adrenaline rush.

"So what's really wrong then?" Lance's hushed tone triggered her in all the ways she didn't want to be triggered. She wanted to kiss him and hit him at the same time. This was her Lancelot. "Aren't we both on dates, Amanda Barnes?"

Amanda's stomach flipped. "How did you find out my name?"

"I did some digging of my own. You're not the only one who's paying attention." Lance leaned into Amanda and whispered in her ear, "You're not the only one who's completely spooked by the intense chemistry between us."

"Keira, can we go?" Jerry pulled on Amanda's skirt like a child and she kicked him away.

Focusing back on Lance she said, "All right, I'm going to throw it all out on the line. You get rid of Supermodel. I'll get rid of Deadhead. Meet me back at my place in half an hour. Either you're in or you're out. I need to know for sure. I can't be one of your flings."

"I'll be there."

"We'll see."

****

At his request, Amanda dropped Jerry off at the liquor store, and then hightailed it back to her apartment complex. She washed the smell of patchouli off her hands, refreshed her makeup, and waited. And waited. Fifty-five minutes after she left the Spur. She dejectedly shut off her porch light and bolted her door. She kicked off her sandals, peeled herself out of her skirt, and walked into her kitchen wearing only her tank top and underwear to search for any alcohol, and proceeded to polish off the vodka. Fifteen minutes later, the doorbell rang. Looking through the peep hole, she saw Lance. He wasn't holding roses or a pizza or wine. He wasn't holding anything. He looked bedraggled and weary, and not at all like he had the other two times he'd appeared at her door. Amanda opened the door.

"I told you I'd come."

CHAPTER 31

Amanda whacked her phone, maybe a little too hard, when the morning alarm woke her from a deep sleep.

"Watch it, you wild woman!" They laughed, Lance put his arms around Amanda and pulled her on top of him.

"I wish I could wake up in your arms every day."

"Well, babe, for the last ten days you have."

"I'm so glad I found you."

Amanda kissed him, knowing how deeply meaningful that thought was and wondering if there would ever be a day that she could share the truth with him. There had to be. Someday.

"Me too. So, what do you say we try and clean ourselves up before going to work?"

"Deal. And can we hit Jumpin' Java on the way?"

"Yes, we can stop at Jumpin' Java, my caffeine hound. Why don't you buy a coffee maker? Wouldn't it be easier and cheaper to make it here?"

"I only drink lattes."

"You're high maintenance."

"It's Starbucks's fault, I've been well-trained."

****

Amanda and Lance pulled into the parking lot at the same time as Baldwin the Fool — Baldwin the obnoxious Fool, Amanda liked to add the extra descriptor.

"Good morning, lovebirds," Baldwin sang as he made mocking kisses into the wind.

"Knock it off, Baldwin!"

Amanda giggled at Lance's outburst. She'd quickly learned it was no use getting frustrated with Baldwin.

"Don't give him any ammo," Lance berated Amanda with his eyes. "We'll be news across the whole Faire in an hour."

"We already are."

"Dammit!"

I hope his tone is satirical, but what if he means it? And if that's true, then what? It would certainly be confirmation that this is only a summer fling, "What do you care? It's not like we have anything to hide."

"It would just be nice to have some privacy once in a while."

"At this place? Ha!"

Maybe he's simply feeling protective of our relationship. Maybe.

"So you're going out with Claire tonight, right?"

"Why do you always say her name with a hint of disgust?"

Lance shook his head.

"No, really, I like Claire a lot. I want to know."

"She's a bit annoying ... it's nothing."

Lance wouldn't make eye contact with Amanda, *is there some kind of sexual history between them?* she wondered. *But, sometimes, you don't want to know.*

"Should I call you when I get home? We're just going to a movie," Amanda asked.

"Have fun." Lance kissed Amanda deeply on the mouth before running off to the men's side of the Costumery. *Does his lack of reply mean he's already made other plans? Probably, with Supermodel from the Spur.*

Claire entered the women's side of the Costumery and spotted Claire not far off.

"Morning," Amanda called, brushing her way past a mass of dresses and wafting waves of patchouli.

"Hey, chica, are we still on for our girls night?" Claire held up a bright orange gown with green lace trim, then turned her nose up and put it back on a hanger.

"Sure are. Are we going to check out that new rom-com?"

"Definitely!" Claire picked up another dress, held it against her body, shook her head, and placed it back on the rack. "So, I have to say, I'm impressed you're willing to leave Prince Charming for a night."

"Why do you say that?"

"You two have been inseparable. I thought I'd lost you forever."

"I can still make time for a friend." Amanda flipped through the costume rack trying to decide what to wear.

"So I presume you've finally mastered getting dressed?" Claire paused, staring to giggle. "God, that sounds funny."

"I knew what you meant. Although it does sound rather strange. I think I've finally gotten it down. I seem to have conquered popping breast syndrome, so that's really all a girl can ask for."

Claire and Amanda looked at each other before releasing a gush of laughter.

"Popping breasts. Love it!" Claire eked out between gasps for air.

"So, I'm surprised I haven't had more warnings from you about Lance lately," Amanda tossed out, finally spotting her favorite purple dress with pink ribbon. She referred to it as her Barbie Doll dress.

"You've already heard it all. I've told you that he's the most commitment-phobic man I've ever met, and that he's more in love with the mirror than he ever could be with any woman. He hasn't emotionally matured past the age of eighteen. He's a narcissist of the highest order. I don't think one woman could ever be enough for him. That's it, Keira. That's all I have to say. So, did I tell you I decided I'm going to be celibate for a while? I've had it with one-night stands. It's time to detox."

"Really?" *I can't imagine choosing to not have sex. Celibacy is just the natural result of not dating for long periods of time. I've been that way since it ended with Ryan, but it sure isn't a state I've entered on purpose.*

"My cousin could stand to try that." Amanda thought of Roxie and wondered if she'd ever willingly taken a break from men. Probably not.

"We all could, from time to time." Claire finished lacing her shoes and then stood to leave. "Sorry, hon. I have to run. Royalty calls. See you tonight. Want to meet here, six-thirtyish?"

Amanda agreed, even though she was still somewhat regretting the decision not to spend the evening with Lance. She didn't fully trust him not to go back to that brunette — or Lord knows who else he might have waiting. Melinda and Claire's comments continued to scare her. *I'll just have to trust that everything will be okay. If he's truly my Lancelot, won't it all work out? If only I had Therese to assure me I'm doing the right things.*

****

As Melinda and Amanda were frantically trying to put the store back together after a group of seven-year-old campers came through in a swirl of screaming and bouncing bodies, Amanda's phone started playing *Shut Up and Let Me Go*. She crouched behind the counter to dig through her purse and find her phone.

"This is Keira," she answered without thinking, startled by the ringing and knowing Melinda had clear rules about cellphones. Ringtones broke the magic of the Faire.

"Oh, I'm sorry I have the wrong number."

"No, Mom, it's me."

"Excuse me?"

"Sorry, Keira's my name at the Faire. You caught me off guard. What's up? I'm working."

"I want to talk to you about the Women's Rotary Club. They're having their annual dinner next weekend, you remember, the Banquet of the Roses, the one that serves the retarded ... "

"Developmentally disabled," Amanda interrupted.

"Whatever. Well, you've gone with me every year, so I bought you a plane ticket to fly home for the weekend."

"You bought me a ticket without asking?! Mom, I can't come. I work weekends." Melinda leaned over the counter, shooting Amanda a warning look.

"Ask for the weekend off."

"It doesn't work that way. The Faire only runs for eight weeks. We have to work all weekends. That's part of the deal."

"You are so selfish, you know that?"

Amanda clenched the phone in a vice grip and lowered her voice. "I'm not getting into this with you now. I'm at work. I'll talk to you later."

"I won't be home tonight. It's mahjong night. You can call me tomorrow."

"Okay." Amanda hung up and turned her phone completely off before burying it in her purse.

"Everything okay?" Melinda asked.

"Long story."

"Keira, if you get calls like that again, ask for a break and head off to the woods. Don't spoil the magic spell of the store."

"Sorry. It won't happen again," Amanda assured Melinda, wishing she could believe it.

The end of the day couldn't come soon enough. Amanda was looking forward to her first girl's night out in a long time. *How long has it been? I think it was last April when Roxie dragged me to that god-awful jazz show to celebrate Lisa's divorce? That was a terrible night. Then again, I was still pretty raw from Ryan, so who knows how much that contributed to it. I can't remember a good night out with just a girlfriend, at least not after the mess with Cassie.* Amanda unpinned her hairpiece as she approached her locker. When she got up close, she noticed a note taped to her locker door.

Keira,

Sorry to do this to you,

but I have to cancel for tonight.

Maybe we can try again in a few days.

Claire

Amanda looked around but didn't see Claire; *I hope she isn't sick again, but as disappointing as this is, it also means I may be able to get together with Lance.* She dug her phone out of her purse and texted him that her plans had changed and she had the night free, then she changed and drove home.

By eight o'clock, Lance hadn't returned her text, so she decided to walk to the liquor store, get a bottle of wine, and enjoy it with a movie. *A night alone isn't such a terrible idea. I used to really like them. I've been with Lance nearly every night for several weeks, and maybe he'll still surprise me tonight.*

When she opened the door to the liquor store, she saw Jerry perched on a stool behind the counter, immersed in a book.

"Whatcha reading?" Amanda asked. She hadn't really spoken to him much since their night at the Spur, and was grateful he didn't remember much beyond the fact they had gone out.

"Hi, Keira," he said in his dreamy Jerry tone.

"Anything good?"

"Sci-fi." He held up the book cover. It was a vintage 1950's paperback. A couple was running in terror from a UFO.

Amanda nodded. Walking away from the counter and heading down the wine aisle, she could sense that Jerry never shifted his eyes from her.

"This is all," she said, handing him a bottle to ring up. She already had one hand in her purse, digging out her wallet.

"I get off in a couple of hours, want to enjoy this together?" He asked.

"I'm sorry, I can't," Amanda avoided making eye contact. She felt like such a jerk. Yes, she wanted to know what he knew, but she'd given up on ever getting to the answers. They were buried deep inside his drugged-out mind.

"Is it that guy from the bar?"

"Yes." *I wonder what else he remembers.*

"He'll hurt you."

"You know, that's what everyone keeps trying to tell me. I guess I'll just have to figure that out on my own." *Now Jerry's in on the lecture? I can't believe how the universe is conspiring against me and Lance.*

"I don't want to see you hurt, Keira."

Amanda smiled, grabbed her bottle, and walked toward the door.

"He's not your Lancelot," Jerry called out as she stepped into the Colorado night.

CHAPTER 32

The crowds were relentless. It was one camp group after another. Amanda restocked the dried-flower wreaths twice and the silk ones at least three times. Right before the noon lull, the time when fairgoers sought out their drumsticks and fried pickles on a stick, Lance stopped by the shop.

"Hi, Princess."

"Hi there, Pirate. Did you come in search of a flowered tiara?"

"No," he smiled, dimples flashing and eyes shining. Dressed in his knight costume, Amanda frequently had a hard time distinguishing this Lance from Keira's Miles. "But I think you need a new one," he teased. "Let's try this."

Lance removed Amanda's autumn-colored silk-leaf wreath and replaced it with a glittering band of gold-painted rosebuds. "Now that's more striking — much more appropriate for a princess."

"And gaudy," Amanda added, placing it back on the wall.

"Sorry I couldn't meet up last night. I went to see a show in Denver with Ryan and some guys. Trying to keep myself distracted."

"Worried you'll be tempted away from me?" Amanda teased, although she knew it was completely true.

"How could anyone tempt me from you? No, I'm getting worried. I should have gotten my renewal contract for my teaching job by now."

"Oh," Amanda felt bad for immediately assuming everything was about her. "Maybe they're just late with the paperwork."

"Maybe."

"So how was the show? Good band?"

"Yeah, they're pretty good. Sorta punkish. I actually went to high school with the drummer."

"Small world."

"It sure is. So where's Mistress Melinda?"

"She ran to the restroom. We've been going non-stop all morning. She bolted as soon as the store calmed down."

"What are we going to do tonight?" Lance asked, scooping Amanda into his arms and holding on tight.

"I don't know. Do I sense a kidnapping coming?"

"Perhaps. Does the princess have any requests?"

"Thai food? I'm dying for it. I think it's going on two months since I've had any."

"Thai food, eh? Let me think ... okay, your wish is my command. I know just the place. Might be a bit of a drive, is that okay?"

Amanda nodded yes, and with that, he kissed her on the lips, leaving the taste of him on her as he walked away.

****

Lunchtime turned out to be later than usual because of the crowds, and Amanda wasn't sure she'd make it on time to watch Lance in the jousting tournament — that had turned out to be her normal lunchtime routine. Hurrying along, she walked by The Palm Reader's gypsy wagon *I've always thought that one day I'd love to have my palm read. Is today the day? Something seems to be calling me. I know what I need now is guidance, especially since Therese has gone AWOL. Maybe Natalya will be able to shed some light on what I'm supposed to do next with my life.*

Natalya's wagon was set on the ground; its wheels appeared to be shorn off so it leaned to one side. Whenever she'd passed and looked through the gauzy mustard-colored curtains that framed the worn window, Amanda thought it was odd that Natalya always appeared to be sitting up straight. Red paint peeling off the side of the wagon made it look like it was bleeding, while battered gold trim hinted at a previous luster and brilliance. Amanda wondered, *is the wagon real, or is the whole look simply a Faire prop built for effect?*

As Amanda approached the wagon, she was overcome by the scent of lavender. She hadn't smelt it so strongly since it came on during a regression back in her apartment in Chicago. The aroma guided her in, and for a brief moment, she thought she might regress.

"Hello, love. I have been waiting for you," Natalya said with a heavy Eastern European accent. The fortune teller, Zora, was also from Eastern Europe, and Amanda wondered why all the psychics seemed to be from that part of the world. Stepping into the red wagon felt like being instantly transported to the woods of Transylvania in the 1800s. The lavender scent continued to permeate the air. Amanda broke out in goosebumps. Her heart fluttered.

Natalya's silver-white hair peeked out in spots around the red bandana that covered her head. She was layered in brightly colored shawls that dressed her large, shapeless body. When she made eye contact, Amanda instantly fell into her deep brown eyes and under her spell.

"You've seen me before?" Amanda pulled at her split ends, a bad nervous habit left over from childhood.

Natalya's eyes lowered and she nodded slowly. "Your aura ... " she started, and then brought her arms up and around in a sweeping motion, " ... radiant and strong, it is. You!" she pointed her finger into Amanda's chest. "Very old soul with a very interesting story. I'm pleased you have finally decided to pay me a visit. Sit down, dear."

Natalya had a calming presence that settled Amanda's jangled nerves; she hadn't felt energy like that since her sessions with

Therese. *Perhaps Natalya is Therese in disguise, come to Colorado to check up on me?* Taking a seat in the chair opposite Natalya, Amanda studied her face to see if there were any signs of Therese.

"Twenty-five dollars." Natalya put her hand out, palm side up and looked away. Amanda chuckled to herself at the odd combination of gypsy mysticism paired with old-fashioned hucksterism.

The Renaissance Faire had a low entry price, but was notorious for charging outrageous amounts of money for every little service and ride. Amanda was surprised that they hadn't found a way to charge for the jousting.

"I only have fifteen dollars on me. I'll have to come back another time." Amanda pushed her chair away, ready to leave.

"No, no, no. You leave, you no come back." Natalya grabbed onto Amanda's arm and firmly put her back into the chair. "We settle up later. I take your fifteen dollars now." She extended her palm right into Amanda's personal space.

Amanda handed her the cash. Natalya nodded her head in thanks, pocketing the cash.

"Your hand," she said, taking Amanda's right hand in her open palm. Natalya drew her finger over the criss-crossing lines. Her touch was light and gentle, as though she was blind and Amanda's palm had a braille code that would reveal everything unknown.

"A butterfly is emerging from a cocoon," she said, gripping her hands tightly around Amanda's and lowering her eyes. "I see grey, nappy, hard-to-break cocoon. It's falling to the ground. Oh! A beautiful butterfly's wings are batting in the sunlight." Amanda watched in awe as Natalya's eyes floated to the ceiling. *Does she truly see a butterfly?* Amanda checked the corners of the wagon to make sure she hadn't missed anything. "The butterfly is now free. Its yellow and orange spots soak up the sun." At the mention of "free," Amanda felt a release of emotional weight.

Natalya continued, "It floats away. It's a very beautiful sight. You are that butterfly." Amanda wiped away the tears that were sliding down her cheeks.

"That's exactly what I am," Amanda sniffled. "I'm a butterfly who has finally been released, but can you tell me where the butterfly is going? That's what I need to know." Her tone of desperation brought a motherly smile across Natalya's face.

"Who knows the direction of beautiful butterfly, but those who are it? Tell me child, where do *you* think you're going?" Once again, she gently pushed her finger into Amanda's chest.

If I knew that, I probably wouldn't be here paying you for advice, Amanda thought. "I don't know."

"You need to trust yourself. You're on the path. I see a man," Natalya continued, once again closing her eyes. "You've been searching for this person." Amanda thought back to how Melinda had compared Lance to a butterfly. She saw an image of her and Lance dancing around each other in an open field, free as butterflies.

"And this person is here at the Faire, right?"

"This person has been searching for you too. You must be careful, walk softly. Be true to you."

"Will we end up together?"

"I cannot see."

Anxiety overcame Amanda. "Do you see anything about past lives?"

"He is tied to your past life. You have been together before. You are an old soul, Keira. You have the right name."

That last comment caught Amanda off guard.

"What do you see about my name?"

"You have been too scared to fully be Keira. It is time."

"But I've told everyone my name is Keira,"

"But you don't believe." Natalya reached for Amanda's other palm. "There are others you must confront."

"Who?"

"Only you can know."

Amanda was growing frustrated with the ramblings and decided to bring the conversation back to the beginning, back to why she came in the first place.

"Where do you see me after the Faire? I'm trying to get some guidance around what to do when the summer ends."

"You go with him."

"Where?"

"Go with him. No matter what, you go with him." Natalya dropped Amanda's hand. "That is all we can do today," Natalya said and retreated back into herself, her hands clasped together on her lap. "Be well, dear."

Amanda sat dumbfounded. It was like Natalya was a recording that had abruptly ended.

"Are you sure there's nothing else?" Amanda begged.

"You bring me other ten dollar and perhaps I see more."

CHAPTER 33

Amanda's tired feet could barely carry her back to the Costumery. She couldn't believe the season was more than half over; it was already the end of July. She kept stretching and flexing the muscles in her arches and toes. The period shoes, with their soft leather form, lacked any type of arch support.

Claire had called her earlier in the day, and they'd agreed to meet at the Costumery when the Faire closed. Claire had never explained why she wasn't free the other night, and Amanda figured she'd find out after work. She tried to pick up her pace so she wouldn't be late, but rushing only caused her feet to cramp more.

She was zoning out, thinking about what Natalya had said to her earlier that week, but was interrupted when her phone played *Shut Up and Let Me Go.* Baldwin the Fool walked past her while she was fumbling through her purse, and from the corner of her eye, she saw him give her the thumbs-up sign. He continued smiling and nodding his head along to the music as he walked by. She threw her purse on the ground in frustration, and the phone came tumbling out, as if it had been lying on top of everything the whole time.

"Hi, Mom," Amanda answered while returning the contents to her purse. Once she began walking again, she grabbed a bunch of fabric from the lower portion of her dress and pulled it up, so that the front edge wasn't sweeping the bark chips along while she walked.

"Did you forget you have a mother?"

Amanda sighed. Even with a thousand miles between them, her mother still tried to maintain control over her life. Amanda mustered all the energy she could to stand up to Celia.

"You never called me back about the Rotary weekend."

"That's because I told you I couldn't come. There was nothing more to discuss."

"I have no idea what's going on in your life. Are you eating? Are you safe? Are you associating with the right people?"

Amanda winced at that last question. It was so like Celia to randomly sort people into acceptable piles. Sweat trickled down Amanda's face, even though it was past six o'clock.

"So I've had enough. I've bought us tickets to come to Colorado."

"You did what?! Wait! Who's 'us'?"

"Roxie and me, of course. Who do you think?"

"You and Roxie?" Amanda lost track of where she was going and had to stop a moment to orient herself. "You and Roxie are coming here? When?" She continued walking, but hadn't gathered up her skirt and nearly tripped over it, stumbling on a rock in the process.

"We'll be there Friday around dinnertime. I'll give you our flight information. You can pick us up, and then we'll spend the weekend together."

"But Mom, I work all weekend. And I live in a studio apartment. I have no place for you to stay. Why didn't you ask me first?"

"So here's the information: flight number ... "

"Mom, I hate to be so bold," Amanda took a deep breath and went for it. "But I don't want you to come. Do you hear me?"

"We will be there whether you like it or not. You are an ungrateful daughter with no respect for her family. You have no idea what I'm giving up in order to make it out there on such short notice."

"I can't believe I'm having this conversation."

"Yes, well, I can't believe you've been gone for this long. You never call. You've left me all alone in Chicago. You have no consideration for my feelings ... or for poor Roxie's for that matter. You know ... you know ... "

"What?" Amanda demanded. She had reached the Costumery, but would not go inside while she was on the phone. She stood in a shady corner of the building, under an awning, wiping endless sweat from her forehead.

"No, we're not going to discuss this. I'll see you Friday night." Celia hung up before Amanda could respond.

****

Amanda had barely touched her mojito. Claire played with her mousy locks, untangling the braids while her eyes scanned the bar. "Do you think I should get a perm?" she asked, pulling a small lock of hair in front of her eyes.

Amanda didn't look up. She hadn't looked up since she got to the Spur. "I can't believe they're coming."

Claire dropped her hands dramatically onto the table. "So they come, you have an obligatory meal or two, and then you send them on their way. You can do it." Claire made it sound so simple. That was easy to do when you didn't know Celia and Roxie.

"I can't believe they're coming."

"Okay, stop saying that. They're coming, and you need to get a grip." Claire locked onto Amanda's wrist with her hand and made her look her in the eyes. "You know if you drink that mojito, and then maybe even get another one, you'll feel a heck of a lot better, and you'll be able to come up with a plan. It's the secret elixir for troubled souls. Didn't they tell you that when you ordered?"

Amanda surrendered a bit of a smile.

"So, you know, I was all into the idea of a fun girl's night, but so far, you've been a bit of a drag. Think you can come around and help me out by getting drunk, or am I going to have to find a new friend?"

"No, no. You're right, as usual, wise Claire. To girlfriends!" Amanda raised her drink and clinked her glass with Claire's before downing half of the mojito in one gulp.

After Amanda's second drink, her worries started to ease. She laughed off Celia and Roxie as her posture dropped and her smile turned into a giggly, drunken grin. She shifted her thoughts to Lance and their post-Faire life.

"So where do you go next, Claire?"

"After this, I stumble home and pass out. Then I get up and do it all over again. Work, anyway, if not the drinking part."

"No, I mean after August, after the Faire ends, then what?"

"Oh that! I go to magical, enchanting Wisconsin, of course," Claire said with a straight face, then she and Amanda broke out in laughter loud enough for the people in the adjoining booth to stop their conversation and glare at them.

"Sorry!" Claire waved before turning to face Amanda and pressing her finger to her lips in hushed laughter.

"So do you think I can come too?"

"To Wisconsin? Sure! There's room for both of us. It's a big state."

They continued laughing as their waiter came around. "You ladies need another round?" he asked, sliding his football player's build into the booth, so that he was right on top of Amanda. He eyed her up and down; it made her feel good to be admired, even if she had no intention of following up on the attention.

"I could use another one of these." Amanda held up her empty glass, her arm swaying in front of the waiter.

"And we need some nachos," Claire said loudly, finishing what was left of her drink and slamming her empty glass on the table.

"Is there anything else I can get you?" He hadn't taken his eyes off Amanda.

"No, I'm all taken," she replied.

Claire burst out laughing. The waiter smiled at them both and left.

"You sure are taken!" Claire continued, "I figured you would have woken up by now, but you're really into him. Is he good in bed or something?"

"No." Amanda smiled then shook her head. "I mean, that's not it. I just really like him."

"Really?"

"Claire, did you ever go out with him? It's been really bugging me. I can handle it if you say yes."

"No, I never did. He's not my type. But I did have a good friend who went out with him a few summers ago. He broke her heart in a bad way. I never forgave him for that, and he knows it."

"I keep hearing the stories. Everyone has them."

"Listen, I have strong women's intuition. There's something up here. Nobody falls for Lance the way you have. It's like you're possessed."

She couldn't take the pressure any longer. Her need to tell someone — plus the alcohol — combined to form a truth serum that she knew she would later regret. "I have a confession."

"Ooo! Goody, goody! Now we're getting to the juicy stuff! I knew there was something secret hiding in you!" Claire rubbed her palms together and leaned back in full attention and anticipation.

"You're going to think I'm crazy," Amanda paused. "No, I shouldn't."

"Well, it's too late now, you have to tell me."

"Okay, here we go." Amanda took a big first sip of their latest round of drinks. "Back in February, I started doing past-life regressions with a therapist in Chicago."

"Whoa." Claire's eyes locked on Amanda.

"Yeah, and I would always regress back to this time in the 1500s England where I was a girl named Keira."

Claire sat staring at Amanda whose heart raced. *There, I've done it — screwed up my one good friendship. I should have kept my mouth shut.* She took a huge gulp of her drink. *Now Claire's going to think I'm some kind of freak.*

"So then ... is your name really Keira?"

"We don't have to go into it."

"No, no, I'm curious. Keep going. I've heard about this stuff before. I had a cousin who did it. I find it completely fascinating. I don't think I would have the guts to do it myself, but it's super interesting."

Claire's interest reassured Amanda. She took a deep breath before continuing, "Okay, so my name is actually Amanda. I changed it to Keira when I came to the Faire."

"Amanda? Really? You don't look like an Amanda."

Amanda laughed. "I lived in this abbey where I was being raised by some monks. One day our abbey came under attack and I was kidnapped by a knight."

"Ooh! Love it! Love it! Keep going!"

"So, this knight took me into some magical place called the Forest of Forgiveness. There I met a hobbit-type person who turned out to be my mother. She was the queen of that magical fairyland."

"Then you have fairy blood. How fucking cool is that?!"

"I suppose so," Amanda said matter-of-factly. She looked down at her hands. Their waiter appeared, carrying a plate of nachos and a large stack of napkins. He tried to sit down again, but Amanda body-blocked him. She was too deep into her story to engage in mindless flirting.

"Oh my God, this is wild! So what happened next?" Claire pulled herself to the edge of the booth in anticipation, reaching for a handful of nachos.

"I lived there in the forest, learning the ways of her people, which of course was very different from the abbey. But here's the freaky part. You ready?" *I wonder if I'm ready. What's going to happen once this knowledge lives outside of me, out in the world in Colorado?*

Claire nodded her head.

"The knight who captured me was named Miles, but it was Lance."

Claire was quiet. Amanda wondered if maybe she hadn't heard her. After a few moments, Claire broke the silence. "This is way too bizarre."

"Yeah."

"Lance? Someone's soul mate? I'm not sure, Keira. I think you might have to revisit this one."

"I know it's him."

"Do you think he knows?" Claire's eyes narrowed in deep skepticism.

"No, I'm sure he doesn't. See, I think we do this thing, where in every life, only one of us remembers the other. In the regressions, he knew me more than I knew him. I had a reading by Natalya today, and she confirmed that he was here. In this life, it's my turn to remind him. It's completely up to me, or we'll drift away for another lifetime."

"Okay, okay. This is all super weird, but say it is real, then what are you going to do?"

"Well, obviously, I have to make him realize who I am."

"This is some heavy shit," Claire muttered.

Amanda sobered by the concern of having exposed herself unnecessarily thought, *Yes, it's also a little liberating, but there is a vulnerability in sharing everything, even to someone as kind as Claire.*

Claire nodded. "Does he know anything? Anything at all?"

"No. But he keeps saying that he feels like he knows me from somewhere. I deflect each time it comes up."

"Yeah, okay. Wow. A soul mate. You're soul mates with Steve Thrasher. This is really way bizarre. You picked a tough one, girlfriend."

"No kidding."

"So what happens now?"

"That's the million-dollar question."

CHAPTER 34

Celia had texted all the flight details to Amanda; she had also emailed them to her twice. Amanda was having a hard time bringing herself to respond to her mother's barrage of communication. She re-read the last email: "Where are you? We expect you to be by baggage claim waiting for us. Again, we're on United, flight 952, leaving at 5:10 p.m. (NOT A.M.) and arriving at 6:20. We have not rented a car, so make sure that there's room in yours for our bags. We will discuss this new attitude of yours when I get there."

Amanda cringed for the umpteenth time at reading that last line. *New attitude. Hell, nothing's new about my attitude. It's just the Keira in me shining through.*

****

Amanda stood in Faertyale Fynery, eyeballing the clock. It was 2:15. Melinda had approved Amanda to cut out early, so she could get to the airport in time for their 6:20 arrival. Melinda was so friendly and accommodating that it still caught her off guard. She kept waiting for the erratic, angry, psycho side of her new boss to appear, the way it had with all of her previous ones.

Except for the latté she picked up on her way into work, Amanda hadn't been able to eat anything all day,. At lunchtime, she thought she'd try a turkey sandwich, but she couldn't stomach anything beyond the first bite. She could practically hear her mother: "This is where you live? My shoes have more space in my closet than you have in this apartment."

Is there any way they can support my new life? Be happy for me? Maybe even be proud of me? Will they see any of my change in a healthy light? I've certainly gotten over Ryan. I think I look different, and no longer dragged down with the weight of that failed relationship.

Roxie would be viciously jealous of Claire, just like she had been of all of Amanda's other friendships. *I don't even want to think about what Roxie will do to Lance. Will she hit on him? Tell him the truth? Both*? Celia and Roxie were simply reminders of the life she had left behind. *I knew eventually I'd have to see them, but I didn't think it would be so soon. I'm just not ready yet. I need more time. Truth be told, maybe I'll never be ready.*

Lance had offered to let Amanda stay at his place, so Celia and Roxie could stay in her apartment. She'd already been keeping a toothbrush and change of clothes at Lance's, but somehow couldn't picture her Mom and Celia sharing her futon or fighting over the bathroom. No, they were going to have to stay at a hotel. There weren't any within a thirty-mile radius that were up to Celia's standards, so Amanda had booked them a room at the Hampton Inn, the same hotel where she stayed when she arrived. It was the closest thing to luxury available in Castle Rock.

She checked her watch again. It was only 3:30. Her nervous stomach had triggered two desperate dashes to the Royal Flush but they only left her dry-heaving and dizzy. There was nothing in her stomach to come up.

Finally, at 4:15, she headed to the Costumery to change into her T-shirt and capris. She wanted to get through Denver before Friday's rush hour.

Everything felt out of place as Amanda walked to her car. She was amazed at how packed the Faire became during the course of a day. Inside her car, the air was sweltering and stale. She must have left a banana somewhere in the back seat because the car reeked of rotting fruit. She gagged, rolling down the window and desperately taking in the pine-scented air. *Great, another thing for Celia to rag about,* she thought, peeling out of the dusty lot.

Driving north on I-25, Amanda tried to put the situation into a positive light. She turned the radio dial, looking for something to alter her mood. She found Bob Marley and began singing along: "One love, one heart, let's get together and feel all right ... " *Maybe it won't be so bad after all*, she thought, as her stomach grumbled.

She took I-225 on Lance's suggestion, skirting around to the east of the city. She wished he could have come with her, but leaving early wasn't an option for him since the last joust of the day took place at 4:30. She joked with him that they could kill off Sir Lancelot in the first round so no one would expect him to return, but he said King Henry wasn't much for messing with the script.

She arrived at the airport with plenty of time to spare, and looked for the signs for the cell phone lot. *Perfect,* she thought *I'll park there and wait until it's closer to six o'clock.*

Amanda pulled her car into an empty spot and cut the engine. From her parking space, she could see the planes coming in. They appeared so graceful, sliding noiselessly through the air. She got lost in their easy momentum, picturing the reunion with Celia and Roxie.

She started to plan that she would stand at the top of the escalator, waiting for them to come up as she'd seen other people do for their loved ones. *Loved ones. Eek. But that's what they are though, right?* Amanda looked down at her shirt and wished she had thought to put on a nicer one. *Celia will have a fit, seeing her daughter dressed in an advertisement for a beer. "But it's a microbrew, Mom. It's not the same," I'll argue, and then Celia will say, "Beer is beer. Only cheap and easy girls flaunt such crap."* Amanda shook the comment from her mind. *Roxie will be dressed all in black, but Colorado isn't really a black-clad depressing place. The sun shines 300 days out of the year.* Amanda smiled broadly. *I've really fallen in love with Colorado. At least Keira has. But, is it Colorado I'm in love with, or simply a life that isn't like the one I left?*

Amanda looked at the clock in her car. It was 5:45. Her nervous stomach cranked up again, and she looked around for a place to vomit if the urge rose that far. There was nothing. Her phone rang its generic ringtone. It was Lance. She had to find a good song for him.

"Hi!" she exclaimed into the phone, holding her other hand low and tight across her stomach, begging to keep the nervous energy down.

"Hey, babe. I was just thinking of you. Wanted to see how you're doing."

"Not well. I'm waiting in the 45-minute parking zone agonizing over actually going in."

"Do you have to?"

"I'm here. It's too late to turn around now."

"Is it?"

As Lance spoke, she noticed a car circling the parking lot. All the spots were full. She looked at her watch.

"Somebody wants my spot."

"I'm on my way over to the Spur. Call me when you get back to town."

Amanda's stomach grumbled. *If I turn around,* Amanda told herself, *I could see Lance and get food. A hamburger. A big, juicy hamburger covered in the famous spicy Spur barbeque sauce.*

"I want to see you." Tears trickled down her face. I don't want to go into the airport. I don't want to get Celia and Roxie. I want to keep moving forward." Her stomach grumbled again. She could hear Lance's breath on the other end of the phone. A rage built deep inside her. *What the hell am I doing? I'm letting them run my life again. Keira wouldn't. Keira would have set boundaries.*

"Keira, are you there?" It was the simplest of questions, but its timing couldn't have been better. It played for Amanda on multiple levels. *Is Keira here in the car or not? Is this the same old Amanda I wanted to leave behind in Chicago? Amanda would go through that gate into the airport. Keira would meet Lance for dinner.* Her stomach growled even louder.

"Lance, I'm not going to do it. I can't go and get them. Save me a spot at the Spur. I'll see you soon." She beamed with a new-found energy as she got back on the expressway, turned off the air conditioning, opened her windows all the way, and released her hair from its ponytail holder. She shook her head, letting out a powerful yell from deep inside her. She cranked up the radio and slammed on the gas. *There will be severe consequences to pay, I know that, but this feels like the healthiest decision I've ever made.*

****

At six-thirty, her phone started singing. Then her message alert chimed. Amanda's stomach clenched.

"I can't believe you actually did it. You ditched your mom!" Lance shook his head at Amanda as she sat down in the booth across from him. Her phone alternated between *Like a Virgin* and *Shut Up and Let Me Go*. She released a nervous giggle.

"You will as soon as you meet her." Amanda took a big swig of the beer in front of her, and set it down fiercely. It sloshed over the side, and started trickling down her hand. Regret crept its way back in, but she downed her beer, trying to quickly drown the feeling. "Thanks for ordering for me," she said, licking the beer from her hand. "God, I feel so fucking free! I feel amazing."

"Wow. I didn't think you had it in you."

"I didn't think I had it in me either. Your call triggered it. You're good for my soul, Mr. Thrasher," Amanda winked, taking another huge swig of beer.

"I'm sure it won't be pleasant when you finally see them."

"Fuck pleasant," Amanda said with a fierceness that startled her.

Lance shook his head and looked away.

"What?"

Lance wouldn't look back.

"What?" Amanda pressed, laying a hand on his arm.

"Nothing," he said, finally turning to really look at her. "It's just that I'm excited to see this passion in you. I've only gotten a few rare glimpses."

Amanda felt a powerful energy grow inside her, "Well, that's who I am," she said, taking even herself by surprise. Amanda sat up straight and felt an immense amount of confidence run along her spine and spread across her shoulders, pulling them back, wide and strong. *I am woman. Hear me roar*, she thought, letting out a self-conscious giggle.

"I like it." Lance took her hands into his and brought them to his lips. "I was wondering what personality you were hiding in there. My sweet little Keira isn't always so sweet," Lance released those deep dimples of his that simply melted Amanda to the core.

Her phone vibrated. She turned it off.

"I have an idea, Miss Amazing," Lance continued, lowering his voice in a seductive manner that made Amanda want to rip his clothes off right there in the middle of the bar.

"What's your idea, Mr. Wonderful?"

"How about we go back to my place, leave your phone off, in fact, turn all the phones off, and hide out in my pirate cove. That way, I can keep you free for one more night. I want to get to explore this side of you."

"That sounds like a smashing idea." Amanda finished off what was left of her beer and slammed the empty pint glass onto the table.

Once inside his apartment, Amanda made a beeline for the bathroom. By the time she was done primping, she could see that the magic moment had disappeared. Lance was slumped on top of a barstool at the kitchen counter with his palm pressed to his forehead, either in deep thought or hiding tears, Amanda couldn't tell which. She approached slowly, laying a hand on his shoulder.

"What's wrong?"

He handed her the letter that was lying open in front of him.

"Fuck!" he yelled, walking across the living room, violently throwing pillows from the couch around the room. Amanda read the letter:

> Dear Mr. Thrasher
>
> We have reviewed your renewal application for our National Endowment for the Arts Teachers program. It is our deepest regret to inform you that due to the dramatic cuts in funding we experienced this fiscal year, we are no longer able to award this grant. Please visit our website to learn of other funding opportunities. Thank you for your passion and commitment to the arts.
>
> Mr. Paul Hokum
>
> Chairman, Grants Committee

"Oh honey." Amanda walked over to where Lance was standing and reached out to hug him. He pulled away.

"I'm screwed. I'm totally and completely screwed." He was crying, and Amanda took in his pain as if it were her own.

"We can figure it out. I'm sure there's a way for you to get back to New York."

"No. There's no way. I've already tried to work it every which way. Fuck!"

Amanda tried to hug him again, and this time he let her take him into her arms. She patted him on the back and rocked him.

"You can be a nomad like me. Want to walk the earth together?"

Lance let out a forced laugh.

"Marry me." Amanda couldn't believe she said it. She couldn't believe that the words flew from her mouth. It was like they had been released from a cage. A butterfly.

"You're nuts, Keira. You know that? Completely nuts."

"Perhaps. But reality isn't working well for either one of us. Why can't we disappear together? That's all I've ever wanted."

"So you think we should just check out and run around the country like Claire does, going from faire to faire?" Lance's mocking tone hurt.

Yes, she thought, *that's exactly what I want us to do.* "I'm sure there are worse things we could do with our life."

"But I love my job. I'm just stupid for not coming up with a Plan B."

"We can't always have a Plan B. Sometimes we have to live in the moment." Amanda couldn't believe she was saying this. *I must have had quite an epiphany at the airport to have become so confident, so quickly.*

"Keira, I think I need to be alone tonight."

"Don't push me away, please."

"Sorry, I'm not in the mood."

"It's okay, we can just be together. I want to be here for you."

"I'm not much company."

"Let me be strong. Let me take care of you."

"You're so amazing. How did I find you?"

Amanda's heart ached with the weight of their long history together. She wanted to share everything, but it never felt safe enough to do so. She wondered if it ever would.

"I came looking for you. I wasn't going to stop until I found you."

Lance smiled a weak smile and took Amanda in his arms.

CHAPTER 35

"Hey, hon!" Claire called across the Costumery. Claire was halfway into an emerald green dress with gold trim. It made for a unique look, as the rest of her was only wearing a hot pink Victoria's Secret bra with the VS insignia all over it.

"I think you should go out like that today," Amanda teased.

"You think so? Maybe create a fashion statement? Renaissance meets modern-day woman." Claire struck a model pose, chest puffed up, shoulders back, chin lifted. Amanda jokingly gave her a thumbs up. "So how was your night?" Claire asked, removing her bra and working herself into the dress. "Did everything go okay at the airport?"

"I didn't get them."

"What?!" Claire froze, with one arm in the dress, one arm dangling freely. She looked like a deformed mannequin.

"I almost did. I made it to the airport early and was sitting in the cell phone lot, agonizing about going in. Next thing I know, Lance called. Then I guess I just had one of those epiphanies, you know?"

"No shit!"

"I thought to myself, What the hell am I doing?" Amanda took a seat on the floor. "I got to thinking about what Keira from my past life would have done, and well, I turned around and high-tailed it back to see Lance," Amanda explained. "I'm sure I have a ton of texts and voicemails from them, but now I'm too scared to actually turn on my phone. You know how you do something crazy when you're drunk, and then regret it horribly the next day? I know the minute I hear their voices, I'll lose it. The guilt will crush me, and my self-esteem will crash." Amanda's eyes welled up and a knot moved into her throat. She started shaking, and the tears finally came. "I wish I could blame it on being drunk."

Claire shimmied closer to Amanda, and gave her a hug. "You poor thing, making big decisions sucks."

Amanda clutched Claire's hand as a thank you. "I guess I should get ready for work ... and face my day." She fumbled through the costume rack, trying to find something to wear when really all she wanted was to go back to her apartment and hide.

"Good luck, my friend. Being a grown-up sucks the big one some days." Claire picked up her shoes, and walked in the direction of the makeup department. "Call me if you need me. Seriously, any time."

"Thank you. Oh, and Claire, wait a sec," Amanda called after her. "Lance's teaching contract didn't get renewed."

"Bummer."

"I was with him last night when he got the letter. He's really freaking out. I feel so helpless."

"Yeah, well, he's a big boy. He'll figure it out. We all do." Claire shrugged and continued walking away. "Sorry. That wasn't very nice. I know how much he means to you. I gotta run. Keep me posted on what happens."

****

The morning flew by, as usual; it was nearly lunchtime before Amanda realized she had still not turned on her phone. Each time she saw it lying in her purse, she felt like it was a bomb waiting to explode.

Around lunchtime, Baldwin the Fool came into Faerytale Fynery, skipping and whistling. He and Melinda were good friends, and Amanda was used to him dropping by. Normally, he would pinch Melinda's rear as he was leaving, and give her a wink. He always made an attempt for Amanda's, but she had learned to reposition herself quickly. Amanda often wondered if he and Melinda went for romps in the hay after work. Free love was rampant at the Faire.

"How's it going there, Baldwin?" Amanda sashayed herself out of reach, just in time.

"Fine, my fair lady. How goeth it with you?" Baldwin batted his eyelashes in the direction of Amanda's chest.

"Fine."

"Hark, fair maidens! I have come to call the alarm. There be quite a commotion going on in the park this fine day."

"Oh?!" Melinda exclaimed, immediately dropping the notepad she had in her hand. It was inventory and she was trying to get things prepared for the 'big count,' which was supposedly happening the next week. One thing Amanda had learned was that not much happened on schedule in great King Henry's kingdom.

"There is a lady of wealth and stature strutting around our great land in an ivory suit spun by the gods themselves. She is accompanied by a devil clad in black with hair the color of fire." Baldwin used his hands dramatically in order to set the mood. Amanda felt the blood drain from her face. *Celia and Roxie. They're here.*

"They ask of a fine lass named Amanda. They say she is among us and new this year." Baldwin turned his eyes to Amanda.

She felt her heart plummet. *They're looking for me.*

"Yet no one has known an Amanda of such fair beauty," he jested, letting his eyes continue to walk all over Amanda. "A lass so new and fresh to be picked like an apple off a tree, juicy and sweet and ripe."

Amanda wanted to clobber sick Baldwin over the head.

"Well! Who do you think it is?" Melinda asked, hanging on to Baldwin's every word. A couple entered the store, holding hands with a little girl. Amanda used it as an excuse to get out of the conversation.

"May I help you find a crown, my little princess?" Amanda attempted her fairly pathetic stilted English accent. She never got it down the way others, like Baldwin, did.

"Methinks it could be anyone," she heard Baldwin say.

"I want the one with the pink flowers!" the young girl squealed with delight.

"Let me show you the ones that are your size, sweetie. These are for the mommies," Amanda added, happy to be out of earshot of Baldwin and Melinda's conversation.

After the mother purchased her daughter's headpiece, Amanda excused herself to go to the bathroom. She started walking to the Royal Flush, but really, she wanted to find someplace to hide. She walked past the restrooms, which had a line wrapped around the building, and headed to the Costumery. When she passed the Celestial Stage, she spotted them. They were standing under a pine tree outside the cobbler shop. A wave of dizziness overcame her and she rushed for a nearby picnic table, immediately putting her forehead on her forearms. She knew she was heading for a regression. She breathed deeply and tried to relax.

****

Keira is in town on market day. The cobbler's booth is quite busy, but she has come to town to see Robert. From a distance, she sees him attending to a customer. He is smiling and glowing in the peaceful way that makes her love him. He continually bats away a lock of golden hair from his eyes and a black streak of shoe grease is smeared across his face from where his hand has tried to move the hair. Keira thinks about how she will wash his face when they are married, and how she will be sure to have sharpened shears, so she can trim his locks and see his soft brown eyes.

Robert has never mentioned marriage. It is only Keira who dreams such wondrous ideas. She feels a longing for companionship, and she believes she has found what she has been craving in Robert. Keira knows that he is fond of her, and that one day she will make him ask for her hand. She walks towards him, but a crowd of people move in front of her and block him from her view.

****

Even though the sun beat down on Amanda through the spaces in the pine trees, she was shivering. She hadn't thought of Robert in ages. The market really did feel so much like the Faire.

Celia and Roxie were still in front of the cobbler's stand, studying what looked like a map of the Faire. They did look absolutely ridiculous there, just as Baldwin had described. Celia was wearing a designer suit set: skirt, pantyhose, heels, and jacket. Even her purse matched. Her hair was swept into an up-do, which meant that she had to have stopped at a salon on her way to the Faire.

Roxie wore a green boa, the angriest of her assortment. The fact that Roxie packed a green boa was a bad sign. She looked grossly out of place, in skin-tight black pants, black vinyl boots, a short-sleeve black turtleneck, and a black beret. Her fiery red curls flew out from under the beret in every direction. Amanda saw passers-by in shorts, T-shirts, and sandals staring at Celia and Roxie.

Amanda stood up, but there was nowhere to hide. *Where has the fighter energy I summoned yesterday disappeared to? I started this. I'm going to have to finish it, or I can turn around and run toward the store.* She hesitated. Roxie looked up from the map and made eye contact with Amanda. Amanda's knees locked. She stood doe-eyed, like a fawn caught in a hunter's scope.

"Well, look who we have here!" Roxie exclaimed in a nasty, sarcastic tone.

Why didn't I pick them up yesterday? What did I think was going to happen?

"You little bitch," Celia snapped. "Where the hell were you last night, leaving us high and dry in cowboy country? Get out of those ridiculous clothes, and get us out of here."

"So you all had a nice flight then?" Amanda decided that her strategy would be to pretend everything was okay. It was the only way she felt she could keep her wits about her in this uncharted territory.

"What's your problem, Amanda?" Roxie demanded. "We come all the way to bum-fuck Colorado to see you, and you don't even have the decency to come get us at the airport? What's gotten into you? It looks like you went and joined the circus!" Amanda felt all of her power seep out of her and evaporate into the dry air.

"Sorry," she cowered, triggered back into her old patterns. "Something came up. I had an emergency."

"Oh, and you couldn't call or text? I call bullshit," Roxie spat.

At that moment, Amanda saw Lance walk by in the afternoon royal parade. She saw him wink and blow a kiss. She remembered she had the power to choose who she wanted to be.

"You're right." Amanda took a deep breath and marveled at how the nervous butterflies slowly drifted away.

CHAPTER 36

It was finally time to face the proverbial music. Amanda agreed to meet Roxie and Celia for dinner at the Applebee's adjacent to the Hampton Inn where they were staying. The whole evening felt surreal. She left her apartment and drove into town. She'd told them that she would explain everything over dinner. But now, as she drove to meet them, she realized that she still didn't have any clue what she was going to say or do. She had only said that to buy time and get herself away from them at the Faire.

Amanda walked into the restaurant, and spotted Celia and Roxie sitting in an oversized booth for six. Amanda enjoyed the irony of meeting them in a suburban chain restaurant, someplace they would never have been caught dead in back in Illinois. Thankfully, though, the restaurant felt like neutral ground.

"Hi," she said uneasily, sitting down next to Roxie. Both Celia and Roxie were wearing the same outfits they'd had on earlier in the day, but now they looked even more out of place, set against the backdrop of a restaurant teeming with parents in shorts, T-shirts, and sneakers, and kids running around in grubby clothes with messy faces.

"No Prince Charming?" Roxie asked, her voice dripping with sarcasm.

"No, I thought we should talk first." Lance had offered to come with her, but she'd insisted that confronting them was something she needed to do on her own.

"What's this?" Celia wrinkled her face in disgust.

"I met someone, Mom."

"Oh? I didn't know."

"He's royalty," Roxie snickered. Amanda needed to grab hold of the conversation fast or the next thing she knew, she'd be explaining the past-life regressions to her mom as well. Fortunately, the waitress came to take their order.

"Do y'all know what you'd like to have?" the waitress asked in a thick Texan drawl. Amanda had realized that Colorado was heavily populated with people from somewhere else. It seemed to be the Promised Land, in a way. It had certainly proved to be a salvation for Amanda. Whether she ultimately decided to stay or not, she knew she would always be grateful for how Colorado let her find her true self.

"So, I guess I owe you a proper — well, better — explanation about why I didn't come get you yesterday," Amanda owned up after the waitress had taken their order and left.

"That would be nice," Celia huffed, her gaze drifting past Amanda's. She had barely made eye contact with her, but that had always been Celia's way: temporary disownment.

"I was intending to, but ... "

Both Roxie and Celia glared at Amanda.

"Well," she paused, taking a sip of ice water. "I wanted to make a statement." There, it was out in the open. Simply saying it was a major emotional release.

"A statement?" Celia's tone was perfectly tuned to the same pitch she'd used when Amanda had gotten into trouble as a kid. Amanda fought her sense of inner panic and pressed forward.

"Yes, a statement. I told you that I wanted to move out here to find me, to do something on my own. Since I left, you've both kept trying to pull me back. Mom, you make me feel like a child, and I just needed to do a grown-up thing. Possibly stupid, I agree, but I needed to decide on my own."

"That's the most selfish thing I've ever heard. We came all the way out here for you. You must have been in touch with your father. This is him talking, not the Amanda I raised." Celia reached into her purse and pulled out a lipstick.

"No, I have not been talking with Dad. This is me talking. Maybe you're finally hearing."

Roxie sat quietly. Amanda felt a little bad that Roxie had gotten herself embroiled in their mess, but she was the one who'd chosen to join sides with Celia. She could have stayed in Chicago.

"And you did not come out here for me. You never asked me if you could come. You told me you had already purchased the tickets. You flew out here for you."

"We were very worried about you. What did you expect us to do?" Celia didn't make eye contact, placing the lipstick back in her purse. "Just sit in Chicago, wondering if you're ruining your life?"

"I didn't expect it, but I hoped you'd respect me. Is that so hard to do? I'm not a child. I'm 26! I'm not married, and I don't have a traditional career. I'm not living the life that you think I should be living, but I'm a woman capable of making my own decisions."

"Questionable decisions." Celia played with the sugar and Sweet'N Low packets. She was heading into her silent mode. Amanda could see the migraine beginning to form in Celia's stare.

"We really were concerned," Roxie jumped in, loosening the wrap of her green boa.

"But your collective concern is suffocating." And with that, a pimply-faced teenage boy brought their entrees.

They ate in silence, and even though she wasn't hungry, Amanda forced herself to eat to prove to them that she was fine. When they did talk, the conversation was polite at best, but mostly awkward and stilted.

After they finished their meal, almost on cue, Celia complained of a migraine. Amanda walked them back to the hotel and said goodnight to Celia. She and Roxie got in Amanda's car then headed to the Spur to meet Lance. One down, one to go.

****

"So my mom still doesn't know about the regressions?" Amanda confirmed once they were safe inside the car.

"I told you I wouldn't tell, and I didn't."

"Thank you."

Roxie didn't say anything, and Amanda could tell by her silence that Roxie had been tormented over the decision.

"So you really think you found him?"

"Yes, I think I have."

"Maybe I'm jealous, Mandy." Hearing someone refer to her as Mandy felt comforting and disorienting at the same time. "So I need to tell you about this guy Mohammed that I've been seeing ... " Roxie continued on with her monologue until they arrived at the bar. For once, Amanda was grateful for Roxie's hook-up ramblings.

They pulled into the parking lot at the Spur, and Roxie reached into her purse, retrieving a purple boa. She replaced the green one, and Amanda felt the tension of the day melt away.

"Thanks."

"You're not just my cousin, you're like one of my best friends. I fucking flew to the wild west to check on you." Amanda and Roxie hugged before walking into the Spur.

Once inside, Amanda quickly spotted Lance sitting at a booth adjacent to the bar.

"Roxie, this is Lance." Amanda recognized the glimmer in Roxie's eyes and cringed. *I'm not out of the woods yet.*

Roxie slid into the booth next to him and Amanda shot her a dirty look.

"Nice to meet you," Lance said, looking Roxie up and down. Amanda noticed a twinkle in his eye, and didn't like what she was seeing. He was obviously attracted to Roxie. Who wouldn't be? The woman specialized in oozing sex appeal. If she could bottle it, she'd make a fortune.

"Shall we get some drinks?" Roxie suggested. Lance waved John, the bar manager, over to their table.

"Everyone like margaritas?" Lance asked Roxie.

She nodded her head and tossed her curls around. "Love them." She held onto the "love" for too long and rewet her lips with her tongue. Roxie's actions were playing like a training film – *Flirting 101: The Roxie Way.*

John returned a few minutes later with a pitcher of margaritas and three salt-rimmed glasses.

"So, Keira tells me that you two are really close." Lance poured the margaritas and passed them around the table.

"Keira? Oh yeah," Roxie laughed, "Sorry, yes, we are."

Amanda locked her eyes on Roxie in a scolding manner.

"I'm not used to her being referred to as 'Keira.'" Roxie responded to Amanda rather than Lance.

"Should I call you Amanda, then?" Lance asked, puzzled.

"No, Roxie can get used to 'Keira,'" Amanda answered, not releasing her gaze on Roxie, and thinking, *she'll spin circles around him before the night's over.*

Roxie polished off her margarita as if it were ice water on a hot day, and poured a refill.

"What did you think of our Faire?" Lance attempted to divert the conversation while rolling his eyes at Amanda.

Phew, he isn't entirely captured by Roxie's spell.

Lance reached his foot under the table and rubbed Amanda's leg as a sign of reassurance and support.

"I don't know. Not really my thing. I'm more of a city girl."

"Yeah, you have to just get into the spirit of it. I live in New York during the school year, but I love my summers in the mountains."

"New York, really?"

"Yeah, I teach arts at a high school in the Bronx."

Amanda cringed. Lance still hadn't come to grips with the fact that his contract had been terminated.

Roxie pounded her second margarita and then a third. The conversation continued in a stilted manner for another twenty minutes, in that way conversations do when you have to get all the facts organized and exchanged.

"So you really bought into all this soul-mate bullshit?"

Amanda's face went pale. *This can't be happening. I never thought Roxie would take it this far. How did I not see this coming? She had laid a trap and I fell into it face first. Damnit!*

"Rox, stop," Amanda pleaded.

"What are you talking about?" The look of concern on Lance's face made Amanda want to lean across the table and strangle Roxie. *How dare she strut in and ruin my perfect world!*

"It's nothing, Lance. Roxie's drunk. Aren't you Roxie?"

"She thinks you two are soul mates." Roxie wouldn't make eye contact with Amanda. "That you've been lovers for multiple lifetimes, or some crap like that. She never told you? I'm surprised."

Roxie had been too easy on her in the car. Now it was clear she'd likely been plotting her revenge the whole time. *That damn Scorpio nature of hers, never to be trusted, always with a hidden agenda.*

"Roxie!"

"Let her talk," Lance interrupted, and Amanda knew it was over. The truth was going to come tumbling out on the table.

"She didn't tell you about the past-life regressions?"

"Keira, what's going on?"

"You're a fucking bitch, Roxie. You were just waiting for the perfect moment to screw up my life, weren't you?"

"Looks like you're the one who's been screwing things up. Lying to your boyfriend? Tsk, tsk." Roxie shook her head.

"You're just jealous. You can't stand to see that I might have found some happiness. Or is it that I found happiness that you had nothing to do with?"

"Oh, whatever!" Roxie turned to Lance. "So, Keira here thinks you two were together in England in the medieval times — you saved her from an abbey and took her into a forest full of fairies." Roxie laughed.

Lance's face wrinkled, his brow furrowed. He inched towards the wall.

Amanda felt nauseous.

"What's this all about?" he asked.

Roxie, unrelenting, went on, "She came out here looking for you. She got obsessed. She lost all this weight, turned her back on everyone important in her life, quit her job, and came out here to find you! You must be really fucking special."

"What the hell is she talking about?" Lance asked looking at Amanda with distrust in his eyes.

"Roxie, shut up!" Amanda pleaded.

"Amanda, I'm doing you a favor. You're leading this poor guy on."

"It's none of your business!" Amanda hissed.

"Amanda, tell me what the hell is going on," Lance challenged.

Hearing him say Amanda instead of Keira, the stress of the exchange, and the bursting of her perfect bubble was too much to bear. She didn't know how to get out of it as she burst into tears and tried to run from the booth.

Roxie got up, grabbed her by the arm, and swung her back toward the table. "You have to tell him the truth eventually."

"I have to tell him the truth. Not you!" Amanda screamed, while all the adrenaline of the moment built inside her and she pushed Roxie backward, causing her to lose her footing and fall.

"You never would have done it. I just allowed for you to have an open, honest relationship with this man."

Roxie's self-righteousness pushed Amanda over the edge and she lunged for her on the floor. Thrashing Roxie back and forth, Amanda wanted to shake her out of her life. Roxie was bigger and stronger, though, and she quickly had Amanda pinned to the ground.

"Girls!" Lance screamed.

"Calm down, bitch!" Roxie pinned Amanda's flailing arms to the sticky bar floor.

"Get off me! I hate you!"

"Shut up!"

"Why did you come here? Get out! Get the fuck out of my life!" Amanda tried to wiggle free from Roxie's clutch, but couldn't.

"Roxie, get off her!" Lance demanded, and with that, Roxie loosened her grip, and Amanda was able to free herself.

"What's going on out there?" John, the manager, came running from behind the bar.

"Sorry, dude. Chick fight," Lance answered.

Amanda was mortified. What would Lance think of her now? Everything was ruined.

"Keira, is that you?" John pulled Roxie off Amanda. Amanda rubbed her shoulder, slightly bruised from Roxie's tight clutch.

"No, it's Amanda," Roxie spat out the words.

"I don't care who you are. There's no fighting in my bar. Get the hell out of here. Lance, settle the tab." John physically pushed both Roxie and Amanda out the door. Amanda was dizzy. *How did things get so out of control?* Through the bar's front window, she could see Lance handing John a credit card and shaking his head.

"I think you and Celia need to leave," Amanda demanded, keeping her distance from Roxie.

Roxie nodded her head. "Why doesn't your hot boyfriend drive me back to my hotel?" she taunted.

"Go wait in my car. I'll drive you myself."

"I'd rather get an Uber."

"Fine! I'd rather not have you anywhere near me."

And with that, Lance came outside as Roxie was getting into her ride. There were no goodbyes between Roxie and Amanda, only steely looks and layers upon layers of anger and pain.

"Okay, Amanda, what the hell happened in there?"

Amanda shivered at the steely look in his eyes, his arms crossed, and brow furrowed. *I wish I could peel back time, back to when everything was still good. I know I have to tell him the truth now – there's no other way.*

"What the fuck is going on and who the hell are you?"

"I'm Keira. I'm your girlfriend. Nothing has changed," Amanda pleaded.

"So, you've been looking for me? There's some secret agenda that you have?"

"Most of what Roxie said was true. I just wanted to tell you myself, in my own time."

"Well, now would be a damn good time."

Amanda took a deep breath and went for it. She didn't have a choice. "To try to find some direction in my life, I started seeing a therapist in Chicago for past-life regressions." She paused, checking for any kind of emotional response from Lance. There was none. He stood stone-faced, arms still crossed, brow still furrowed. She could feel him falling less in love with her with every word she said. "I always regressed to a place in England in the Renaissance time, when my name was Keira."

"How do I factor into this, Amanda?"

Amanda cringed.

"You were there in my past lives. You looked the same; you acted the same. I know it was you."

"And we were lovers, you say?"

"Yes." Amanda reached for his hand, but Lance shoved his fist into his jean pockets. "I came to the Faire to find you."

"This is pretty out there, you know." His gaze was averted, lost somewhere off in the distance.

"I know it sounds crazy ... "

"I don't even believe in reincarnation."

Amanda's heart hurt on a whole new level.

"Why did you think I'd be here?" he asked in genuine curiosity.

Amanda took another deep breath. She never thought she'd have to explain why she knew he was in Colorado. Now, she realized just how crazy she sounded. "I saw your picture in a pop-up ad online for the Faire. I saw your face, and I knew it was you." Amanda hoped her quick pace would mask the insanity of what she'd said. "What's so weird is that in our life together in England, you were always trying to convince me that we belonged together. Now, in this life, the tables are turned. Maybe this explains why you wondered so much if you knew me."

Lance's silence scared Amanda. *There's nothing worse than not knowing what's going on inside someone's head.* She braced for the worst.

"So, you think we're like Romeo and Juliet or something? Two ill-fated, star-crossed, whatever lovers who seek each other out time and time again?" Lance looked past Amanda into the distance.

I'm losing him. It's all happening, and I can't stop it. Tears streamed down her face, and she desperately needed a tissue. Panic overcame her. *I can't let him get away.* "You've said over and over that you've never felt anything with anyone as strong as you have with me."

"Keira, I like you. Maybe I thought I even loved you ... "

"*Maybe* you love me?"

"It doesn't mean that we've been lovers for time eternal. You're not going to get me to believe this soul-mate bullshit. It's been a fun summer, but I'm not part of your hidden agenda."

Amanda lowered her voice to a whisper. "I've gone through hell and back to find these things out. You just prance into my life like some kind of knight-in-fucking-armor. Then you go and turn my world into something wonderful. But now you tell me what … " Amanda was sobbing hysterically. "You tell me you don't believe in happily ever after? Well, what the hell am I supposed to do now? You're it. There's no next guy!"

"I don't know what to say, Keira — or Amanda — or whoever you are."

"Please call me Keira. Nothing has changed."

Lance huffed a sarcastic sigh that confirmed that everything had changed.

"I think I should go."

"Please don't." Amanda grabbed his arm.

"Goodnight." He pushed her away, got into his car, and drove off.

CHAPTER 37

"Still no word?" Claire called across the Costumery. Amanda's sadness was palpable, like a sticky sheath she couldn't shake.

"Nothing. Haven't heard from him in four days. I've driven by his place, his car is never there. He won't return texts or voicemails. He hasn't even shown up for work. It's like he's disappeared."

Did Lance and Therese enter some kind of portal into another dimension? Is my life really just a creepy psychological thriller like a movie on Netflix? Maybe all the shows exist because the concept is real, she wondered.

"Well you can't go home and spend another night drowning your sorrows in baby bottles of vodka."

"I can't?" Amanda gave a half-hearted laugh. She didn't know what the hell to do anymore. Chicago didn't really seem like an option, and the last thing she wanted to do was go back and start her old life all over again. She couldn't stand any aspect of who she was when she was only Amanda. She only wanted to go back in time and remove drunk, angry Roxie from the Spur, and revert back to when everything was still okay.

"Let's get out of town. You need a change of scenery. Seeing you like this is making me depressed."

"Am I that bad?"

"You're worse."

Amanda offered a small smile. *Thank God for Claire. I can just follow Claire wherever she goes. Wisconsin? Did she say Wisconsin was next on her list? Okay, fine. I'll go there with her.*

"I know a band playing in Denver tonight. It will take your mind off this mess."

"I don't know."

"I insist. I'm actually not letting you go home."

Amanda smiled. She needed Claire. "Okay."

"Way to go, girl. Suck it up and let me force you to have fun."

****

The band was called Slim Cessna's Auto Club and they blended country and punk, two of Amanda's least-favorite genres. The lead guitarist and lead singer were slam dancing and yodeling simultaneously, something Amanda would have never thought possible. Apparently, Claire was a huge fan. It made Amanda realize how little she actually knew Claire.

"Not so into them?" Claire screamed into Amanda's ear as she gyrated to the music.

"They're okay. It's good to be out. Thanks for dragging me here."

The band performed what must have been one of their hits because the crowd went crazy. Amanda thrust her hands into her jean pockets and swayed along to the music, letting her mind wander to the idea of Florida and escape on warm, sandy beaches. If she closed her eyes, she could almost feel the sensation of the hot sand between her toes.

****

"So what are you thinking is next for you?" Claire asked as they turned onto the highway and started their drive back to Castle Rock.

"Well, I know what I can't do. I certainly can't go back to Chicago after the whole fiasco with my mom and Roxie."

Claire nodded in agreement.

"I feel sorta homeless."

"Why don't you come to Wisconsin with me?"

"Thanks, Claire, I've actually thought of that, but you know I really came here to find Lance. I'm not sure how I would feel being at another Renaissance Faire without him. There's always Florida."

"Florida?"

"I got a brochure for some condos there when I was still in Chicago, back when I was first thinking of leaving. It sounded like a good idea then, and maybe it really is. I like the concept of living in perpetual summer. I've always wanted to live in a place where pools never have a 'Closed for the season' sign."

"I once had a friend who moved to Boston because she grew up loving the show *Cheers*. Can you believe it? I guess you can go anywhere, for any reason."

"None of it really matters, though, if what you're looking for is someplace else."

Later that night, Amanda awoke to her phone playing the Ed Sheeran song she'd finally picked for Lance's ringtone. For a groggy moment, she wondered if she was still dreaming. She looked at her alarm clock. It was 2:20 a.m. The concert was a late one, so she'd only been home and asleep for about an hour. *Did he really call? Surely it was only a dream.* Amanda fumbled around her apartment in the dark, but by the time she found her phone, it had stopped ringing. She called the number back, shielding her eyes from the brightness of the screen. Her heart raced so fast, she didn't know if she'd be able to talk at all.

"Lance? Did you just call me?"

"Keira. Thank God you're awake."

"I wasn't, but I am now. What's wrong?" Amanda's blood pressure rose in response to the tension in his voice.

"Can I see you?"

"Of course."

"I'm almost there."

Amanda sat on the edge of her futon, rubbing her eyes and wondering what happened. *This is a good sign*, she told herself. She stumbled around her apartment, trying to find some shorts to wear under her nightshirt. She washed her face and took a good hard look at herself. *Don't screw up this time*, she scolded. *This may be your last chance to get him back. He wouldn't come by to break-up. He already did that.*

****

When Lance arrived, he had bags under his eyes and looked like hell. He was wearing scruffy shorts, a ratty T-shirt, and had such thick stubble that he barely looked like himself. Amanda was glad, in a way. She liked the idea of him suffering without her.

It was stiff and formal between them in a way it never had been before. Lance took a seat on the edge of the bed as though he were poised to leave at any moment. He wouldn't touch her. Not knowing his intention in coming, she didn't know how to react.

"I just got down from Vail," he began. "Literally, I called you from the highway. I've been up with my sister for the last few days. I had to get out of town."

Lance stopped, and an awkward silence filled the room. Amanda didn't want to say anything until he had divulged what was hiding in his heart.

"Do you want something to drink?"

"Sure. A soda or something, whatever you have." While Amanda was in the kitchen, Lance continued. "So I had a chance to do a lot of thinking up there. Something about the mountain air helps put my life in perspective."

Amanda nodded, walking back with two glasses of ice water. "No soda."

"That's fine, thanks." He took a large gulp.

Lance's bouts of silence were killing her, but she held her tongue. He had to do the talking this time. "It was nice to see my sister. Her kids are doing really great. I was able to help her husband out with a project on the house, and we ... "

"Lance, why are you here?"

"Sorry." He lowered his head. "I had to see you."

"Because you missed me, or because you want to end this?" Amanda took a huge gulp of water herself and ran a hand over her knotty hair.

"Keira … " he said a bit awkwardly. "Can I still call you Keira?"

"Please. Only call me Keira."

"I had a lot of time to think up there. Not getting my teaching job renewed was a big wake-up call. I feel like my life is being turned upside down. I can't go back to New York without that grant, and New York and teaching are my life. Then I met you this summer, and you fill my every waking thought like no woman ever has. You scared the living shit out of me that night at the bar. But then I wondered, do I care? I mean, I like you, you like me, who cares how we met, right? If you believe that we're soul mates, then maybe you're right. I'm just glad that you found me, and I don't want to fuck this up like I have so many other relationships."

Amanda's heart raced with anticipation. "Say it. Say you want to be with me. I need to hear it."

"The reason I came down tonight is … " He stalled for a minute, looking away. Amanda felt like time was moving backward. "Sorry, this is hard for me." He took a sip of water. "Keira, I love you."

Amanda could almost see little cartoon blue and pink butterflies circling the two of them in a wave of love that was pure magic. Lance leaned in close, took her face in his hands, and kissed her. It was a timeless kiss that felt just like her first one from Miles, back in the Forest of Forgiveness, so many lifetimes ago. Amanda felt dizzy with an oncoming regression, but she willed it away. *No more sleep-walking through life. I have to be awake for this kiss.*

EPILOGUE

Amanda made a last-minute pass through the apartment to make sure she hadn't forgotten anything. The Faire had ended with a big wrap-up party the night before; she hadn't made it home until after midnight, and then she'd had to finish packing. She could hear Lance's car horn honking for her. She knew that if she rushed, she would end up leaving something behind.

She couldn't believe the day had actually arrived. She and Lance were off to spend the fall in Wisconsin with Claire. They were going to work another Faire, and put real life on hold for at least one more season. She wondered if they would end up like Claire, lost in a time warp of make-believe. It reminded her of her breakdown her sophomore year in college when she'd been pressed to declare a major. She didn't know what she wanted to study, and Celia threatened to stop sending Northwestern her tuition payments if she chose anything other than a business degree. On her way to enroll in the marketing program, the degree that Celia was pushing her to get, she passed the recreation department. On a whim, she walked in and registered as a recreation major. She would go and work at Club Med in the Caribbean. Why lead a traditional life? But then the reality of what she'd done began to weigh on her heavily, so the next day, she undeclared her recreation major and headed over to the business school. She had never once used her marketing degree.

Amanda hadn't talked to Roxie and Celia since that horrible night at the bar weeks before. She knew she was getting stronger each day, and she hoped that soon she would be able to email them and begin to repair some of the damage.

Amanda said goodbye to her apartment, turning off the light for the last time. As she reached down to pick up her last carry-on, she saw something glitter from an outside pocket. Therese's bracelet! The same one she'd thought she lost in the hotel, back at the beginning of the summer. Amanda rolled it over her fingers and onto her wrist, remembering how grounding it felt to have it on. She shed a tear, wondering if she would ever see Therese again.

Walking down the stairs, she saw Jerry standing on his balcony. He was waiting for her. They hadn't spoken since that night at the liquor store, when she'd explained that she was with Lance. She wondered if he would still be living in this complex ten years from now, still hitting on women by the pool, still abusing his body with drugs.

"Goodbye, beautiful one," Jerry whispered. "This reminds me of our lifetime in Rome. We must be doomed not to be together. Don't worry; we'll meet again in another life, my darling Keira. We can't always be together. 'For this is all a dream we dreamed one afternoon, long ago ... ' he sang as he stepped back into his apartment and shut the door.

This isn't happening. "No," she told herself over and over, the word echoing in her head. Amanda looked down to see Lance, waiting in the car below, waving at her to hurry up. Her feet wouldn't move. She was paralyzed. Lance stuck his head out the car window and called to her.

"Are you okay, Keira?" and in that instant Amanda didn't see Miles, she saw Robert, full and clear. It was Robert's caring voice, wrinkled brow, and innocent eyes that looked up to her.

"I'm coming!" she smiled, picking up her bags and running down the remaining stairs to him.

ACKNOWLEDGEMENTS

Work on this book started over 15 years ago, and as with so many creative projects, it would not have come into being without a lot of support from my writing community and friends. I would specifically like to call out my Colorado writing group: Ann, Laurel Suzanne, Monica, Susan, and Gye who helped hold me accountable and provided wonderful guidance on my first draft; and a special thank you to David, my critique partner, who helped through endless revisions.

Thank you to all the friends who read early and late versions offering quick feedback and deep critiques, and especially to my tribe sisters Jessica and Allyn, who went above and beyond with the detailed attention and support they gave to this book.

A big thank you also to Beth for the initial full book edit, and to Catherine for another gorgeous cover. And huge appreciation to Judith for the final edit and formatting, and for tirelessly bearing with me to make sure the story was told just as it needs to be.

To my family: Mom, Dad, and Rebecca — thank you for your encouragement and support. I am blessed to have such a great built-in fan club.

To my amazing girl, Elizabeth, and to my 'Lancelot', Rob, you two keep me grounded and are my ***everything***.

ABOUT THE AUTHOR

Tamara Palmer knew she was going to be a writer before she could even write. As a young girl, she created elaborate dramas with her Barbies for days – even weeks – on end. Later stories made their way onto pages via her typewriter. Tamara is the author of *Missing Tyler*. She leads writing retreats and virtual writing programs through her writing community, *Tami's Tribe*. Tamara lives just outside Chicago with her husband, daughter, and an assortment of pets. Find her online on Facebook, Instagram, and at www.tamarapalmerauthor.com.

MISSING TYLER

Tamara Palmer

Available as Kindle or Paperback

on

Amazon.com

www.tamarapalmerauthor.com

www.facebook.com.tamarapalmerauthor

e-mail: tamara@tamarapalmerauthor.com

Made in the USA
Middletown, DE
13 October 2020

21848232R00157